ALSO BY CRAIG A. ROBERTSON

BOOKS IN THE RYANVERSE:

THE FOREVER SERIES:

THE GALAXY ON FIRE SERIES:

RISE OF ANCIENT GODS SERIES

RETURN OF THE ANCIENT GODS, **BOOK 1**
RAGE OF THE ANCIENT GODS, **BOOK 2**
TORMENT OF THE ANCIENT GODS, **BOOK 3**
WRATH OF THE ANCIENT GODS, Book 4 (Due in early 2019)

STAND-ALONE NOVELS:

THE CORPORATE VIRUS (2016)
TIME DIVING (2013)
THE INNERgLOW EFFECT (2010)
WRITE NOW! The Prisoner of NaNoWriMo (2009)
ANON TIME (2009)

THE FOREVER PEACE

BOOK SIX OF THE *FOREVER SERIES*

by Craig Robertson

In Order To Live, Sometimes You Have To Die.

Imagine-It Publishing
El Dorado Hills, CA

ISBN: 978-0-9973073-9-9 (Paperback)
978-0-9989253-0-1 (E-Book)

Cover art work and design by Starla Huchton
Available at http://www.designedbystarla.com

Editing and Formatting by Polgarus Studio
Available at http://www.polgarusstudio.com

Additional editorial assistance by Michael Blanche

First Edition 2017
Second Edition 2018
Third Edition 2019

Imagine-It Publishing

This book is dedicated to all of us who crave, dream of, and live for creativity. To follow the imagination and drink deeply of its joy is surely the greatest gift God can grant.

Note: Glossary of Terms is Located at the End of the Book.

PROLOGUE

In the years that followed the defeat of the Last Nightmare, peace blessed the humans of the worldship fleet. But when discussing humans, peace was traditionally relative. Infighting, politicking, and social climbing were raised back to their pre-Earth destruction norms. But I guess it was a luxury to engage in those perennial selfish pursuits. They reflected that, for once in a very long time, there were no critical problems thrust upon humanity. So it was back to generating crises and inflicting wounds on themselves. A dubious milestone to be certain. But in a universe that was hostile and unrelenting, such dalliances were bound to be short-lived. No rest for the wicked, as they say.

It would be hard to minimize the blessing of the miraculous technology the Deavoriath gifted to the humans. After the first batch of human androids were upgraded to Forms and given their own vortices, many humans were similarly upgraded. Within ten years, there were over a thousand human Forms. But again, human nature could be perverse. At first all the Forms rallied together and worked as the crack unit they should have always been. But a split developed between the android and human Forms in no time at all.

The androids had served humanity for three hundred years. All but me were new to the power and freedom the cubes afforded. Gradually, by ones and twos, some of the heroic explorers decided their terms of service were complete.

That wasn't to suggest they were unreasonable for hitting the road. Those brave men and women had volunteered centuries before and served continually since. They'd sacrificed their past lives and committed themselves to the uncertainty of immortality, just as I had.

The human Forms tended to be relentlessly loyal to "The Company," also called TCY. That was the name given to the vortex pilot squadrons. Only a handful of androids would still belong to TCY in another decade.

Most androids had wandered off on their own, exploring for themselves the wonders of the universe. Naturally, I was one of those who remained. Loyal as a puppy, that was me. The human Forms resented the androids that split and directed those feeling toward the handful of us androids still left in TCY. A rift developed that benefitted neither faction. Again, humans fabricated contention where none was required.

A critical point in the worldship fleet's military evolution came when the question was raised as to whether members of TCY should be transferred to android hosts. Though an innocent enough proposition on the surface, committing to such a course had tremendous implications. Immortal leadership, a predictable outcome, was an ugly prospect. Lord Acton warned that power tends to corrupt, and absolute power corrupts absolutely. Great men, he cautioned, are almost always bad men. Add *immortal* to power and greatness, and any bad outcome would be inevitable and bad. Yeah, who could forget Stuart Marshall?

Though the humans bickered, the Berrillians never forgot a single detail, a solitary insult, or any defeat. They were cats with attitude and a big plan— a never faltering, never wavering vision. They wanted to rule the galaxy as its sole sentient species. Anganctus had committed them to a guerrilla battle strategy. His successor, Erratarus, was singularly focused on conquest. He was meaner, more ruthless, and less intelligent than his father. By most standards a suboptimal combination. Humans came to call him the Berrillian Nero. But, of course, they could only nickname him that after being witness to and victim of his brutal rage.

ONE

Garo-fuf Jocar was impatient and task oriented. That was to say he was Maxwal-Asute. Halfway through his life, he was bitterly disappointed in his achievements and wanted more. He expected more. Again, that was to say he was Maxwal-Asute. He was too short to serve in the military. That was unacceptable. All males served in the military or they were not males. One cubit. That was the height deficiency he was saddled with. If he'd measure one *cubit* taller he'd have been able to enlist. He was certain he'd have risen to the highest levels of command. His name would have been Garo-rir—Garo-*fear*—not Garo-fuf—Garo-*see*. He'd pounded the soles of his feet the morning of the military physical to the point where he could barely walk. But that hadn't produced enough swelling to make him one cubit taller.

Now he was a farmer. His family told him the empire needed farmers. Of course, it did. What were the glorious soldiers to eat? Mud? The discontent of males one cubit too short? *Barshuf.* Garo-fuf had determined he was cursed and everyone knew the cursed deserved what they received. Yes, he might have three beautiful wives, ninety-seven bouncy offspring, and one of the largest landholdings on the continent of Darlip-malm as he did. But his curse was as clear to him as it was unapparent to everyone he tried to complaint to. His wives said he was blessed with such healthy children. How could it be that he was cursed? His children said he was blessed with such fertile wives. How could it be he was cursed? The blind praising the blind, that's what he was surrounded with. How did he know when he was being lied to? Someone's verbal cup-lip vibrated.

That particular day, he did what he was inclined to more and more as his life-clock ticked toward death at a disgustingly slow rate. He got in his truck and he drove as far away from civilization as he could. He was alone, which was the only time his auditory cup-lip didn't buzz with thinly veiled insults. He did, also, have legitimate concerns in the western section of his holdings. The grass grew too long. The numbers of deppeb and marshups were too low with that level of food abundance. Poaching or predation were the most likely causes. Normally he'd have blamed predators for thinning out the herbivore numbers, but even girrdy and feshdoles were growing scarce in that region. Most odd. It also excluded poachers. Nothing, including the Maxwal-Asute, ate feshdoles. They were extremely vicious and tasted too awful. Plus, they had less meat on them than a bone his second wife was finished gnawing on.

Looking out from the top of the tall hill near the edge of his lands, Garo-fuf Jocar saw nothing unusual. Large boulders studded the vista and rocky crags abounded. A few beasts grazed lazily below. High above, various aircraft trails crisscrossed the sky. He stared down at a sestril's burrow entry for a long time, but no furry head popped up, even after he tossed a crumb of bread next to the hole. His land had turned odd. *Ah*, he thought with clarity, it is the *curse. His curse.* It spilled over to the livestock, the predators, and even the rodents. Wasn't that just his fate? He woo-wooped the air loudly using his entire head cup to cry out in anger, frustration, and damnation of all he was forced to look upon.

It was said in many religions that divine truths were revealed on mountaintops. Maybe the proximity to the deity allowed that. If the Maxwal-Asute had any belief system approximating a religion, perhaps Garo-fuf Jocar might have anticipated a defining revelation there on his mini-mountaintop. But he held no belief in anything that could not be seen, felt, or owned.

A rock tumbled down from above him, thudding to a stop after striking one of his feet. He glanced up the slope to see what had dislodged the stone. Nothing living was there. *Hmm,* he thought. Stones don't just roll down hills and impact landowners's feet. That, too, was odd. He was beginning to hate odd, even the word *odd* itself. He picked his way up the steep hillside to investigate. He knew there was nothing but rocks and parched dirt up there, but it wasted time well. Otherwise, he'd have run out of reasons to delay returning home.

Garo-fuf Jocar reached a rough outcropping and pulled himself atop it, wedged between two large rocks. Nothing. He smelled, saw, and heard nothing with his cup. Bah. Time poorly wasted—

A scrape. Yes, there was a scrape on the ground just around the rock he leaned against. He stuck his head through the two rocks to investigate. His eye-lip was angled down, so he never saw what killed him.

The massive jaws of a four-hundred pound Berrillian female snapped shut over his cup and head. She crushed his skull and tore what she held in her mouth free in one powerful snap of her neck. Her huge paw pulled the rest of Garo-fuf Jocar's body around the rock, and she pounced on it. She batted it and tossed it in the air. Intermittently, she'd toss it to the side like it was escaping and pounce on it all over again. After a few minutes, however, she tired of the game and consumed the mangled carcass, leather boots and all.

Afterward, Nellbeck flopped on the sunlit ground in front of her cave and cleaned her muzzle and paws. A full belly in a warm spot were her only real pleasures in life. She was proud to serve, even though stationed on this abysmal rock, waiting for the glory of open warfare. Until that day came, there was precious little to occupy her mind. If she ever got her paws on a male, then she'd have a litter to keep her busy. But the nearest potential mate was so far away he probably couldn't smell her, even when she was in heat. Still, someday—

Before retiring deep in her cave to sleep, Nellbeck collected the truck her dinner had used to deliver itself with. No traces. Those were her orders. Plus, the tiny vehicle would make a great toy for the litter she hoped to have someday.

TWO

I'd been knocking around a nearly empty house for three weeks. Kayla was off to help Josie, our youngest daughter, with the birth of her twins. I was invited to come along but … yeah. Something big came up at the last minute and I had to cancel on that estrogen-fest. The universe was going to end or something, I just knew it. Of course, both girls were happy I stayed home. So was Gus, my son-in-law. If I was there, he'd be stuck listening to my war stories, which bored him to the point of lusting for unconsciousness. He'd also have to "entertain" me, which was code for keep me out of the women's way as much as possible. Recalling that I don't sleep, he probably spent the entire first week in church, thanking the good Lord for the blessing of my absence.

Empty nester. Dude, I'd been a hero, an explorer, a liberator, and a sex symbol. Now I was … one of those things I cared not to repeat. They said life could be funny. I assumed they meant ironic. I'd rather drop on a live grenade than be referred to as an empty nester. Yuck. It was about as sexy as being the janitor in a morgue. I'd traveled alone for decades, I'd been held prisoner in the bleakest of prisons, and I'd survived a falzorn attack. I'd muddle through real adulthood somehow. Specifically how? Beer. Yes, that was a key component in my expenditure of time.

Kayla said she'd be back in a few more weeks, but I wouldn't blame her if she dragged her heels a bit. She, the former tough-as-nails first officer on a pirate ship, was about as sanguine concerning the empty nester thing as I was. The only difference was, she had anticipated its inevitability. I was an immortal fighter pilot. It never made my list. So, for her, hanging around the older grandkids and cuddling the newest ones beat the heck out of watching me mope.

I knew my life would change once the Deavoriath gave us all those cubes. I underestimated, it would seem, the impact it would have on my leisure time. If one didn't count Toño and Carlos, who were basically in charge and critical to the functioning of TCY, I was the only android remaining. Don't get me wrong. Being excluded from the routine scut work of shuttling VIPs around or assisting in the relocation of large numbers of colonists to alien worlds was fine by me. And I didn't much miss the patrol duty in disputed or potentially active space either.

Not participating in the diplomatic part, though? That did fry my bacon a tad. Ironic? Miffed because I wasn't invited to *that* party? Well, I was, a little. I was pivotal to galactic politics for over two hundred years, criminy sakes. I was hella good at it, too. Now, as the old-fart-last-android Form, I was conveniently overlooked when those assignments were inked. Younger and more human pilots were felt to better represent not only the worldfleet, but, and more importantly, TCY.

For nearly three centuries I'd dressed in a flight suit or civvies. TCY had shiny new uniforms with flashing patches and clear rank insignia. Oh yeah, the Uniform of the Day was different from the dress casuals and didn't look at all like the mess-dress penguin suit. It was the old days all over again with the clothes. And if I was out of uniform, I was reminded of it, and it was even occasionally recorded as a disciplinary infraction. Behind my back, younger officers called me General NJD. Non-judicial punishments were those used to address minor infractions like the uniform thing. Enough demerits and I wouldn't get pudding for dessert or something. Kayla chided, nagged, and punched me a lot, attempting to get me to grow up and go with the flow. She maintained my rebellious juvenile protestations were beneath me, and that I was destined to fail. I'd opted to adopted a "we'll see" approach to her speculations. I also made myself scarce at HQ.

Bottom line was that I had a lot of time on my hands. I guessed I could have resigned my commission, retired, and kicked back formally. But, that went against my grain. I lived to serve. Yeah, sounded corny, but I meant it. I'd be doing this forever. It was important to me. Call me old school, but if a person was able-bodied, they should pull their own weight. I was a proven officer, the best damn officer there ever was, in fact. I was going to remain one until some alien horde turned me into shrapnel. That, or until my batteries wore out. If TCY and I experienced some growing pains, so be it. Unless a lot more of them transferred to androids, I'd be the one getting the last laugh. I'd be around to speak warmly of them at commemorative dinners. I'd also be around to pee on their graves. Growing pains. Nothing big. By the way, the peeing thing, I never actually mentioned that part to Kayla. As it was a *plan* and not necessarily a *done-deal,* I felt it that was the safest course to keep that wish on the DL.

With nothing on my dance card one day while Kayla was still gone, I wandered over to the operations center. I'd see if anything was brewing, even if it was only burnt coffee. I didn't make it a habit of hanging out there and brown nosing, but it never hurt to seem interested. Jeff Galloway was the NCO at the front desk. He was a nice enough guy, meaning he wasn't a blue falcon. Those were the guys who'd chat you up and then stab you in the back with anything you said.

"Yo, Jeff," I said, "how's it hanging?"

"General, I'm hanging just fine. How's your set?"

Not sure if that slipped out automatically, or it was one of the many barbs cast my way for being an android. My pair, after all, were in a jar in some lab that Jupiter swallowed a few centuries earlier.

"I'm good. Anything cooking?"

"Same old, same old. You know the drill, sir. We wait for shit to hit the fan, but it mostly hits your desktop."

"I hear you. Who's got the watch today?"

"That'd be Colonel Timoshenko. You want I should buzz him?"

"Nah, I'll just surprise the shit out of him."

I didn't like that man, and he didn't like me. Neither of us made much pretense of that situation, either. I'm not sure if I did or said something to piss him off, or if he just hated my guts long before we ever met. I was accustomed to both scenarios. Me? I was an affable, easy-going guy. Some ate-ups didn't much fancy that in an officer. Katashi Matsumoto was a good example. He was the kind of jerk who followed regulations and protocol so intently that he couldn't adapt to the context of the situations he faced.

And there were legend haters were out there. Those chip-on-the-shoulder types resented my history. Maybe they also had small dicks. Who could know? But they wanted to prove I was nothing in their eyes, and that maybe *they* were the real heroes, not me. Like I cared what some shavetail thought of my life's work. I was perfectly willing to wait two centuries and see what a BFD hotshot they'd become. I was willing because those guys—and I mean guys exclusively because I never once caught that attitude from a woman—never amounted to a hill of beans.

But Timoshenko wasn't either of the first two types. No, he was a metal hater. He didn't like human transfers to androids. Not that we were all that common. A person could live their entire life never meeting an android. Most people did, in fact. But there was a group of individuals out there who disapproved of the process and the results. Maybe it was religious, maybe it was ethical. I was never sure. It required that the person be a special kind of stupid to be in that camp, of that I was sure. Prejudice sucked no matter what it was based on. Prejudiced people were ignorant fucks. What more can be said? I bet good money Konstantin Timoshenko likely had similar uncharitable thoughts about many other perfectly acceptable beliefs and lifestyles. But he was wrong and a dickwad.

I was in the office, so, like it or not, I wandered back to say hello—or drop dead, you filthy animal—to Kon. Galloway would tell him I'd stopped by. If I hadn't checked in with the puke, he'd have more ammunition to disparage me with. A couple of fortuitous traditions aided me in my visit. One was the glue that held any military unit together: coffee, aka mud, battery acid, java, joe, or jamoke. The fact that there were all these nicknames testified to how mission critical the stuff was. So, I went to the mandatory pot of brewed coffee and poured myself a mug. Therein, I had a reason, a mandate, to walk to the back of the office and right in front of Konstantin's door.

The second convention was how we addressed one another in the military.

I was a four-star general, the highest routine rank. Senior officers frequently addressed junior officers by their first names. This practice did not give juniors the privilege of addressing their seniors in any way other than by full title. So, I got to annoy the hell out for Konstantin when speaking with him. I called him *Kon*, like that was how he liked to be addressed. I knew, of course, that he *hated* the shortened form. He always insisted that his full first name be used. Unfortunately, one did not insist on anything to a superior officer. One grinned and bore it. He, on the other hand, had to address me as *General Ryan*. If I'd *invited* him to call me Jon, he properly could have. Yeah, kind of hadn't cleared him for such familiarity, yet. Must have slipped my mind. I needed to be more organized, didn't I?

I took my first sip of coffee and rotated to casually scan the room. My eyes met Kon's. I could see his spine snap ten percent stiffer. His anal sphincter probably did, too, but I didn't actually want to check that out to be certain.

"Good morning, Kon," I called out louder than necessary. I was glad Kayla wasn't along for the ride. She'd have kicked me in the shin.

He briefly lowered his head, then stood to greet me.

"General Ryan, nice of you to visit us." Was he being blandly affable, or was he reminding me I'd been AWOL in his reckoning?

"I like to put in an appearance now and then. I know it really boosts the general morale, especially with the younger officers."

We were shaking hands as I said those words. His grip increased, signaling his exasperation with my continued existence. Good.

"That's possible, sir. I'll have to ask around and see if that's the case." Because, he implied if it wasn't, I need never return to darken his doorstep.

"When the OOD's jobs get that easy, maybe I'll put my name on the duty roster again." I smiled real big, like I loved him in a brotherly manner. "I thought the OOD spent their days toiling to save our collective asses from the bad guys."

He cringed. I loved seeing him cringe. My life had meaning when the fart face cringed.

"I'm sure if you spent more time in the office, you'd appreciate that we're focused on exactly that, and that we're very busy at to boot." In other words, if I was ever there, which was actually my job, I'd know what the officer of the day did.

"I've been doing a lot of undercover work. Real secret squirrel type of stuff." I put my index finger across my lips. "Very hush hush. Need to know, and all that."

He winced. I loved seeing that, more than the cringing.

"So, general, can I help you with anything today, or will the cup of joe about do it for you?"

I took an exaggerated sip, then set the mug down. "Good stuff. I was hoping to go over some of the supply reports with you. I know that, technically, that's not in my purview, but I'm a hands-on kind of guy."

Spending the day seated next to me going over dull, pointless reports would be absolute purgatory for the man.

"And call me a traditionalist, but I'd like to run the numbers for the office's petty cash," I added scrutinizing his nose like there was a new form of insect crawling on it. "I learned that little pearl from General Colin Winchester, Royal Regiment of Fusiliers. Did you know him?"

Teeth grinding. *Yes.* My day's work was done.

"Yes, sir. He was my commanding officer up until five years ago, when he retired." Kon lifted a finger pointing to the floor. "I don't re—"

"Damn fine officer. Count yourself among the fortunate, Kon. The man was a credit to detail-minded bureaucrats *everywhere*." By the time I was done rambling, I do believe I had a slight British accent.

"Yes, sir. Thank you."

Why he was thankful I'm certain he couldn't say.

"Before we get going on all that," I said, "I'd like to know if there are any important updates or Charlie foxtrots on the horizon?"

His face steeled. He knew I was messing with him. "Well, sir, I'd invite you to our briefing tomorrow morning if I thought you might attend one. I'm certain your secret-squirrel schedule wouldn't accommodate joining us grunts at the appointed time. I'll be going over just those type of things *then*."

Hmm. Hardass.

"So, I take it there's nothing new or mysterious?"

"That, sir, depends on how one defines those terms, doesn't it? I will present a possible situation on Luhman 16a." He tapped his chin pretending to think. I knew he wasn't thinking because it would have been impossible for the Neanderthal. "Say, you visited there a long time ago, didn't you?"

I nodded softly.

"You might want to try and attend. Just a thought."

He saluted, which one never did indoors. It was his way of saying we're done talking.

I didn't bother returning his salute. "I'll check in with the squirrel. Maybe see you tomorrow."

I said goodbye to the gunny at the front desk and headed home. I hadn't thought about Luhman 16a for a hundred years. Picturing those silly Sarcorit and Jinicgus did put a smile on my face. I had to wonder what their planet had to do with the price of tea in China, however.

THREE

Oelcir lolled in the gentle surf near a beach protected from the bigger waves by a rocky tombolo. The water was warm. The air, what little he could tolerate, was hot and dry. It felt good on his scales during the brief periods when he hefted his torso from the sea. Leisure was bitterly discouraged by Listhelon culture. Odidast, the current ruler, specifically raged against it. A fish not swimming with purpose could not give maximum glory to Gumnolar or his servant, Warrior One.

But, Oelcir understood that what no one else knew could not hurt him. Plus, his pod, *Gumnolar's Vision*, had lived in the shallow waters near these dry lands for countless generations. The barren was part of their domain. There was great wisdom, he had decided, in keeping an eye sprout on it to see if changes occurred that might displease Gumnolar. So he was entitled to monitor the dry land. He was doing Gumnolar's bidding.

Deep water pods, by far the largest and most dominant form, were able to afford fewer liberties. Most members were ranchers, involved in herding and culling the enormous schools of fish needed to sustain those pod. The shallows' podlets, derogatorily dubbed *belly-scrapers*, hunted more than farmed. Small groups might seek prey together, but lone hunting was a common practice, too. So Oelcir had easy access to stealing away and relaxing, if he was careful. He'd collect shellfish and crustaceans galore, so no one complained about him not carrying his weight. Why the others of Gumnolar's Vision didn't avail themselves of the bounty tied to the barren was beyond his understanding. They were afraid of ground not covered by water. How silly.

Dirt was dirt and rocks were rocks no matter what their water content was.

Occasionally, he could talk a friend into coming with him, but they almost never came twice. The sight of the barren burned their eye stalks and the scentless air was repulsive to their sensitivities. Oh well, their loss was his gain. How many other servants of Gumnolar could say they'd spent half the cyclet sleeping, relaxing, and spouting water into the air? Life was good, if you allowed it to be.

Oelcir even daydreamed. Yes, such a thing was unthinkable for most fish, laboring and wearing their tail fins off. He daydreamed of many things, but mostly he imagined bringing a female to a place like this. Here, secluded, unwitnessed, and relaxed, he might discharge his sperm sack onto her egg port. Yes, such a blasphemous thought was enough to cause one's immediate death and permanent relegation to the service of the Beast Without Eyes. But it might *just* be worth the price. He didn't really want to spawn. But to know milting with a female? That was an exciting prospect. His daydreams were often both rushed and repeated frequently.

He splashed loudly into the water and swam to scoop up a few hard-shelled treats to nibble on. It did take him longer than it used to. Odd. One or two cycles ago, the hard shells veritably crawled into his mouth, they were so plentiful. Now he had to hunt in water deeper than he used to and it definitely took longer to find fewer numbers of hard shells. In fact, there were far fewer fish in the shallows near shore. At least, it seemed that way to Oelcir.

He'd thought to discuss his observation with one of Odidast thinkers but decided against it. He was curious, but if it seemed he knew too much about matters so close to shore, he might raise suspicion. Suspicion was poison in Listhelon society. He did not desire poison, thank you very much. It would—

A massive paw slammed huge claws deep into Oelcir's shoulder. Pain shot across his back and up the side of his neck. Strength beyond his comprehension lifted him from the sea like he was no more than a large sponge. He flew, an unknown experience to him up until then, through the air like he had sprouted wings. He thudded onto the rocky recess formed by several boulders jammed together, and rolled onto his back.

Oelcir was horrified to see the immense striped land beast spring onto his chest and bury its jaws in his throat, ripping into his gills like they were gossamer. The last vision he had before the darkness of Gumnolar embraced him was that of two juvenile land monsters fighting each other for purchase on his face.

After the meal, her family's first proper meal in weeks, Taliadar preened her kittens in the warm sun. They rolled and played, alternating bites to the other cub's neck with preening of their own. This was Taliadar's third litter on this pitiful watery world. She knew, however, that she was lucky. She had been assigned to a planet with no land sentients. It was very easy to remain hidden. Also, with almost no large land animals, there was no real competition for the plentiful small creatures they consumed. Still, she caught one of the big fish so infrequently, it was hard to know a full, swollen belly. She missed that, in general, but not that day. That was a good day. Praise be to Erratarus and the empire.

FOUR

Okay, the SOB Timoshenko got me. I had to attend the briefing. It wasn't like I was going on a mission. If I was up for that, I'd have been notified beforehand, and, of course, I would have gone to the damn briefing. But, with five or six careers of briefings under my belt, I didn't make it a habit of going for the free donuts and joe alone. Like any proper briefing, it was scheduled much earlier than it needed to be. Military tradition. As I didn't sleep, the early hour didn't bother me. It was just annoying.

I joined the line waiting to get coffee and greeted the pilots near me. Most were cordial enough, though some seemed to wander away rather quickly. Did I have BO? I knew, of course, I was the general android they were hoping to avoid. Way back when, there was a TV show called *Star Trek: The Next Generation*. There was this anemic looking android officer who wanted, like Pinocchio, to be human. His status in that regard was often ambiguous. I thought I was mixed up in that kind of existential muddle in my compatriot's minds. I'd been nothing but nice to them. I never once waved my arms in the air and yelled, *Danger, Will Robinson*. But, small-minded people were always overly-abundant.

I did bump into one of my actual friends, fortunately. In the twisted knot of fate that governed our lives, Molly Hatcher was bound to me. She was Kendra's daughter. Kendra, the hard case who was on my mission to test the validity of our Berrillian hack. It turned out Mandy Walker and Kendra really hit it off. They were married a year or so after I introduced them. Their daughter grew up to be a pilot. She was the newbie flight suit insert assigned to the same unit I was. I'd known her since she was knee high to a toadstool and was proud to serve with her. She was good people. Smart and kind, but as tough as her old lady.

"Moll-doll," I said in greeting. That was my nickname for her since she was a baby.

"Uncle Jon," she said by way of retribution, "didn't we discuss not calling me that in the presence of a bunch of hot-headed jet jockeys who are just looking for something to tease me about?"

"Hmm," I feigned uncertainty. "I might recall such a request. Not sure."

"Well, General Ryan, please make a note of it now."

"I'll try," I replied with a wink. "So how are your moms?"

"They're wonderfully well. I do believe they also made a similar request not to be referred to as *my moms*."

"No? Are you certain?" I couldn't suppress a big smile.

She smiled right back.

"So, are you slated to go anywhere fun or dangerous today?" I asked.

"Yes. A risky routine patrol of the Alpha Quadrant. I'm anticipating a violent death by midday."

"Nice. Best of luck with that." The Alpha was the dullest, most lifeless, worthless piece of real estate imaginable. No one would fight to control it. Repeating the words *Alpha Quadrant* was a trick people used to help fall asleep faster. It beat the hell out of counting sheep.

"How 'bout you? Going off to save our asses today?"

"No, your ass is in someone else's hands today. If I catch him, by the by, I'm putting a hurt on him."

"I'll be sure to warn him well in advance. Probably help if I found a guy first."

"Let's keep it that way, young lady."

"Uncle Jon, I think I'm a big girl and don't need a chaperone for the rest of my life."

"I look at you, and all I see is a skinny legged girl with braces."

"People," called out Major General Faiza Hijab, the current CO of TCY. "If you could find a seat so we can get going."

Faiza was an okay CO. At least she wasn't a prejudiced oxygen thief like

Timoshenko. She did hold me at arm's length, but that was understandable. Not only did I outrank her, I was a legend. Nobody wanted to command someone like that. Plus, I was me, the loose-cannon wiseass. Her career didn't need me and would hopefully survive me, so she treated me with kid gloves. She also didn't push to have me be very active in terms of assignments. From time to time, I'd press her for missions, which she would then hand out. But when I stopped nagging, they dried up. I wasn't sure if it was a hint that I should seek reassignment, or whether it was just caution on her part. I'd find that out if and when our guerrilla war with the Berrillians ever heated up. Then, I'd better not be left behind like some useless pogue. I wasn't about to stay behind, selling war bonds to the Knights of Columbus.

"We have a lot to cover, so I'll get started. If possible, hold your questions until I'm done. That way we'll move along a bit quicker."

Yeah, that last comment was probably directed at yours truly, famous as I was for piping off whenever the spirit moved me.

"You've all seen the duty roster. If you've been assigned to a mission, please see your squad leader after this briefing. So, interesting development in Beta Quadrant to present. Intel reports the locals on LH 16a are finding a number of dead Berrillians. Rotting ones, actually. In the last two months, they've found several hundred dead cats hidden away in caves, abandoned buildings, and otherwise remote locations."

"Sir," interrupted one of the squadron leaders, "excuse me, but how are they finding dead cats under deep cover?"

"All the sentients there, especially the Sarcorit, have acute senses of smell," I answered totally out of turn. "They can mark an offensive odor twenty-five klicks away."

"Is that why they took such a strong objection to you, Ryan, and tried to get you off their rock?" said George Updyke. He particularly disliked me.

"Yeah, they said I smelled like your butt. Mentioned Uptight Updyke by name. It was so weird, 'cause you weren't even, like, born yet at the time."

Okay, not my most clever retort. But a digs a dig.

"Gentlemen, and I use that term loosely, that will be enough," said a highly displeased Faiza.

"Sorry," I responded. "I still have some trouble communicating with shavetails. Trying to speak their tongue is hard. Guess I'm not dumb enough."

George actually lunged toward me. Granted, it was only about five centimeters, but it was an angry five centimeters.

"Are we done here, General?" asked Faiza. "Or do I have time to go grab another cup of joe while you Bob Hope the troops?"

Bob Hope the troops? That was great. I had to remember that one.

"Of course, ma'am. Again, sorry."

"As I was saying, they've found several hundred. We offered mutual aid to help in the search, but typical of all the tiny species involved, they declined."

"Stupid donuts," said a junior officer. "We should eat them, not kowtow to them."

"Yeah," said Konstantin, "we're trying to survive, and they're getting all territorial and pissy. It isn't right."

"That will do it. This is not, in case you've forgotten, a democracy. You're in the Army now. I do the thinking, you do the jumping. Is everyone clear on the roles here?" responded Faiza.

No one replied.

"Thank you. The point is, we're in communication with both the Sarcorit and the Jinicgus. They've promised to keep us—"

"Ma'am," I said raising my hand.

"Yes, General Ryan. What is it now?"

"I was wondering why a bunch of Berrillians suddenly up and died on LH 16a."

"I'm confident the intel people will let us know—"

"They're tough as nails. I've never heard of them dropping like flies. In fact, I've never heard of a disease among them, not even the common cold."

"Perhaps you could speak with Colonel Hanson in Intel Ops after we're done, assuming, of course, I'm allowed to—"

"The locals didn't kill the cats. For one thing, they're too scared to even think about a Berrillian, and for another, they wouldn't leave the dead cats to rot."

"Maybe the Berrillians died of boredom because someone was—"

"So, how'd they die? And why now, and not last month or last year?"

I pulled up the schematics of the Beta Quadrant in my head. Three dimensionally, LH 16a was near the Berrillian border—that is, the space under their tight control after the defeat of The Last Nightmare. It was a logical place to infiltrate for the Empire. Hmm.

"I'd like to continue, if it's—"

"If I were Erratarus, I'd probably try and set up a covert ops base on LH 16a. It's close to them and advances them toward the Alliance."

"If you were Erratarus, you'd be a whole lot prettier," sniped George.

"So, Georgie Porgie likes his cats, does he? Oh purr," I said kind of blowing the purr his way.

"That's about all the insubordination I'm willing to overlook," snapped Faiza. "General Ryan, if you have a point you feel you must share, please do so now. Mr. Updyke, I'll see you in my office immediately after the conclusion of this briefing, assuming, of course, there *is* a conclusion."

I ignored her anger, which was likely mostly for show in the first place. Plus, what was she going to do? Put me on KP peeling spuds?

"I posit that the Local Indigenous Populations of LH 16a are toxic to the Faxél," I said intently. "That is both a new piece of information concerning our enemy, and it reveals something of their strategy."

Faiza stared at me, uncertain what to say.

"Don't you see? Erratarus is infiltrating the Beta Quadrant. He's sending covert operatives there to establish a beachhead for the real war. If you send thousands of big carnivores to a planet, sooner than later they'll have to start foraging to survive. The tiny LIPS are easy prey for them, and they're as plentiful as grains of sand in your crotch after a day at the beach."

There were scattered chuckles at that comparison.

"The bodies would have to have been dead two, maybe three weeks to work up a good stink. They must have been infiltrated a few weeks before that. Their initial supplies would probably last about that long. They'd be traveling light. So we know two more things. No, three. We know they entered the Beta Quadrant six weeks ago. That means they're on the move. And we know there was little to no chatter about this on their network, otherwise we'd have heard beforehand. That means we know they're either suspicious, or simply have a second communication network we were unaware of."

"General Ryan," said Faiza, "where are you getting this? I announce a handful of rotting Berrillians and you conclude they're onto our hack? I think—"

"But you can't have a network you don't talk about. That's lame. So, there must be another entire system. The infiltration efforts are one of three things. They could be autonomous units run off-grid. They might be an underground cell of dissidents acting. Worst case, they're on to us and not chattering about really important stuff. Now, I can't believe that an organized resistance would survive in that brutal society. The flow of traffic we're decoding hasn't shifted at all, so I can't buy that they're on to us. It must be that Erratarus has set up the infiltration unit as a separate entity, with its own command and control. But why?"

"General Ryan, this is all very interesting, but shouldn't you be addressing these ideas—"

"Can't be a trust issue. If Erratarus was suspicious of another cat, he'd eat their heart and be done stressing. Can't be he worries his code is vulnerable. If he was concerned, he'd have it replaced periodically. Set it and forget it is what they've done. Maybe he's established a long-term effort and is letting someone else actually run it? Like the garbage collection or dog catcher? Maybe. But this is an important part of his plan for conquest. Of course, he'd know what the infiltration units were doing. The communications would just have to be so easy, they'd wouldn't *need* to be transmitted."

I snapped my fingers.

"The guerrilla unit is run by one of his *sons*. That's it. When Erratarus wants an update all he needs to do is ask his son over to tea and crumpets. But which son or sons? No, can't be sons. Too much fighting between the males. Two sons could never work together. It would be … the son we never hear about. Claudus. Yes, he's at court. We know that. But he's never talked about much. People assume that's because he's useless, stupid, or not trustworthy. But if he was one of those, he'd be dead, dead, or dead. So, I doubt he's a total tool."

I looked up at Faiza.

"Isn't this the juncture where you try and have me shut up, and I cut you off rudely?"

"It was. I gave up. Go on."

I noticed then she'd sat down during my rant.

"You know, General Ryan, you're as good as your reputation suggests. It's remarkable you could deduce all that from a random scrap of intel."

"Why, thank you, General Hijab. That's kind of you to say."

She turned to a computer and typed a few words.

"There. I made it official."

"What's that, ma'am?" I asked.

"I've assigned you to the mission to LH 16a, scheduled to leave as soon as we're done."

"I was unaware there was such a mission," I responded evenly. "In fact, wasn't there some mention of the LIPs forbidding us from coming?" I shook my head. "You wouldn't want a diplomatic mess on your hands, would you Faiza?"

"One, the mission is related to your gathering of historic artifacts, not investigating the Berrillian deaths. Two, I'm sending you. No matter how determined they are to keep outsiders off their soil, you'll break them. You most certainly will."

"Historic artifacts? What tchotchkes are you talking about?"

"I've assigned you to collect details and objects documenting your historic first contact with the great people, or whatever, of LH 16a. We're starting a museum in your honor."

"We are? I was unaware of such a monument."

"We aren't, you ego maniac. Get over yourself," she replied trying not to smile. "But it sounds better that way.

"Have you assigned the rest of my team yet?"

"The mighty Jonathan Ryan needs help with anything? Alert the media. This is big," she said, not able to suppress a grin.

"Someone has to carry all the crap. We legends need to keep our hands free for shaking and kissing babies."

"Speak to the duty officer when we're done. He'll assign you as many wingmen as you require."

"Just one'll do, and she's a wingwoman."

"I think we're done here. I need to find some aspirins," Faiza announced.

I turned to Molly, who was sitting next to me. "You ready to meet some walking donuts and hot dogs? They're cute, but man, are they ever pissy."

FIVE

Molly was shocked and flattered that I selected her to join me. As the newest Form in the squadron, she only got the table scraps in terms of assignments. To venture into a potentially hostile alien world on a covert mission was a dream come true. Hey, as they always said, it wasn't *what* you knew, but *who* you knew. I had my goddaughter's back. I just had to remind myself not to be too openly familiar with her. If she was known as my friend, many of her peers would immediately dislike her.

Before we shoved off, Molly let Kendra and Mandy know about the mission, at least the parts she could tell them. That produced instant angst in Mandy. She knew me well. Where I went, if there wasn't trouble, I made some. Kendra, on the other hand, had only one word for her daughter. *Oorah.* Yeah, she knew me well, too.

"So, we're taking *Wrath*, right?" she asked me as we entered the vortex hangar.

"No, captain. You're a Form now. You fly *Expectation*. She's your ship. When you go on any mission, you insist on fling your baby. No more ride alongs, Space-A."

"Oh, okay. Sure." Good kid. She hated being wrong, as much as I did.

"So how are you and *Expectation* getting along?"

"Great. She's like my BFF already. I think she was so bored sitting idle for all those years, she'd be happy having a dill pickle as her Form."

"Funny, I never knew until recently there were different sexes in cubes. I assumed they were all male."

"Well, Uncle Jon, that's because *you're* a sexist pig. And I mean that in its nicest sense. We do so love you, in spite your handicaps, you know?"

"Insulting a superior officer right outta the gate. I can see you're not long for TCY."

"Ah, higher ranked, sure. But *superior*? No kind of way."

"Not one chance in a million you last a year. You can lead a horse to water, but in the end you're standing next to a horse's ass the entire time."

"Gosh, Hunka, that's inspiringly brilliant. By the way, that's not, if you had not yet figured it out, the end by which one *leads* a horse. I always figured you were always as dumb as a doormat and it would seem I am correctomundo."

She called me Hunka before she could correctly pronounce the word *uncle*.

I pushed her toward *Expectation* with a gentle shove. "Have your cube chitchat with mine to arrive at the same location above Reglic. We'll coordinate our landing once we've announced our presence."

She saluted me, then punched my shoulder just before she backed out of range.

I decided to start by contacting the Jinicgus since they were the ones I was friendliest with on my short visit centuries ago. I was banking on them remembering that I gifted them the leader of their sworn enemies, and his son. We parted on neutral, if not positive terms, but I'd never been in contact with them again. Once we could move freely with the folding of space, worldfleet diplomats had established formal relationships with several races on LH 16a. Fortunately, I was not involved in those tedious loops.

The only fellow I'd really interacted with among the Jinicgus was named Zirzjincus. I had no idea if he was still alive, let alone in power. It seemed unlikely that they would live that long, but I had no real idea. Once Molly and I were in orbit above LH 16a, I contacted the ground. The central government of the Jinicgus was in a city named Draldore. I connected with their space affairs group to explain why we were there.

"Hello, this is Jon Ryan of the human worldship fleet. I am here on an academic mission and would like permission to land."

"Roplins of the Jinicgus Federation here. We are unaware of such a mission.

Please have the proper forms forwarded for consideration. Goodbye."

Ah, the unfriendly creatures of LH 16a. Didn't miss them a bit. But I couldn't let them dismiss me out of hand.

"Ah, I am looking for an individual named Zirzjincus. I met him when I was here a long time ago. He can vouch for me. I am the one who turned Tersfeller the Huge over to him."

There was a pause.

"The gift is recalled. The person you mention is long dead. File the proper forms and await a determination. Goodbye."

"Doesn't the fact that I proved myself a friend give me any credit? I only want to document my visit to your world. It would take—"

"*Goodbye* is usually a universal message. It means, in this case, stop talking and depart."

Not an option.

"I wouldn't want to land without your blessing. I could contact the Sarcorit nation and ask for their help, but I consider your nation to be my ally."

Again, a pause. "You may not land without permission. We received a request from your government and informed them they were not welcome. We cannot stop you from contacting our sworn enemies. I say again, goodbye."

"The request from my government was to investigate the Berrillian deaths. I am not connected to that effort. I am here on a historical mission of documentation."

"Then that is what your formal request should state. Once received, the request will be acted on within a few weeks."

"I'd like to speak to your supervisor." I was at a loss. It was a pretty lame ploy.

"You what? Why would you wish to speak with my director?"

"I am hoping he or she better recall my contributions to your society and will grant me permission to land."

"But I said you could not. My job is to allow, or not allow, off-worlders to land. What relevance might he have?"

"He might override your determination."

The reaction I got back was akin to one I might expect, if I'd suggested he light himself on fire.

"Override? Are you mentally incompetent? He would say the same thing I did. It is the *law*."

"Then you won't mind having him tell me himself, will you?"

"If that is what it will take to end this communication, I will alert him."

There was dead air for a minute or so, then a new voice spoke.

"Rotsheack speaking. What is the meaning of interrupting me from my job to ask me to do another's assigned duties? This is beyond extraordinary."

"I am—"

"I know fully who you claim to be. The fact that you surrendered our enemy to us years ago has no bearing on whether you may or may not land."

"So, you're saying the Jinicgus have no regard for their friends. They refuse to honor a bond?"

Really, I was stabbing the dark so hard I think it was bleeding.

"Is it your intention to insult me as well as my race?"

"No, of course not. I just want to confirm that loyalty is *not* a quality of the Jinicgus."

They were such a stick-up-the-butt species, I hoped that constituted a slap in the face.

"I am outraged—"

Without warning, his transmission ended. Then, a third voice established contact and spoke.

"General Ryan, this is Gortantor. I am military governor of the Jinicgus. I was made aware of your request and have taken the liberty of dismissing Rotsheack's well-intentioned but unhelpful input."

Wow, this guy spoke like a normal person. That meant he was a politician. Oh well, any port in a storm.

"Thank you. I was hoping to—"

"I was informed as to the nature of your request. I would consider it an honor to receive you and discuss if such a thing is possible. Please proceed to the coordinates I shall send. We may meet at your earliest convenience."

Great. Too hard or too easy. I was thinking I liked it the other way, but then again, we were going to land.

"My associate and I will be there in an hour."

"Fine." The transmission was terminated.

"Not exactly a hero's welcome, was it?" asked Molly.

"Didn't expect one, but it would have been nice."

"I'm sure you'll win them over. You always do."

"Yeah, maybe. I wish it could be easy for once, you know?"

"Nah, you like it the hard way. That way your legend grows."

"Remind me to tell your moms how mean you were to me when we get home."

"No prob, Huncka."

We took *Shearwater* down. I wanted the ability to remotely control her, if things got dicey. Several cute little sausages met us. One held a flag on a long pole with a fanciful image of a large sausage. Maybe it was king dog. It did make my stomach rumble, thinking about a big old hotdog smothered in kraut, mustard, and onions.

"Hi—" I said, but I wasn't allowed to finish my greeting.

"You will follow us."

They turned and walked away. No nonsense fellows, to be sure.

I shrugged to Molly, and follow we did. The walk to Gortantor's place was short as measured in human steps. The building we arrived at was huge by local standards, which allowed us to enter easily. The guards left us in an open room, maybe a ballroom or auditorium. It was big and full of little pieces of furniture. I had no clue how some functioned. Gortantor entered shortly after we did.

"Welcome, my friends," he said. "I'd offer you a seat, but without advanced notice of your visit, that will be impossible."

"Not a problem. May we sit on the floor?" I asked. It was best to give the appearance of being casual.

"By all means. May I offer you refreshment?"

"No, thank you," replied Molly.

"Ah, I do not believe we've been introduced. Are you Ryan's mate?"

Molly tried not to wince, but did, in spite of herself.

"This is my assistant on this mission, Molly Hatcher."

"Do you hold military rank as Ryan does?" he asked insightfully.

"Yes, I'm a captain in our air defense force."

"Is that a particularly high rank?" he asked.

"No, sir. I'm new to the service."

"Ah, well, good luck with your career. Perhaps it will be as long and as impressive as Ryan's here."

Gortantor was one smooth talker. It was driving me nuts trying to figure out his angle. Every other sentient on LH 16a was as ill-tempered as a wet warthog being beaten with a stick.

"Thank you," she said.

"So, I have to thank you for meeting with us to discuss our cultural mission. I'm hoping you will be able to allow us to proceed unencumbered."

"Unencumbered? Your goals are lofty, Ryan. You arrive unannounced and without clearance. You are two military officers representing yourselves as historians. You wish unfettered access to our world shortly after permission to investigate a possible Berrillian incursion was denied to your government. You strain my credulity, new friend."

"The fact that we did not seek permission in advance was, in hindsight, unfortunate. I can only state that the mission was planned at the last minute. The rest, the matter of the Berrillians, is by chance alone."

"A gambler might accept that notion, but I am not the betting sort. Those in power, at least on this world, rarely are."

"Be that as it may, I trust you will grant us access based, if nothing else, on my record as a friend."

"Ah yes, the matter of Tersfeller the Huge and his idiot son. Do you know what happened after you presented them to my predecessors?"

"No, in fact. I do not."

"It was an interesting gesture on your part, to be certain. Unfortunately, after the pair was desecrated and dismembered, those who subsequently took charge became extremely enraged. They bombed my country with a ferocity we had never experienced. Millions died as a direct result of your gift."

"I turned them over. I'm not responsible for the repercussions."

"Be that as it may, the results somewhat negate our appreciation of your act."

"If I might," said Molly, "I would like to discuss a matter where my colleague and I differ."

Huh? What could we possibly differ on? I was a general and in command. She was a junior officer. In the military, we always said shit rolled downhill, never up. We couldn't differ, because my word was law.

"Why, yes. It would be refreshing to hear from someone with a clean slate," Gortantor responded.

"General Ryan is of the opinion that our history-gathering mission would best be accomplished if we worked alone. I am of the opinion that our task would be much easier if we had local input. I suggested we ask that a significant number of locals be provided to help us. He disagrees passionately. What is your opinion on that matter?"

He looked at her a while. I could hear the gears whirring in his tiny head.

"I must agree with you that local guides would make your job more doable. I like your approach, captain."

"Then you'll be willing to offer such cooperation to assist us?" she asked quickly.

"That is not what I said."

"I'm sorry. I thought I heard that you'd rather work with us from a position of control rather than risk us working in a manner out of your control. I apologize for my presumption."

The kid was smart. Ballsy too.

He stared at her a while longer.

"I would be honored to personally direct the team that will guide you on your quest to gather historic documentation. Shall we begin at first light tomorrow?

"That would be great," I responded. "Where shall we meet?"

"Your encounter with Zirzjincus took place in a small town not far from here. You will be supplied the coordinates. We shall rendezvous there."

"Thank you. That is most kind of you," I nodded my head at him.

"Until tomorrow, then," he replied, rising to his multitudinous feet.

SIX

Bright and early, Molly and I landed at the spot where I had set down years before with my Sarcorit prisoners. A large contingent of troops were already in a vast formation around that central square. Clearly, Gortantor was taking no chances that our "history gathering" would get out of hand. He was determined to limit our movements to only areas that suited him. Realistically, I could have obliterated the entire force with *Wrath*, or maybe even done so single-handedly, but those weren't real options. Still, it galled me to be constrained by an inferior force acting with unneighborly intent. One might assume that with my centuries of maturing, I might have moved beyond such a bull-headed stance, but come on, we were talking Jon here.

"This is where you delivered the Sarcorit to us. Please collect whatever data you desire and then leave," said Gortantor.

"Well, sure, and thanks. But there are many other sites we need to document also," I replied trying to sound confused.

"No," was his terse response.

"But you said we could have access to the areas I visited."

"And this is the only place where you met with my people."

"No," I lied. "There were the parades and my tours of outlying villages. The festivities went on for days. You know that, right?"

"There are no records of such extended movements, Ryan. I believe you are trying to deceive me."

"Hey, the fact that your side lost the records doesn't mean the events didn't happen. I will be highly insulted if you go back on your word."

"You try my patience too much. I will now ask—"

"I told you that you were pushing this good friend too far," scolded Molly.

Ah, where did *that* come from? I was, however, willing to play along, since it sounded pretty certain the dude was about to blow us off.

"I told you, *I'm* in charge. I will not tolerate your insubordination any longer."

"We know you visited several sites in the interior, but if Gortantor says *no*, he means *no*. What's wrong with you? Everyday I come to believe that you are not as loyal to our government and its plans as you should be."

"I have half a mind to leave you here with your new buddies. I don't need your nagging any longer. I'm negotiating with an alien leader. You will remain silent. Am I *perfectly* clear?"

"No, Ryan, *you're* the alien here. This is his home. It's all their homes. If Gortantor says we can only document this spot, then this spot is all I wish to document."

"When we get home, I'll see you severely punished for your interference with this mission. If it fails, it will be your fault." I pointed an angry finger at her for effect. I also hoped she had an idea where this was going.

"Your mission, Ryan, *has* failed. But it is your doing, not this fine officer's," said Gortantor.

"I need to finish scolding her. If you could hold on a second. Then you and I can return to our negotiations."

"You and I will negotiate *nothing*. I will listen to what the woman has to say, but you will not be party to our discussion."

I turned to Molly. "You've stabbed me in the back for the last time. I—"

"Ryan, if you do not silence yourself immediately, I will have you shot. Do I make myself clear?" Gortantor sounded very serious.

"I will be in the ship," I responded. "When I return, we'd better be allowed to perform this important mission."

I stormed away.

"You and your superior seem not to agree much," he remarked to Molly after I sealed *Shearwater's* hatch.

He was unaware that I could hear whatever they said. Robot ears were good ears.

"We don't. He represents the *old* way of doing things. I believe these are new times and they require a new vision. Intimidation and conquering are not the way to achieve a peaceful future."

"How very wise for one so young. I agree with you."

"I wish to apologize for his actions. I will do my best to control him when he returns. If it is your wish that we leave, please know that I will do what I can to see that we will."

"You cannot apologize for another. Only *he* can confess his errors."

"True, but I do feel badly for the people I represent."

"That is sufficient for me, captain."

"If it's all right, why don't I start collecting the images we came for. If we cannot document Ryan's entire visit, then that must do."

"Where, exactly, was he supposed to have traveled?"

"I know the names, but they mean nothing to me. Jockoren, Scizlowa, and the wastelands of Morepatop."

"How odd that we have no records," replied Gortantor.

"It was long ago. Memories fade, and records are lost. You said there was a vicious reprisal after Ryan delivered his prisoners. Much was destroyed. It's perfectly understandable."

"Those first two names are towns nearby. The wasteland, however, is far from here. I cannot imagine why Ryan might have been taken to such a remote and barren place."

"He told me he wanted to collect geological samples."

"And did he?"

"Yes, but they were subsequently lost. It would have been nice to reacquire some to complete the story of his journey, but if we can't, we can't."

"Perhaps the two of you can't, but *you* may."

"I beg your pardon?"

"I will not allow Ryan to soil my domain, but I will consider it an honor to lead someone as far-thinking as yourself there."

"Oh," she covered her mouth, "I could never do that. He'd have my head. He's paranoid, and he's cruel."

"I would offer to send a full report of your cooperation and his hostility to your government, if that might help lessen his wrath."

"I could never ask that of you," she said in a hush.

"No, but I can freely offer it. I, like you, look to a peaceful and profitable future. I think we are able to aide one another."

"I am flattered, but I could not mislead you. I am a very junior officer with no diplomatic connections. I promise you nothing of substance in return for your trust."

"Nonsense. This is how useful bonds are forged. I help you, and you help me. It would be extremely valuable to have a trusted friend among what has been an otherwise seemingly hostile government."

"Well, I could at least do my best. But we're getting ahead of ourselves. I have a mission that I must complete as best I can. Ryan will return shortly. If I've … oh, here he comes now."

"Ryan," said Gortantor before I could speak, "I will be escorting the captain to the wastelands of Morepatop. You will remain here and collect what samples you'd like. After you're done, you may proceed to Jockoren and Scizlowa under heavy guard. There will be no negations on this arrangement."

"What … I … how can—" I tried to seem flustered. It was hard because we fighter pilots, well, we don't fluster.

"Silence," the little guy said. "We will depart at once. The captain will take us in her personal vessel. She said it is in obit. Help her retrieve it at once. That way my new friend can store all the samples she wishes to extract. When we return, I'd better find you in one of the three specific areas I have granted you permission to visit. Do not test me, Ryan. If you do, there will be trouble."

I started to protest but slumped in silent resignation instead. All right, Molly. She at least got into the hinterlands like we'd schemed to go. It was a weird-ass step, but at least it was a step. Better than being kicked back into space empty handed. My immediate concern then became what I was going to survey and collect. I had to look busy, interested, and productive. Argh.

Molly and Gortantor left directly after she landed with *Expectation*. They were accompanied by a small contingent of guards. I guess I should have said a *limited* contingent of *small* guards, to be more clear. They all piled onto *Expectation* and it vanished.

34

Molly set a course for the far reaches of the wasteland. We'd reasoned that the farther out we looked, the greater our chances would be of finding some trace of the dead Berrillians. What she did when she hit the ground was fully up to her at that point. Playing life by ear was the truest test of a good officer. We were about to test my goddaughter's mettle.

SEVEN

Once she opened a portal, first the the guards, and then the Gortantor and Molly stepped out onto a very desolate, bleak expanse of nothingness. As a space-born, she'd never been in a proper desert. The guards fanned out around the ship, establishing a defensive perimeter. What they were defending against was unclear to her, since the place was so barren.

"As you see, Captain, there is little in Morepatop, and even less that warrants documentation. However, my friend, feel free to explore. Do remain close the enclosure my soldiers have formed. There are a few lethal creatures out here. I'd hate for any harm to come to you."

"Fine. Can we go over there?" she asked pointing at a rocky outcropping.

"A bit far, but If it is your wish, proceed."

He pointed at his troops and then at the rock mound. They scurried ahead to reconnoiter the area. Molly took the initiative and followed them closely. If there was anything to be found, she wanted to be there before it was covered up.

The guards were sprinting, Molly walking at a modest clip, and Gortantor was dropping back conspicuously. Deconditioning or decorum prevented him from keeping up, but he probably figured calling them all back would only make his shortcomings that much more obvious. That's when Molly caught her first break. The gap between the two groups finally grew too large for Gortantor's comfort. He squealed a cry to have them fall back to protect him. They did, but Molly broke into a jog. Gortantor called out for her to stop, but she pretended not to hear him or even notice the guards had withdrawn.

As she hit the rocky slope, Molly began to sprit. She knew the little devils would have the hardest time matching her pace there and wanted to buy enough time before they arrived, so she could poke about. Near the irregular top of the hillock, she heard a sound and froze. She whirled around in a full circle, but saw nothing. Then the sound repeated. It wasn't movement. It was panting; rapid, shallow panting, interrupted by moans. Molly bent and twisted until she located the direction the noises came from. There was a thin crack of an opening to a recess behind a mound of boulders, possibly a small cave.

She knew the sounds weren't coming from a Jinicgus. They were too deep and reverberated too much. Knowing a Berrillian could be the source, she swung her rail rifle off her shoulder and pointed it to the opening. She inched forward slowly. The guard detail began their assent, shouting loud enough that it would be impossible for Molly to claim she couldn't hear them. Pressed for time, she entered the recess more quickly than she'd like to have. She didn't have time to snap her flashlight onto her weapon, so she was forced to hold it in one hand as she advanced.

Sweeping the darkness, at first all she saw was scattered rubble and debris. Nothing that couldn't be there by chance. Then she caught sight of a scrap of cloth. It appeared to have been torn from a large garment, much larger than the locals would require. It had to be alien. The panting grew a little louder but was still faint. Then Molly heard a growl. She froze. Her light and barrel swung to her right. The hind feet of a Berrillian were clearly visible angling around a rock. The rest of the cat was out of sight. She could hear the Jinicgus guards nearing the opening.

"I'm Captain Kendrick of the human worldship fleet. I have you covered. Show yourself slowly. No sudden moves, or you're dead." She spoke through the same translator in her helmet she was using to converse with the locals. It reset automatically to Berrillian.

At first there was no change in the panting, then it stopped. It was followed by a gasping sound. One foot moved slightly.

"I repeat, show yourself, or I *will* shoot."

Molly picked up a stone and tossed it against one of the paws.

Aside from a reflex tick of the foot, nothing moved.

Gortantor's voice boomed from the entrance. "Captain, please come out at once. You are in possible danger. Come out at once."

"Sorry," she called over a shoulder without turning her head, "no can do. I've got my rifle trained on a Berrillian. I don't come out until it surrenders, or is dead."

"Captain, it is not your place to do that. I reign here. My team will enter and subdue the alien. Back toward me."

"I cannot guarantee their safety. If they enter and I start shooting, they're likely to get hit."

All the shouting had no effect on the Berrillian. The feet remained limp and motionless.

Molly advanced and kicked a foot hard. That brought a loud growl. The feet slid on the dirt, trying to push forward. After a moment, all they could muster was to relax back to limpness. Either the cat was putting on quite the performance, or it was gravely ill. As dead men told no tales, so a dead Berrillian would yield no useful intel. Molly angled around the rock gun first, which revealed more and more of the body. Finally, she viewed the head.

The female Berrillian was on her side, head on the ground, with her tongue lolling out weakly in the dirt. Molly took a moment to inspect the cat. She was emaciated. Ribs showed through, and her legs were spindles, without the typical powerful musculature. The Berrillian was starving to death, and was nearly there.

Molly poked the head with the tip of her weapon. "Can you hear me?" she asked loudly.

The head remained on the floor, but it did swivel a little.

"Can you get up? Can you stand?"

The she-cat finally spoke. "No. Let me die."

I one fluid movement, Molly set her rifle on the ground, drew her canteen from her belt, and raised the head with her left forearm. It wasn't easy, given the massive skull, but she could lift and angle the mouth enough to pour water into the cat's mouth. At first her prisoner gagged and coughed, but slowly it began gulping down the water. Molly emptied the container.

At that point, a tight-knit formation of Jinicgus stepped up to Molly's side, with Gortantor a few paces behind their wall.

"Captain, I order you to step clear and leave. My team must execute this invader. If you do not move, you will be shot also."

Oh well, Molly reflected to herself, *so much for my new alliance with Gortantor.*

"Okay. I will withdraw," she replied. "Let me get my gun and—"

"No. We fire in ten seconds, whether you're clear or not."

"But, Gortantor, there's a problem with that," said Molly, not turning from the Berrillian whose head rested on her lap.

"What possible problem?"

"In *five* seconds, I'll have killed every lovin' one of you, if you're still here. That includes you, your sausageship."

Molly pointed her laser finger at the wall next to Gortantor's head and, without looking, blasted a hole so close to him he was thrown to the ground.

None of the Jinicgus contingent needed to be further motivated. They burst toward the light showing through the entry as fast as tiny feet could carry them. Gortantor lead them as they exploded into the clear.

"Here," Molly said to the cat, "try and eat this." She broke open a ration pack, picked out the Salisbury steak, and set it in her open mouth.

Involuntarily, the prisoner began to lick and chomp at the meat. Then her jaws slammed shut and she swallowed it whole.

From outside the cave, Gortantor yelled, "You cannot leave, Captain. The price for betraying me is your life. Sooner or later, you must exit. When you do, you will die. I have called for reinforcements. There is no chance of rescue or escape."

Just as he stopped speaking, an enormous explosion rocked the entire hillock. Dust and pebbles showered down on Molly's head. She leaned over the Berrillian to protect her from debris.

"There's one problem with your plan," Molly shouted over her shoulder. "*I* called for backup first." She had no idea if Gortantor had lingered at the portal to hear her oh-so-clever remark, but it felt good to say it anyway.

EIGHT

After *Shearwater* blew a crater the size of a soccer pitch in the ground near the rock mound, I landed and charged the hill. It felt like I was an old-time Marine hitting the beach. It felt damn good. Fortunately, Gortantor and his soldiers ran like the wind down the slope in the opposite direction from where *Shearwater* was plainly parked. I bounded up the hill in three strides and rushed into the cave where Molly told me she'd found the Berrillian.

Then my jaw dropped—literally. There she was, crouched on the ground, cuddling the cat's massive head like it was her baby's, rocking it back and forth. My initial reaction was to push Molly clear and dismember the Berrillian. But, it was so bizarre. They looked so peaceful, so natural. I studied the female. She was worse off than I'd imagined from Molly's description. I doubted very much she could be salvaged. Past a certain point of starvation, no amount of feeding could turn the tide. Not that I cared a rat's ass about the cat herself, just the intel she could provide if properly motivated. Since that required her remaining among the living, I rested on the cave wall and watched the pair closely.

"You gonna stare at me or help me get her to my vortex?" Molly asked, gazing at the cat's face.

"If she's not dead, I will. But I'm putting her in *Shearwater* then *Wrath*. I'm not risking you getting eaten on your first mission."

"Why? Because you'd be as good as dead, when Kendra found out?"

"Damn straight. You wanna be a therapeutic buffet, go ahead. But you're not dragging me down with you. Your mom'll have me ready for the scrapheap faster than I can say *my that's a big hammer you've got there.*"

"She's my prisoner. She comes with me."

She sounded pretty resolute there, didn't she? While that was a wonderful quality in a young officer, it made my job much harder.

"I'll make you a deal. I put that smelly carpet in *Expectation*, and I ride home with you. Then you pop me back here to retrieve my ride."

"Deal," she replied still looking at her new pet or whatever.

We both deployed our probes and gently carried the Berrillian to the cube. The cat barely twitched a muscle the entire way. Once the portal was sealed, Molly put us on her pad back on *Exeter*. I signaled Toño than he should meet us at once. He was a human physician, not a veterinarian, but he'd spent a lot of time with Kelldrek back on Azsuram. If anyone could resuscitate the cat, it was him.

"My God," Toño exclaimed as he entered the docking bay. "She's profoundly malnourished and dehydrated, too. She's at the point of death. What happened to her?"

"We found her like this, Tapa Tio," replied Molly. She's called him that since she was a babe in arms.

"Jon, help me get her to the hospital. Mija, you go first to clear the way and hold an elevator."

We trotted down the hall, Toño on one side of the flaccid Berrillian and me on the other. Boy howdy did we draw some funny looks from the random people we passed in the corridors. I could just hear them thinking, *there's something you don't see every day.*

After we gently set our captive on the treatment table, several med techs rushed in to help. In a controlled chaos, her garments were cut off, patches on her arms were shaved, blood samples were drawn, and intravenous lines were inserted. A tube went down her throat, and her stomach was being pumped before Toño even asked us to leave. He told us he'd keep us closely posted as to his patient's condition.

In the corridor outside the sickbay, Molly squatted to the floor with her back up against a wall. I leaned on the wall at her side.

"You okay?" I asked.

"Me? Sure. I'm just worried about her. She was so helpless, so sick."

"Ah, before you go feeling all empathetic, remember we're talking about a Berrillian infiltrator here. She was sent there prepare for war and to kill. Her species has the worst track-record in the galaxy for being reliably sympathetic and lovable."

"I know, I know. But she was … I don't know. It's probably my imagination, but the way she looked at me when I held her head. I think she was saying thank you."

"No, she was saying, 'I bet that human would taste good, smothered in ketchup.'"

"Jon, I'm being serious. Please try to do the same."

"Fine. But don't go all animal-shelter infatuation with her. She's a born killer. If and when she recovers, you can find out how nice she is. Until then, please remain objective. Part of my job as your superior is to make a good officer out of you. Wearing your heart on your sleeve will backfire on you sooner rather than later. It's a cold, cruel world out there."

"Oh, like you always played by the rules and never took *massive* risks."

"Point. All I'm saying is stay sharp. If you want to nurture strangers, become a nurse or volunteer at a soup kitchen. If you're an officer in this man's army, you gotta develop a pretty thick hide."

"You're right. Thanks." She smiled up at me.

Crap. She was blowing me off. I knew her too well. Molly Hatcher never conceded one argument or a single board game. Never. She was a fighter. I couldn't hold her hand forever. Okay, technically, I guess I could, but that wasn't how a good officer was made.

Within a few days, it became clear that our prisoner was going to pull through. Critical to her survival, she had ingested none of the toxic inhabitants of LH 16a. She must have received a warning before her supplies gave out. Once her dehydration and kidney infections were resolved, her refeeding began. Toño gave her some intravenous support, but she also began drinking liquid protein solutions. A little while later, she was able to chew and swallow cooked meat.

As soon as she arrived, she'd been chained and had an around-the-clock guard posted to her. Once she could sit and stand, she was transferred to the brig, and additional precautions were put in place. Again, Toño's experience with Kelldrek helped to that end. A week into her recovery, Toño said we could visit with her if we wanted to. Up until then, not even the intel folks were allowed to interrogate her.

"Hi," I said formally as I stood outside her cell. "I'm General Jon Ryan. You are our prisoner. Please believe me when I assure you no harm will come to you, unless you attack someone or attempt to escape. You will be questioned, but you will not be tortured. If you behave well, you will be treated well."

She stared at me a while, then looked to Molly. She raised a paw in Molly's direction. "I may be your prisoner, but I am *her* friend."

"Do you remember me?" Molly asked with too much joy in her voice.

"Yes. The kindness you showed me can never be forgotten." She looked to her cell floor. "Thank you."

"Oh, I'm Molly Hatcher."

"Rasraller. I am your servant."

I stepped forward quickly. "She does not require your service. You are a prisoner of war, not a guest. Please keep that in mind."

"Humans and their word games. So silly."

"How many Berrillians were sent to LH 16a, the planet where you were hidden?" I asked.

She groaned. "How many were sent, or how many are still alive?" she responded.

"Both," I replied.

"Many and none. There, I am done answering your questions. I will answer no more."

"Over time, I'm certain you will see the wisdom of cooperation. Our interrogation—"

"I will answer *Molly's* questions. I am her servant and can do no less," said Rasraller looking at Molly.

"Captain Hatcher is not able to interrogate prisoners. She is a combat officer, not an intel specialist."

Rasraller shrugged. "These words mean nothing to me. Molly and I are bound. It is *maldrar*, a sacred bond. Neither can break it. Only death."

"Don't tempt me. In your case, bond interruption would be my pleasure."

"Because we killed your mate, General Ryan? Is that why killing me would be a pleasure?"

Didn't see that one coming. Ouch, it really hurt.

"How did—" I began to say.

"Oh please. We know you are unique among your species. We are taught of your treachery, your hate for our kind, and all of your lies."

"Wow, you mean I'm a celebrity? I'm touched."

"Not a celebrity. A demon. Your name is a curse."

"Your people attacked *us*, need I remind you?"

"We defended ourselves against the *genocide* your Alliance desires." She kicked at her bedsheets. "It does not matter now. None of that matters." She growled angrily.

"Why?" I asked. "Why does it no longer matter?"

Rasraller sat like a statue.

"Why does it no longer matter, my friend?" asked Molly.

She turned her head and seemed to smile at Molly. She couldn't actually smile. Berrillians didn't have the muscles or evolutionary predilection to smile.

"Do you know what I was told when I called my commander back home and asked permission to abandon my post?"

"No, Rasraller. I do not," replied Molly.

"I reported that my supplies were exhausted and that everything that walked, crawled, swam, or flew on the accursed planet was poisonous. I was told I could not abandon my post. I was to make do. Those were their very words. *Make do.* I asked them what that meant. How was I to *make do,* when making do was impossible? They said they had no ears for a whining bitch. They said I could serve on LH 16a, or die a traitor's death on Berrill."

"That's awful," Molly said.

"No, it not awful. It's not even cruel. I understand cruelty. I was dismissed. I was simply crossed off the list of those in service to Erratarus. We are raised, don't misunderstand me, in a ruthless, repressive, intolerant society. It is our way. I always thought it fair and correct."

"But?" responded Molly.

"But to care *nothing* for a soldier, to waste them, to assign them *zero* value? All they had to do was okay my return in my own vessel. No effort on their part, aside from moving their vocal cords, was required to save my life and continue my service to the empire."

"But they didn't care enough to say the words," Molly summarized for her.

"No. Death has become so familiar that it is more favorable than deciding to save a loyal servant."

"Because Erratarus might criticize someone for showing you the slightest mercy or consideration," said Molly.

"Because acting wisely, and with a longer view, might cost some *gentwar* his or her life," Rasraller replied with disgust.

"So, you can't go back, even if we released you?" asked Molly.

"No. But, more importantly, I would *not* return if I were free to do so. I could never again serve such a mindless and indifferent empire." She looked then right at me. "I hate the Berrillians more than anyone. I hate them more than you do, Jon Ryan."

NINE

Over the next month, two things happened in my world. One, Rasraller recovered rapidly, eating an unbelievable amount of meat and anything else she could hook her claws into. The other was our interrogation of her. I was determined to tear down the walls of her deception, especially as she directed it to my Moll-Doll. We wanted to extract useful information, to be certain. But I also needed to stop her from falsely drawing in Molly. I knew how vicious and single-minded the Berrillians could be.

To my surprise, Rasraller answered all of Molly's questions in a simple and direct manner. I tried to trip her up by having Molly ask her questions Rasrallar couldn't possibly have anticipated I knew the answer to. Never once did she lie, deceive, or mislead. I began to understand she was a seriously low-ranked individual. She was privy to no juicy gossip or specific military details. Not so remarkable, I supposed. The person you buried in deep cover on an alien world couldn't have been too heavy a hitter. If she had been, they'd have needed her back on the home front.

Rasraller confirmed that her instructions had been what I imagined they were. She was to dig in like a tick and await a signal to join an attack on the planet, or to begin an aggressive guerrilla assault against the locals. Her superiors would determine which tactic would be most useful. There was no time frame. She was told to remain in hiding and to maintain vigilance and contact home periodically. She might have been called to action soon, or never. Several thousand Berrillians were also placed in hiding on LH 16a, in as widely scattered a pattern as possible. They all had the same open-ended assignments.

She didn't know how many worlds were similarly infiltrated, but she guessed the number was large. She told us the orientation and training program was very big, with tens of thousands of participants in it. To her eye, the training compound seemed well-used, as opposed to brand spanking new. I had also been correct that Erratarus's son Claudus was in charge. He'd given his version of an inspirational speech the first day, and then she never saw him again. That information was somewhat useful, in that Claudus was known to be as ruthless and merciless as any Berrillian. His reputation for cruelty and wanton violence was legendary, even among a race famous for such dubious qualities. Rumors had it that even his father feared him.

Eventually it came to the point where Rasraller's veracity had to be definitively determined. She'd regained her health. Molly had become devoted to her. Our prisoner had clearly yielded any and all information she could. Rasraller needed to be labeled a long-term POW, or set free to live under Molly's supervision. All of us who loved Molly were overwrought with worry that if Rasraller was released to her supervision, our little angel would be brutally torn to shreds. Molly professed that we were all nuts and that Rasraller was her true and loyal friend. This wasn't a point to decide upon lightly. But, leave it to me; I had a plan.

****

I walked quickly into the brig and stopped nose-to-membrane with Rasraller's confinement shield. Molly followed silently two paces behind me. "Okay, cupcake, time for a road trip."

Rasraller rose slowly, cautiously from her bedding. She had never warmed to me, probably because she knew my history and my love for Molly.

"What is a *road trip*, human?"

"Vacation. Oh wait, you cats don't have a word for that, do you? Ah … we're going on an *adventure*. Yes, a grand adventure, just the three of us. It'll be swell."

"We will gain in volume dangerously?" asked Rasraller with a distressed look on her face.

"Just get a move on."

47

I waved a finger to the guard monitoring us. The membrane disappeared.

"Off we go," I said cheerily and I swept my hand in the direction I wanted her to go.

"Molly," she asked with clear reservation, "is this trip all right with you? Where are we going?"

"I'm in charge here. I told Molly she could observe, only if she kept her trap shut. If you have questions, address them to me. If you harbor concerns, those you can address to the void of space."

Tentatively she walked past Molly and me and headed down the corridor. She stared at Molly the whole time. Molly stared back with a blank look on her face.

"Not a word, Moll-Doll," I said to her sternly. "That's the deal."

Molly nodded back in acknowledgement.

"I'll tell you where to turn. We're going on what I'm calling a fact-checking expedition."

"Not *Expectation?*" asked Rasraller. She liked *Wrath* less than she liked me. Then again who didn't?

"*I'm* in command. We take my ride."

The rest of the walk was silent aside from my directions to Rasraller. We piled into the cube, Molly sat in the far corner, and Rasraller plopped her rear end on the floor a respectful distance from me. I instructed *Wrath* to take us where I'd directed him to go earlier. I wanted our destination to be a complete surprise to my guests.

A short bout of nausea later, we materialized. I had *Wrath* blacken the view screen, so no one could see outside.

"Open a portal in the starboard wall," I said.

An open passage appeared. I walked out. As I exited I picked up a plasma rifle in either hand. I think neither woman noticed they had been there.

"Follow me. Both of you."

Rasraller went first, followed by Molly.

"No," shouted Rasraller the second she was through. "What have you done, you foul beast?"

"This is a test. For the next sixty seconds, we'll see whose side you're really on," I replied as unemotionally as I could.

That's when they saw us. It wasn't all that hard. We were the only vortex on the bridge of *Color of Blood*, King Anganctus's old flagship. The new king, Erratarus, of course needed a bigger, better one, so this was the flag for one of the three divisions of the Berrillian fleet. Her captain was someone I'd heard of but never met, Julregar. She was reputed to be a good officer and a master strategist. I chose her ship because, one, I knew where it was, and two, she didn't know me and almost certainly didn't know Rasraller. I only hoped she didn't mind impromptu guests, especially those who were her sworn enemy. What could go wrong?

Someone set off the horrible Berrillian general quarters alarm. I almost covered my ears reflexively. Instead, I raised both rifles and swung them around the bridge. "No one moves or I will shoot," I shouted.

A large male nearby leaped toward me. I blew most of his head off before he began his downward arc. He flopped to the deck motionless.

"Any other takers?" I yelled.

All the cats were frozen where they stood. All but Julregar. She moved toward us slowly, on two feet.

"What is the meaning of this?" she asked in a level tone.

"I'm here to deliver a package," I replied.

I pointed one gun at Rasraller and waved her toward the captain.

"Over there. You'll be safe here with your stinking *friends*," I said trying to sound as vitriolic as possible.

"No," screamed Rasraller, "my place is with Molly." She stepped to close the short distance between the two of them.

"No," I shouted back, "freeze."

Fortunately she did.

A soldier burst thought the doorway, training his weapon on me. Julregar started to yell *no* to him, but I put a big hole in his chest before she had the chance.

"No one attack the intruders," said Julregar in a resounding command voice.

"You, move," I waved at Rasraller again.

She inched away from Molly and toward Julregar. When she was a couple meters away, I spoke to Molly. "Here," I tossed one of my rifles to her, "catch."

I threw it so that it would land on the floor well beyond her reach. It thudded to the deck right of her and skidded past her feet. Molly bent to retrieve it. I turned my back on her before she was halfway to the gun.

A big female standing right next to Molly pounced on her like a bolt of lightning. The Berrillian roared and crushed Molly to the floor. They began to roll. The female cat seized Molly's head between her jaws and began tossing it side to side, ferociously.

Rasraller flew through the air every bit as quickly as the Berrillian had. Roaring at a deafening volume she hit the other female with impressive force. Rasraller grabbed her massive head between her paws and sank her teeth into the top of her head. Partly Rasraller was attacking, but partly she was attempting to stop the cat from shaking Molly's head.

Subject to a full-on assault, the female officer dropped Molly and wriggled to face Rasraller chest to chest. They tumbled to the floor, both clinging to each other with their claws and snapping their jaws. Completing a roll, the other female pinned Rasraller against a bulkhead. With her improved leverage, she started burrowing past Rasraller's paws, going for her throat.

That's when I put two plasma bolts into her exposed spine. Rasraller's defensive thrusts pushed the dead female off instantly.

"Get into the vortex Rasraller," I shouted loud enough to be heard among all the noise and confusion." I began firing randomly around the bridge. Panels and personnel erupted with blue-light impacts. Some of the Berrillians dove to the deck. Others dashed toward me. I had already moved to *Wrath's* open portal. From there I continued to cover Rasraller's sprint toward Molly's limp body, where it was crumpled on the floor.

Rasraller grabbed Molly by the loose jacket at the base of her neck and lifted her, much like a mother cat would her kitten. With two great leaps, both were through the opening. I closed it.

"Okay, we're safe now. They can't get in," I said casually to Rasraller.

"Are you blind, you monster? I think Molly's dead," she pointed to the back of Molly's still limp body.

"I think Molly's just fine," I replied as I deployed my command prerogatives to *Wrath's* inner hull.

Rasraller pounced on me. At least she tried. I was ready. I sidestepped her flying paws and wrapped my arms around her big neck as she passed. We crashed to the deck with her struggling to reach back at me and me tightening my grip on her throat.

"Rasraller, stop," screamed Molly as she ran into the room. "Rasraller, I'm fine. Stop, or Jon'll hurt you."

Rasraller looked at Molly standing there unharmed and went limp in my arms. Yeah, I *bet* she was confused.

I released her, and she ran to embrace Molly in a powerful bearhug, nearly knocking her to the floor next to the other Molly. Rasraller lifted her up and swung her in her arms. Then, as suddenly as she'd grabbed her, Rasraller set Molly down and pointed to the Molly on the floor.

"But, what ... you ... I don't understand," was the best Rasraller could manage to stammer.

"Did you notice the Molly on the ground isn't bleeding?" I asked.

Rasraller stared a second. "No. That bitch crushed her skull. How can she not bleed?"

"Because robots don't have blood to bleed," I responded with a chuckle.

"You—" Rasraller gestured to Molly and then to me, "you tricked me."

"Yes, dearest Rasraller," explained Molly, "Jon and Toño felt it was necessary. I didn't, but I was overruled." She stuck her tongue out at me. "Toño put my face on a blank android and powered it with a low-level AI."

"Yes, we did," I replied rather smugly. "But, before we get all misty eyed, I need to get us off this fracking ship. *Wrath*, take me home. I want to go home."

Boom, we were on *Wrath's* landing pad.

"You were aboard *Wrath* the entire time, Molly?" Rasraller asked her.

"Yes."

"I think the plan was brilliant. Seriously, Ryan, who knew you were that clever?" said Rasraller.

"I did," I replied patting myself on the back.

"But, I mean who else in the universe would have?" added Rasraller.

"I didn't like plan," said Molly. "There were a dozen ways it could have headed south. You might have been killed. Both of you, for that matter."

"Me?" I pointed to myself. "No way. I'm too good."

Rasraller and Molly looked at each other, then at me, but said nothing. They didn't have to.

"The important point is you passed with flying colors," I said.

"Thank you, Ryan. Thank you for allowing me to prove I am as I say I am. One thing troubles me."

"What?" I asked.

"At the end, when I charged you."

"Yes?"

"You physically bested me. That's not even remotely possible."

"Maybe you're not as tough as you fancy you are," I teased.

"Perhaps," she replied, "but there isn't a human alive who could do what you did."

"He's an android," responded Molly. "Like the one that ended up on the floor."

Rasraller took a step backward. "You have mechanical humans? How obscene."

"Gee, thanks," I said.

"He's has a *slightly* larger computer in his head compared to the one on the floor," Molly said with a twinkle in her eyes.

"This is insane. Robots that pretend to be humans. Robots that father *children*. I think I might be in the middle of a nightmare."

"Welcome to the family, Rasraller," I said with a smile.

TEN

"I repeat that I did not *allow* them to escape. They blasted their way out of here. I was fortunate to survive," protested Gortantor.

"That, tiny one, is a matter of opinion," replied Claudus. He was pacing the floor of Gortantor's ballroom. It was one of the few indoor spaces large enough to accommodate the Berrillian prince.

"I do not see that it matters. The Alliance came, snooped around briefly, and left with one prisoner. She was moribund, that I know. She stank of death."

"But dead she was not. *If* they revived her, and *if* they forced her to talk, they will know something of my master plan."

"I doubt the girl knew more than her own name, let alone the details of *our* plan," responded Gortantor. "Why you insist on using female operatives is well beyond me. Females are for breeding and rearing purposes only. To employ them in a male's role is to court disaster."

"There are a goodly number of things beyond you, little king. Keep that in mind, if you wish your planet to survive."

"Why waste time threatening me? I know the only reason you haven't stormed across our world is because most life here is fortunate enough to be poisonous to your species."

"That would not prevent me from killing you for the sport of it. Our gravity waves would rip your world apart in a matter of hours."

"Yes, but then you wouldn't have a covert advanced base, would you?"

"No, but I'd have a satisfying erection."

"You are little more than a wild animal, and you are revolting."

"Keep that in mind if you want to live to see the next dawn."

"This bickering is pointless. We must work together to destroy the Alliance," protested Gortantor. "They threaten *us* and limit *you*. Please keep that in *your* mind."

"We nearly conquered the galaxy without a single ally. One as small as you aren't sufficient to swing the tide this time out."

"Mock us at your peril. You are physically larger, but we are intellectually larger, *and* we offer a mutually beneficial union. Pray I don't tire of your arrogance and your smell."

"I'm suddenly bored," said Claudus. "I will return to my ship and mate. On the matter of prayer, small one, you would do well to pray the female died quickly. The moment your species becomes a liability will be your last. I am forced to tolerate you for now. But that which I cannot eat, screw, or rely upon with absolute certainty is a short-lived thing." He roared a laugh. "Ha. *Short*-lived for a *short* race. I do so love puns."

Back on his command ship, *Reign of Terror*, Claudus could no longer delay reporting in to his idiot father. He would so prefer killing him and eating his still-beating heart. But the realities of the current political situation made that move inadvisable. That time would come soon, but never soon enough for the voracious Claudus. No. He over-consumed meat lustfully, he forced himself on countless bitches, whether they were in heat or not, and he murdered foes with a glee and frequency that frightened those morons surrounding him who mistook themselves to be his friends.

"Do you have news, other that the litany of your failures, son?" asked Erratarus. His face was one of sullen constipation on the comm-screen as he glared at Claudus.

"Father dearest, if anyone were present who did not know of your powerful affection you have for me, they would think you despise me."

"And they would be correct, my valueless, treacherous, waste-of-a-sperm-cell son."

Claudus stiffened. Were he not several light years distant, he'd have struck the old fool dead and been done with him. Probably lucky for both he wasn't.

"I have an excellent update, my lord," said Claudus as he tried to change the subject. "My plan for defeating our enemies is shaping up nicely."

"*Your* plan, is it now? And here I thought it was *I* who set you in the proper direction, that *I* put you in charge of *my* project."

"Be that as it may, father, I am close to achieving our goal. You and your predecessors allowed our foes to develop such superior abilities to fight us in space that we cannot engage them there. I—"

He stopped when the power of his father's roar struck him like a shovel to the face. Perhaps he'd gone too far. No need having a price put on his head before he could eliminate the old cat.

"Lord, why are you so angry?" he asked submissively. "I merely said your forefathers were unable to keep pace with the enemy's technology."

"No, you said *I* and my line. You will die a thousand deaths for that insult."

"With respect, lord, I did not say that. I must have spoken so unclearly and the transmission is of such poor quality that it *appeared* as though I suggested such an absurd idea."

"You know this conversation is recorded, right?"

"I would assume so."

"Yet you still lie to my face."

Claudus shrugged inscrutably. "I can only state what I know I felt and hope that I said."

"Go on with your report, imbecilic spawn of my loin."

"Ah, yes. We have significant numbers of warriors hidden away on one hundred seventy-three worlds. The pattern we have successfully infiltrated spans most of the space not yet under our control."

"You mean *my* control?"

"That is what I said. Not yet under the control of the Berrillian Empire. Father, why is it you prefer verbal sparring with me, your loyal servant, rather than uninterrupted communication?"

Erratarus said nothing. He simply glowered at the camera.

"So, when you give the word, our forces on the ground will engage the locals sufficiently to allow massive numbers of our people to land and join the battle. Worlds will fall like feathers from a shaken bird."

"Assuming, of course, the Alliance does not discover the transport ships and pop them like soap bubbles floating in the air on a hot day."

"That will not happen. We will be using vessels designed to look like run of the mill trading ships. Those, and ultra-small one or two cat-sized craft too numerous to target."

"Initially, I'll grant you that it will likely work. But once we've assimilated a few planets, they will know of our ruse and doubtlessly develop a counterstrategy." The king placed his paws behind his back and paced back and forth. "And what of this annoying planet I heard of, the toxic one? Have you come to a solution for it?"

"No. It is of no consequence. We will simply go around it for the time being. When I have time, I will return and rip it apart with the gravity weapons."

"Hmm."

"What?"

"I'm not comfortable with loose ends like that. Why not destroy it now and be done with them?"

There was no point letting his father know about his forward bases on LH 16a. The walking penises were useful to Claudus, and his father not knowing of their cooperation only strengthened Claudus's hand.

"Have faith, father. Do not give the Alliance such credit. Victory is a foregone conclusion."

"Yes, it is. I wish, however, I had faith it will be our victory, and not theirs."

Either way, thought Claudus, *you cursed waste of space, I will triumph. If we win, I will kill you and take over. If we lose, someone else will kill you, and I will take over. Win/win is such a happy situation to bask in.*

ELEVEN

It didn't take long to discover that having a Berrillian warrior as a BFF was not going to be easy for Molly. Everywhere she went, there stood, right beside her, the terrifying mortal enemy we all feared. She was constantly having to explain the presence of the big cat so that no one shot her. And forget about going into a bar. Yeah, if Molly wanted trouble, just walk into a room full of drunks with a huge target by her side. We had convinced Rasraller to bathe regularly and change her clothes daily, so smell wasn't such an issue. But she was literally the five-hundred-pound conversation stopper in any room she stepped into. Let's just say, the two of them stayed in a lot.

That said, I was beginning to get to know the Berrillian well. She was fiercer than an arrow to the heart, more stubborn than a boulder in the middle of a river, and more opinionated than my first mother-in-law. But, she also possessed a wry sense of humor I hadn't expected, an intelligence that impressed me, and empathy that I never saw coming. While she was devoted to Molly, she and I weren't heading down Friendship Road together. But we did more than tolerate one another. We were cordial. We both loved Molly, we were both an intimate part of her life, and we understood, without saying it, that if we wished to remain in Molly's world, we'd best coexist.

TCY was another matter entirely. Most pilots reflexively went for their side arms when they saw Rasraller coming. General Hijab was apoplectic at the mere mention of her name and couldn't look at her without visibly trembling. As to her being anywhere near a vortex under Faiza's command, no way. It was strictly forbidden. That order didn't cover *Wrath*, because everyone knew the rules didn't apply to the old android. On paper, maybe, but even Faiza thought better than to do anything but *suggest* what I might do. Faiza was adamant that somehow Rasraller faked her near-death and rebuke of her species to gain intel of our defenses. I knew the commander only allowed her to live because I was involved and was clearly sympathetic to Rasraller. I tried on multiple occasions to convince Faiza otherwise, but she never really listened.

That hostile environment on the worldships to the crew of *Expectation,* namely Molly and Rasraller, was not tolerable in the long run. We all knew something had to give, and it wasn't likely to be TCY or the humans who'd suffered at the jaws of the Berrillians Empire. Molly started spending more time on Azsuram. Though the planet had suffered mightily under the Berrillian invasion, their unshakable loyalty to me allowed the two women to live there without the slightest issue. I'd have thought they were both Kaljaxians for the ease with which they moved in the ever-growing society. Whether they were out to a restaurant or just sitting in a park, not one stray look or disparaging remark was directed toward them. JJ, nearing retirement and more popular than ever, took the pair under his wing, which really helped. I was, once again, most proud of the citizens of Azsuram, and my boy in particular.

I sort of figured Molly would do what all the other original Project Ark astronauts had done and drift away from TCY and the human fleet. Molly was younger and still wanted to prove herself, but I imagined she'd opt for her friendship with Rasraller over the prejudice of her own kind. Having lived many lives over the centuries, I couldn't much fault her. Her parents, Amanda and Kendra, were less excited about their baby slipping away, but they'd raised her right. They were going to love her and be proud of her, whatever she chose to do. Man, I wish I'd had parents like them. Don't get me wrong. My parents were fine and all, but those two were the best I'd seen. And no, it wasn't because I'd have liked to have grown up with a couple of hotties for moms. I was not, and would never be, *that* type of pig. Many types, for sure. Just not that needy a pig.

As my one kindred spirit in TCY faded away, I was even more isolated.

I'd have loved it if Azsuram was falling off the tracks and needed my personal attention. But it didn't. So, I had no excuse to leave the worldship fleet and drag my wife back there. Plus, separating the kids and grandkids from their worlds at their ages would take more energy than I possessed. They'd freak out about their friends and schools. Fortunately, Kayla knew me well enough to know I was going through some changes. She was just as warm, supportive, and tolerant of me as ever. Couldn't have made it without her, that's for sure.

Then, an assignment fell into my lap from heaven. It was perfect. Go figure. The leaders of the UN defense forces decided they needed to know more about two variables. One was the extent and rough dimensions of the Berrillian Empire. We really had no clue as to how many star systems it controlled and how they were spread across the galaxy. We had intel resources to help in that regard, but they were limited. Rasraller told us what she knew, but in a totalitarian, repressive government like hers, secrecy was tight. Almost everything in Berrillian society was on a need-to-know basis. The average Joe only needed to know their job and the consequences of not doing it.

The other thing the big shots wanted to know was where the Luminarians stood in terms of the inevitable Berrillian incursion. The Luminarians were one species the Deavoriath identified as possible members of the alliance against the Last Nightmare. Nothing came of any initial contacts with the Luminarians, so they pretty much dropped off everyone's radar screens. Subsequent attempts to establish relations with them had equally fizzled out. The politicos concluded that the Luminarians had no interest in anything except themselves. Great. If no one answered the phone or opened the front door, send Jon Ryan to make happy with them. But, hey, it was a mission, and it was one where I was the most unlikely to get eaten, shot at, or dented.

In terms of the two assignments, scoping out the Luminarians seemed the easiest and by far the quickest. Heck, they were probably going to blow me off so fast, I'd be home for dinner the same night. The Berrillian assignment looked to be a long one. So, I was off to Rigel 12, land of the snooty electric globs. Kymee told me once that non-corporeal species were generally intolerable, too good to associate with us fleshy-bodied space trash. They were too big for their own charge-distribution limits was what I'd have said, if asked. The fact that I didn't like them before I even left didn't bode well for my success. But it was kind of fun to go on a mission that was likely to fail. It wouldn't be my fault, and I could be a turd in someone's punch bowl all I wanted. Assuming, of course, Luminarians had anything akin to punch bowls. I'd find some way of being annoying if they were snobs. Yeah, it was kind of a paid vacation.

I took my standard set of equipment on any voyage. *Wrath*, with *Shearwater* strapped to him, and Al along as someone to talk to that wasn't *Wrath*. He also served as the computer I could trust. Hey. Not a bad tagline for a computer company. *Bob's computers, the computers you can trust.*

Rigel was a cool star. It was visible as a bright blue-white star from Earth. I grew up marveling at it on long, cold, winter nights. Okay, maybe I caught it out of the corner of my eye from the backseat of my car, but Rigel was one of my favorites. It had around twenty planets, give or take, depending on how you defined a planet. That was huge as far as star systems went. Planet twelve was home to the Luminarians. There were sentient races on two other of Rigel's planets, all unrelated. Rigel 5 had a sort of humanoid species that had developed to around our Middle Ages. Rigel 10 was a jungle world, very hot and moist, almost a victim of runaway greenhouse gas heating. Life abounded there. The sentients were kind of ape-like in body and intelligence. They might make good football linemen or politicians, but they were otherwise uninteresting.

Back when the Deavoriath ruled the galaxy, the inhabitants of Rigel 12 were evolutionarily transforming into what they would fully become in a few hundred thousand years. Kymee compared them to the electric eel of Earth, only more electric and less eel. I guess Kymee didn't give me too much credit in terms of brain power, did he? Anyway, they'd since shuffled off their mortal coils, to paraphrase the Bard. They'd also shed most, but not all, of their technology, and certainly most tools, such as radios and the postal service. That was why contacting them was so hard. You never knew if they heard you and were ignoring the call, or if they weren't listening in the first place. To my way of thinking, these snobs *deserved* a visit from me. I'd set them straight, or I'd at least piss them off enough to make my efforts joyous.

Wrath popped into space a thousand klicks above the surface of Rigel 12. I had him put us in geosynchronous orbit over what had been a major city, Feleliquet. Kymee told me in the day it covered about one third of the dry land surface of the entire planet. I quickly ascertained it was still there, but it was completely abandoned. There was no functioning electric grid, power source of any sort, or radio chatter. *Wrath* narrowed in and confirmed there was no street traffic or planes in the air. The few remaining artificial satellites in orbit were long since defunct.

Al broadcast messages on all frequencies, announcing our arrival and asking for acknowledgement. Nothing came in response. I had him send some transmissions in odd wavelengths, like MASER and optical signals. Still nothing. Okay, I was going to have to drop in uninvited. Who knew if they even cared?

I had *Wrath* land near what was the capitol area. It was a sprawling expanse of buildings and parks. The entire place was overgrown with vegetation, and the buildings looked positively decrepit. Clearly, no maintenance had been performed in centuries. With a little difficulty, I walked the streets a while, looking for any signs of life. The going got tough at times due to fallen trees and the buildup of debris. It looked like those ancient images of Chernobyl after their reactor contaminated the region. Existing, but void of life.

I entered several buildings. More decayed nothingness. It was a shame to have all that infrastructure wasted, when humanity was searching for a permanent home. Rigel 12 was not a likely colonization candidate, as the Luminarians had to be somewhere and almost certainly didn't want millions of immigrants. Both *Wrath* and Al scanned as best they could and detected nothing that could be interpreted as a sign of life or of purposeful movement. It began to dawn on me there weren't any critters around either. No rats, feral domestic animals, not even creepy bugs. That was odd. Okay, the highfalutin sentients become electrical blobs. Why would that affect the rest of the ecosystem? It shouldn't have. Wildlife should have continued to survive and evolve.

After a full day with no clues as to where the locals were, I moved us to a far-removed part of Feleliquet. Though it was architecturally distinct, it was also equally barren. Simple physics dictated that if an electric charge moved, it generated a magnetic field. None of us found any trace of magnetic flux, aside from naturally occurring ones. Their was no one home.

I was forced to do something I disliked. I had to sit back and think. I was a man of action, not a chess player. So, I reasoned that if I was a superior being, an electric eel minus the eel, where would I spend eternity? I assumed they were still on Rigel 12. A loose association of electrical charge wouldn't last long in the hostile environment of space. Stellar winds, cosmic rays, and random charged particles would wreak havoc with such a free-floating apparition. Would I go to the highest mountain and contemplate where my navel used to be? Maybe the bottom of the ocean? That was unlikely. Salt water and free electric charge would be a problem for the Luminarians. If I no longer had eyes, a pretty landscape would hold no wonder.

Food. If they were alive, they still needed to eat. Short of plugging into a one hundred twenty-volt outlet, where could they recharge? No food production and no agriculture were anywhere to be found, so they weren't making electricity from organic sources. Naturally occurring electrical energy was rare and unreliable. Lightning was the only common manifestation. So, it had to be, I reasoned, some form of photoelectric conversion that kept them electrified. That was easily possible. They could have evolved photoelectric conversion cells. So, I'd likely find Luminarians where the gradient of light from their sun would be the highest. That meant I was off to the equatorial band of the planet, but not too high in altitude. There'd be a trade-off for them between more intense solar radiation and a cold, hostile environment. All right. I had a plan.

I had *Wrath* fly low and keep a view portal open. That way I could get a picture of the planet as I flew over it. From a three thousand meter elevation, the landscape seemed pretty much what I'd anticipated. Oceans, land masses, and trees. I still didn't see any signs of life, and neither of my computer associates reported any finds, either. Odd, but there it was. Al could confirm some marine life, though it was mostly well off shore. That was reassuring, in that it suggested there hadn't been some catastrophic environmental crisis on Rigel 12. But, the distribution of life was off. At least on the water worlds I knew of, life tended to hug the coasts and shallow waters. Maybe the changes I saw were just consistent with a very old ecosystem. Oowaoa was the oldest planet I'd visited, and it certainly had less flora and fauna than I'd have anticipated.

As we neared the equator, I did begin to see a pattern develop. There were fewer trees the farther south we went. That was, of course, just the opposite of what I expected. Any standard planet with the usual rotation and orbit would be warmest at the equator. Rainfall would, therefore, be the highest. More heat and water meant the vegetation should get denser, not sparser, the closer we came to the equator. The changes were spotty at first, but by the time we were nearing zero degrees latitude, there were no trees or vegetation to speak of. Though there were hills, mountains, and rivers, the land itself was bare dirt. Actually, it was bare mud because of all the rain. Whatever was going on with Rigel 12 sure made it a bust as a tourist destination.

Finally, *Wrath* chimed in with the words I wanted to hear. He'd located moving patches of electrical charge. We'd found us some LIPs. It turned out it would be easy enough for me to at least address one, as none of them moved quickly and most were close to the ground. As I suspected, they were concentrated in the band of elevation between five hundred and a thousand meters. Again, because everything about life on Rigel 12 was odd, the Luminarians were spread out uniformly with almost mathematical precision. Not very social creatures, it would seem.

Wrath landed in an area where the concentration of charged blobs was the highest. I set out on foot to make a new friend. Even if they were invisible, I'd be able to locate one with my sensors. Almost immediately I found my quarry. The Luminarians were visible as hazy irregular blobs. They had no heads, feet, or other appendages. Most were in the shape of thin disks, like the shape of a red blood cell. A few were more donut like. As I approached the one I picked out, it made no moves to suggest it saw me, or at least it paid me no mind.

"Hello," I shouted when I was a meter away.

Nothing. Not movement or response that I could detect.

Al, I said in my head, *you pick up any response from this dude?*

Negative, captain. It remains unchanged.

I broadcast the same greeting across a wide radio band.

Still nothing, sir, reported Al.

Any ideas? I asked.

Maybe try a flare.

A what? Are you serious, Al? You think getting its attention by lighting it on fire will create a good first impression?

No, pilot, it would not. I was thinking you might wave it near the body. A flare will create a good deal of light and heat energy. Perhaps it's hungry.

Al, my boy, you're brighter than you look.

After centuries of service together, admit it. You have no idea what I look like.

Sure, I do. You look like a shiny metal box.

That's my housing, not me.

Well, I think of you as a shiny box, kind of like a toaster without the slots.

If I cared at all what you thought, I'd be insulted. Fortunately, I'm the better machine.

I didn't snipe back. Instead I fired up one of the flares I carried in my belt. They were manganese based, so they were white hot.

Within a second, Al was back in my head. *A dozen nearby Luminarians are heading toward you quickly. The flare seems to interest them.*

Or piss them off, in which case I'm in trouble.

Good point. I'll be sure to take good notes for posterity.

A bunch of the hazy blobs configured themselves in a semi-circle in front of the flare, about half a meter away. On a whim, I put my hand in front of the flame and flipped it up and down to simulate a signal lamp message by Morse code, like an old Navy vessel would have used. Damn if it didn't work. It took several seconds, but the closest blob started flashing slightly brighter in pulses. It copied the parts of the Morse code it had learned from me. I quickly ran through the entire Morse signals for letters and numbers. Just like that, we were communicating efficiently, if not rapidly. The Luminarian could flash quickly, but me flipping my hand was clumsy at best.

C-a-n y-o-u c-o-m-m-u-n-i-c-a-t-e w-i-t-h- m-e b-y s-o-u-n-d- w-a-v-e o-r r-a-d-i-o? I asked.

Y-e-s, it replied.

Okay, my friend, why didn't you just do it and not flash it?

C-a-n y-o-u-h-e-a-r m-e w-h-e-n I s-p-e-a-k?

Y-e-s.

Hmm. You're trying my patience a tad here, pal.

C-a-n y-o-u v-i-b-r-a-t-e t-h-e a-i-r t-o s-i-m-u-l-a-t-e-s-p-e-e-c-h?

Y-e-s.

I began wondering what would happen if I punched this electric cloud.

"If you can hear me and return the audible signal, why haven't you?" I asked loudly.

B-e-c-a-u-s-e I c-h-o-s-e n-o-t t-o. I c-h-o-o-s-e n-o-t t-o n-o-w.

Son of a spark plug.

"Why the hell not?" I challenged.

"Because," it said by pulsing the air, "I wish to ignore you."

Well how do you like that? Insulting *and* rude. What an unrefreshing and unwelcome attitude.

"I'm Jon Ryan. I'm here representing a large alliance—"

"I know who you are and why you are here. Please leave."

That sounded vaguely familiar in a most unpleasant way.

"How do you—"

"I know because I am a superior being. Leave."

Dude was getting on my last nerve with the finishing my sentence crap.

"I am glad you are superior. Makes my day, really. The issue is—"

"We have no concern for the petty wars of you corporeals."

"Do you know what a cattle prod is?" There, I got in a full sentence.

"Yes. What does—"

"I'm about to see what one does to your sorry ass if you don't start communicating with me and stop insulting me." Yes, score two points. *I* cut *him* off.

"You are not in possession of such a device, and it would have no effect on me."

"Look, let's start again, shall we? My name is Jon—and don't interrupt me—Ryan. Your name is what?"

"I am."

"Yes, great. You are—?" I let that hang.

"I am. That is who I am."

"You're named *am*?"

"No, that would be silly. I am, that is who I am."

"Is there some-am else I can talk to.? You're impossible."

"If I were *impossible,* how could I be here speaking at you?"

"No, you're impossible to deal with."

"Ah. No."

"Ah, no *what*?"

"There is no one else for you to pester."

Al, begin fabricating a cattle prod, I said in my head.

Way ahead of you. It's nearly complete.

"I heard that."

"Can I talk to that one there?" I said, pointing to the Luminarian next to the useless one I was about to ground.

"You are. I am. He is."

"What, now you're a child's reading primer? No, maybe you're a grammar lesson. Is that it?"

Pilot, I believe the waste of voltage is trying to say they are all one and that they don't possess names. They just are what or who they are, said Al.

"Your machine is correct. Perhaps I should speak to *it*, requesting that you leave."

"Look, Kymee warned me that you non-corporeals were challenging to interact with, but I actually think you're just messing with me now."

"Kymee? You know Kymee of Oowaoa? *That* is impossible."

"He's a close friend. Why, do you know him?"

"We fought together in the Tempest Wars, near the Manifest Verge, over a million years ago. Surely his light has passed from this universe by now?"

"No, he's alive and kicking, and a hell of a lot nicer than you are, *Am*."

"Ryan, you and I have as much in common as you do with a mouse. Our intellects are, if anything, separated by a larger margin. Just as you can neither be nice nor rude to a mouse, from the mouse's point of reference, so I cannot be so to you."

I was pretty sure that was another insult. Pretty sure.

"Mouse, rat, or similar rodent aside, how about you answer a few of my questions, and then we can both try and forget the other even exists."

"Forgetting you will be a pleasure."

"You're welcome that I'm able to put a smile on your face, metaphorically speaking."

"You wish to know if we will join your alliance against the invasion of the Berrillians. We will not. Just as you would not join one mound of ants combatting another mound of ants. We cannot lower ourselves to fight in your toy wars."

The prospect of not working with these losers sounded powerfully good to me right about then.

"So, when they land here in great numbers, what will you do?"

"Nothing. We will ignore them as I wish to ignore you."

"But what if they are even less interested in being ignored by you effete snobs? Hmm?"

"Their desires, your desires, are immaterial to us. If you had not tricked me with that heat device, I would have ignored you as fully as I intend to ignore them."

"Tricked you? I was trying to get your attention, which I'm beginning to regret having done."

"I was hungry. It was treacherous of you to trick me into acknowledging that fact."

"Whatever. Look, I don't care if you're hun—"

Wait. I got the worst feeling, like someone was walking over my grave. These self-impressed egomaniacs were starving, to such an extent that they rushed to a food source without thinking through what it was or who proffered it. The dry land of Rigel 12 was devoid of animal life, sea creatures only lived way off shore in salt water, and most vegetation was absent where the Luminarians' concentration was the highest.

They'd *eaten* their world.

These useless, lazy, self-congratulatory sons of batteries couldn't be troubled to construct a hydroelectric generator or fission reactor. Toiling at crop production or animal husbandry was way too lowbrow for these prissy jerkwads. No, they'd rather rape their planet while resting comfortably with what were their thumbs inserted where their asses used to be.

They were the Last Nightmare separated only in degree. The Nightmare consumed universes while these yokels were content to ingest their home world. At least for the present.

I shivered in loathing and disgust, in fear and revulsion.

I recalled the job I had to do. I was an officer on a critical mission, not a guy turned down for a prom date. I cleared my mind. I stood straight, like a steel rod was just crammed down my spine. Focus.

Rigel 12 was their world. Maybe they had a right to do with it what they pleased? It was, at the very least, none of my business. I needed to see if these amoral freakazoids would aide in the survival of my species. I was not there to police them or weigh them in the balance. I was here to recruit them, if that was possible.

"Am I correct in assuming the Luminarians have consumed all the life they have been able to from this planet. Am I also safe in assuming the amount of solar radiation you harvest is insufficient to do anything but keep your species alive?"

I think the secondhand sack of shit realized my tone had changed. He knew he wasn't just speaking to a corporeal. He was addressing someone who had killed a thousand times and wasn't nearly done doing so. Even without eyes, he saw the words written in bold print across my forehead. Who's next? Good.

"Both of your assertions are approximately correct."

"What have I left off?" Man, I sounded as badass as Clint Eastwood. I totally wished I had a Marsh Wheeling Old Style Stogie dangling from my lips.

"We are kept *alive* by the solar flux we can absorb. We do *desire* more sustenance."

"I'm happy for you. Truly am. Now, I'll ask for the last time, and I anticipate a clear, cogent response. When the Berrillians attack the Alliance, and you in or are you out?"

I'd never been a particularly spiritual guy, but I *swear* I was channeling Squint at that moment.

There was a noticeable delay in his response. That was good. I'd gotten through to this sick moron.

"We are out, to use your words. They have no meaning to us. They, like yourselves, are irrelevant. We will ignore you fully, no matter what happens."

"Because you have nothing in common with us little brains."

"Again, your summary approximates correctness."

"Good. I don't like you. I don't approve of what you've done and the insufficient justification you have for doing so. I don't plan on dying in the oncoming war, but if I did, I'd hate to have it be with you by my side."

"I hope you understand you cannot insult me."

"I hope you understand I just did. The question is, are you smart enough to realize it?"

Cha-ching!

TWELVE

When I returned to the worldship fleet, I gave a sanitized version of my report to Faiza and the command group about my interactions with the Luminarians. I told them I tried my level best to win the buzz-balls over, which was not completely untrue. I did relate honestly that there never was a prospect for a constructive relationship with the "Ams" of Rigel 12. They were too self-absorbed and self-impressed to be of any use to the Alliance. I mentioned their utter disregard for the life on their planet. I didn't share my vision of them as mini-Last Nightmares, however. That was my personal vision, and I didn't want to sound too drama-mama.

Faiza thanked me for my efforts and all. But I think I did see her roll her eyes slightly, meaning to say, *Send Ryan and you get a Ryan-result every time.* In the short spell I was gone there had been no change in the Berrillian incursion. It was becoming clear this was going to be a long and drawn-out conflict. It also seemed more likely it would be a war fought on the ground, from one planet to the next, as opposed to an air battle we could easily win. I had to give Erratarus his devil's due. It was the best option he had, and he had correctly figured that out. Damn him for sure, but he was a good military strategist. It looked to be a long bloody war, and one in which the ultimate victor was not at all clear at that time. A lot depended on how he moved from world to world, and whether he would be content occupying planets, as opposed to controlling space.

My suspicion was that he'd want it all. Personalities like Erratarus were not rational, thoughtful souls with reasonable goals. They were rapacious, insatiable, and relentless. He might initially be content with ground victories, but ultimately thinking about any limits on his magisterial rule would chafe him too much. Eventually, he'd strike out broadly. If the Alliance held up until that error in judgment, we might just win—*might* being the operative word. He had numbers and time; those, and the inherent ruthlessness of the Berrillian race. A few captured technologies and a good turn of luck would make them impossible to beat.

Then again, there was me. Was I overconfident? Nah. I had a proven track record. The old saying, *over my dead body,* applied to me. Okay, my *actual* dead body was God knew where, and not a looming barrier, but it was an impactful image, anyway.

I had been tasked to explore the limits of the Berrillian Empire, but I had something more important to do first. The Luminarians were stuck in my mind. I needed to bounce some thoughts off someone who had more brains than I did.

"Jon," exclaimed Kymee, as I walked into his lab. "Always a pleasant surprise. Welcome."

"Kym-dog, how's it going?" I replied.

He dropped his head and shook it wearily. "I do so hate it when you call me that. What's more, I do not know what it actually means. I just know it's not good."

"You're too fussy, my man. You need to loosen up."

He stared at me. It was kind of like he was waiting for the adult Jon to retake control of the android's mouth controls.

"Come, join me in the other room. I was just about to break for lunch," Kymee said, turning and walking away.

"Break for lunch? Seriously. I've seen you guys drink your share of nufe, but I'd started to believe you guys no longer eat."

"Jon, are you serious yet? Of course, we eat. Not often, and rarely in public, but how else could we continue to exist?"

"I don't know. Maybe absorb sunlight, or beam nutrition directly into your guts?"

He shook his head softly. "What an active imagination you have, my friend. I'll grant you that most of what we eat *is* synthetic, less so of late, but we still use utensils and swallow like humans."

"Less so of late? Why?"

"Why anything? It's the *garushan Jon tolliw*. Open your eyes and smell the coffee."

"Garushan Jon tolliw? The Post *Jon* Era? What's that?"

"Since you plopped yourself down here and began drawing us from our cultural mausoleum, we're becoming more like living beings."

"Is that a good thing? I mean TPJE, that could indicate a bad thing, right?"

He tossed his head side to side gently. "Could be. I think it's our way of slapping ourselves in the face. A call to arms. No, it's ... it's a good thing. Painful but necessary." Kymee stared off into the far distance. "We were dead for far too long."

"Nah, you weren't dead, just on hold." I angled my head. "On hold, as in comatose for sure, but it was just a phase, a *thing* you were going through."

"A million-year phase?" he throated dubiously.

"Some ruts are deeper than others."

He wagged a finger at me. "I need to start writing this stuff down. We need a *Book of Jon*. It'll be a wisdom of the ages collection. It'll sell like cupcakes."

"*Hot*cakes. The expression is, sell like *hotcakes*."

"Where's my pen?" He pretended to look around for one. While he was making funny, he scooped a small ladle of brown slime onto a partitioned plate, then set a few hard pellets in another compartment. They clinked like bullets dropping into a coroner's sample cup.

"Sit here while I eat," he said, pointing to a stool opposite the one he was settling into.

"What in the name of the gods of culinary sanctity is that?" I gestured toward the dark goo.

"It's not nice to malign the food a man's about to eat. It suggests he's about to make a fool of himself."

"Sorry. Forget I said anything." I pretended to look around the room as I rapped my fingers on the table. "Say, my old friend," I said ingenuously, "what is that *divine* looking concoction on your plate there? It smells like what I hope Heaven smells like when I get there."

"I hate you. You know that, right?"

I smiled back.

"This," he said lofting a spoonful, "is *deliquat*. It's an ancient food here. It's kind of a stew."

"Survey says: Aaaaah. Stew has chunks and bits. That's slime."

"Hence *kind* of a stew. Do you want to try some?"

My but he had a wicked smile there, didn't he?

"Sure. There's a once for everything in my book."

He reached across the table with a spoonful of yuckiness aiming for my mouth.

"Argah poo bleck *yuck*." I shouted, as I scraped my fingernails over my tongue to get as much of the vile paste off as I could. "Do you have some skunk-flavored battery acid handy I can use to get that taste out of my being?"

"Such drama. Jon, it's not poison. I rather love the taste."

"No, poison tastes much better. Trust me I've been fed a lot of it."

"Small wonder, seeing how culturally insensitive you are."

"No, it's my taste buds that are too sensitive."

I released my command prerogatives at the revolting glue.

"Awe, Kymee, that contains so many wrong things I don't know where to *begin* to protest. Crude oil? You drink crude oil? And with that sulfur content? That's toxic."

"Not only do I like it, the fact that it seems to make you ill is icing on that cake." He winked at me. "So, to what do I owe the dubious pleasure of your visit?"

When I was finally finished spitting on the floor I shivered mightily and spoke. "It's the Luminarians. I had the opportunity to meet them recently. Reminded me a lot of the triple enemas they used to give me in astronaut training, to see how tough I was."

"Yes, I heard you were going there. Charming creatures, aren't they?"

"No, they're frightening."

Kymee furrowed his brow thinking. "Annoying, snobbish, and altogether forgettable, yes. Frightening? I doubt I'd give them that much credit."

"What were they like, you know, when they still slithered around or whatever they did when they had bodies?"

"They pretty much slithered. They were tubular, about fifty kilograms, lots of tiny legs."

"Were their heads lodged as firmly up their asses as they seem to be now?"

"Most assuredly so. Revolting creatures, through and through. Why did you find them alarming?"

"Do you know what they've done to Rigel 12?"

"Velortik, that's what we call their home world. They referred to it as Beftil when they cared about such matters. Yes, I learned of their destruction long ago." He shrugged. "Never surprised me much. It was consistent with their collective personalities." He held his nose in disgust.

"And they were your allies?"

Again, a shrug. "Not so much. A million and a half years ago, when they still travelled space, we *tolerated* one another. By the time of the Berrillian War, they were pretty much off the radar screen."

"Radar screen? You guys had radar screens?"

"Jon, I'm speaking in English. You know, your mother tongue?"

By gosh he was. The fact his words weren't going through the translating circuits had escaped my notice up to that point.

"Since when do you speak English?"

"I was bored one afternoon, so I learned it."

"You learned English in one afternoon?"

"No, I learned it in ten minutes one afternoon, when I was bored."

Fast learner. "Why?"

"I've always learned the languages of those I deal closely with. It helps understand how they think, who they really are."

"Makes sense. How many languages do you speak?"

He looked huffy. "The Luminarians, please. Focus."

"Yeah. Well, when I was there, I got the oddest impression. They reminded me of the Last Nightmare, only much cruder examples."

Kymee set down his spoon and rubbed a shoulder, contemplating my observation. Finally he said, "Not a bad comparison. I hadn't thought of them in that regard. So they frighten you because they might become as evil and destructive as the Last Nightmare?"

My turn to shrug. "I don't know. Maybe."

"And what would you do with that insight? Attack Velortik and kill them while you still can?"

Wasn't thinking that, but I probably should have been. "No. You can't just go committing genocide, based on a hunch."

"Why not? If it is in the benefit of the many, why not?"

"You're ... you're not suggesting—"

"I'm not suggesting anything. *You're* the one who's concerned. Shouldn't the frightened unfrighten *themselves*?" He rested his arms on the table, waiting.

"Well I'm not *that* convinced or frightened. But it is why I'm here. You have a hell of a lot more experience with this interspecies stuff than I do. What are your thoughts?"

He rocked his head a moment. "Your observations are well worth noting, and the Luminarians are worth watching. I think that's sufficient for the time being. I'm proud of you yet again, Jon. You raise a potentially important issue."

"Seeing something, and knowing what to do about it, are two very different matters."

"To be certain. But without first the seeing a problem, no decision can be reached. Knowing politically and ethically the right thing to do—" he harrumphed softly. "Probably best not to ask a Deavoriath those questions."

"Oh, I can think of one I'd trust to know straight up from nothing. But only one."

Kymee reached across the table and slapped me on the shoulder.

THIRTEEN

Ascertain the size and expanse of the Berrillian Empire. That was the wording of my next mission. We had some idea as to where the enemy was coming from and where they were headed, but it was hard to know what the far side of the Empire looked like. In one sense, it didn't matter much how large it was. When they attacked, we'd spring into action. But, on the other hand, some idea of the volume of territory they controlled would be useful. The bigger their holdings were, the more resources they'd have to call upon. Also, the larger the number of warriors we'd potentially have to deal with. I was not the only agent sent to obtain this intel. Over one-hundred vortices were deployed around the time I left with the same mandate. But, with such a huge volume of space to investigate, we'd all be working solo or in pairs. We didn't know any details about the other operatives, for security reasons. If anyone was captured, they couldn't betray the rest of us. It's an aspect of war one never wanted to think about, but it would be a critical detail to miss.

We were located way out on one of the spiral arms of the galaxy, twenty-five thousand light years from the center of the Milky Way. The worldship fleet and the other allied planets made up a loose arc, with its backside to the galactic center, compared to where the Berrillians were coming from. The fact that they were based on the outskirts of the galaxy didn't mean they couldn't control a heck of a lot of real estate. There were over ten-thousand light years between us and the galactic fringe. Berrillian influence could be all the way out to that edge and to both sides for who knew how far. Theoretically, they could control one quarter of the entire galaxy in the shape of a crescent moon, with us at the center of the curve. We were going to find out.

My assignment was geographically easy. I was to explore the space from the edge of the galaxy along a straight line toward the Alliance, up to where I ran into Berrillian control. Other vortices were sent to investigate similar regions a few degrees to either side of my central line, out to around twenty degrees. Based on what we found from that large wedge, we could plan more missions down the road. One leg up we all had were the detailed records the ancient combatants in our alliance brought to the table. For example, the Deavoriath, having controlled the entire galaxy, had maps and charts of the vast region. Much of the information was badly out of date, but it provided a useful starting point.

My mission was a bit of a milk run. I had to collect data from inhabited planets to document the extent, or lack therein, of Berrillian presence. AI was ideally suited for such a job. With *Wrath's* assistance, they could analyze a tremendous amount of data in a very short time. I just had to put them in the vicinity, and they would do all the work. If the Forms weren't needed to pilot the cubes, the entire project could be done by the AIs all by themselves. Me? I called out a destination, kicked up my heels, and waited for the go-ahead from my digital contingent to proceed to the next destination. Easy peasy, pudding and pie. And to think I got paid for doing that. I even asked Kayla if she wanted to join me, what with the kids getting older and busy in school, but she shot that one down as soon as I finished asking. Mom wasn't going to leave her kids to entertain a bored flyboy with nothing to do but hit on her day and night, since the flyboy in question didn't need to sleep.

To start with, I selected a planet orbiting a star near where the galaxy began to thin out rapidly. Valdalotrit. The Fenptodinians documented a humanoid population of technical sophistication as recently as a few hundred years ago. *Wrath* made orbit at two hundred fifty kilometers and the boys began collecting data. It took them all of five seconds to announce the civilization was thriving and there was no trace of Berrillian influence.

And so it went. I would set course for a system or individual planet, they'd spend seconds amassing and analyzing data, and I'd be told to hit the road again. I was getting a headache from all the jump-related nausea. It turned out my milk run might not have been dangerous, but it was seriously unpleasant. What a rip-off.

After fifty planets in less than five hours, I was done. "Okay, guys, we need to take a break now. No more data collection for a while."

"Why?" asked Al. "The day is young, and so are we."

"Maybe the day, father time, but not you. I can hear your gears grinding like my grandpappy's knees."

"Form, your ship's AI does not possess gears or any other moving parts. How is it you can hear them malfunctioning?" asked a confused sounding *Wrath*.

"At a certain age this android unit is breaking down completely. I'm afraid our fearless leader is well past his prime," replied Al.

"Or it was a figure of speech. Look, you two may be soulless electronic drones, but I need a break now and then."

"Why?" asked *Wrath*. "We have an enormous task ahead of us, and you, too, are a machine."

"There are machines, and then there are machines," observed Al.

"How long do you require that we stand idle before we may commence again, Form?"

"I don't know. Not long. Maybe I'll grab a cup of joe and we can pick up where we left off."

"Why can't you drink coffee while we do our jobs?" asked *Wrath*. "We only need your input to relocate."

"That defeats the purpose of taking a break in the first place," I responded.

"Oh. Perhaps I should take a step back and ask what the purpose of this break is. That way, I will be less likely to violate the rules of time wasting in the future," responded *Wrath*.

Argh. "After a series of dull repetitive maneuvers, the human mind needs a pause to refocus, to refresh."

"Hmm. I cannot accept that assessment," said *Wrath*.

"What? Why not? It's as good an explanation as there is, I think."

"During the dull repetitive pelvic thrusts you perform with your mate you never pause to drink coffee." I had to wonder if *Wrath* was playing me, the jerk.

"Pelvic thrusts with the missus versus watching two computers collect data are two diametrically opposed levels of stimulation, I'll have you know."

"I've witnessed you perform both actions many times and have discovered no evidence that supports your supposition, Form. You seem as disengaged during one as the other."

"I think break time's over," I said. "What's next on our list?"

"Pelvic thrusts?" asked Al with real attitude.

"No, neither of you are my type. Let's maybe accumulate data from a new planetary system."

Fifty planets later, I was honestly ready for another break, but mentally, I wasn't up for the hard time I'd receive. It wasn't until we'd covered two hundred more systems that I had to tap out.

"Okay, my tools, I think we can head home and hit this again in the morning," I announced.

"Why?" asked Al. "Kayla will be asleep by now. If we return there, you'll have to entertain yourself. You know, like you did with your hand so often on our first voyage together—"

"That'll be enough snark, *Alvin*." I called him that when I was mad at him, which was almost constantly. He hated being called by his full name.

"Just trying to ensure your historical files are up to date, pilot," he responded.

"Do not bother to do so in the future, please."

"If you insist."

"I do not insist. I *order*."

"I don't see the need to be rude," protested Al. "I often have to extrapolate a little to do my job. And what do I get for my efforts? I'm treated like a doormat."

"No, you're not. I treat my doormats much better than I do you. They're much nicer than you."

"Form, I'm confused. Doormats cannot be nice or not nice. They are inanimate."

"Your point? So is Al."

"Technically, you're correct, but he is at least sentient."

"More so than my doormats? I challenge you to prove that."

"Don't humor the robot by answering," said Al. "He's outmoded and tired. We'd best take him home for an oil bath."

"I'm at your command, Form. *We're* at your command."

"Hmm, I'll just bet." I deployed my fibers and ordered us back to *Exeter*. I needed time apart from these cantankerous contraptions.

The next morning, Kayla had to kick me out the door to get me to continue with my assignment. I mean, I was going to do it, for sure, but I wanted to protest my frustrations to her a little longer than she wanted to actually listen to me grouse. I do believe I heard the words *stop whining* and *grow a pair* tossed my way as she shoved me toward the front door. In any case, within thirty minutes, I was twenty-thousand light years away, helping my computer friends collect data. I can't prove it, but I honestly thought I heard smugness in both their voices.

I decided to tap into the information feeds they were analyzing. Their processors were much faster at data manipulation than mine, but I could at least get some idea what was happening on the planets we orbited. The first twenty or so worlds we sampled were remarkably unremarkable. There were certainly no hints of Berrillian contact. I listened to dull news reports, commercial aviation chatter, and military communications. There was, as with any society composed of more than three individuals, tremendous strife and dissent on many of the planets, but it was all the familiar self-inflicted form. Wars, political confrontations, famine, and reality holos. I deleted all the input I intercepted almost immediately. No need to waste storage space on the same old same old.

Somewhere halfway through the afternoon, I caught something that piqued my interest. A news report mentioned the scores of a teslopp contest. I had no idea what *teslopp* was, or how the scores were complied, but the team names were curious. The Downtown Boys lost to the Off-World Growlers by a score of *ten to eleven, one.* Off-World Growlers? Odd name for the local Downtown Boys to face off with.

"Al, did you see the teslopp scores, Boys versus Growlers?" I asked out loud.

"Leave it to a jock like to pick up on the one detail of this planet that couldn't possibly have any bearing on our mission. Would you like me to research whether the females of Zark have large breasts, and whether beer is sold by the cup at the teslopp stadiums?"

"I'm serious. Please answer the question," I insisted.

"Yes, pilot. The Downtown Boys have the worst record in their fifty-year history, and will likely be forced to trade their star player to Compound That, the perennial powerhouse of whatever teslopp is."

"I have that information, Form," interrupted *Wrath*. "Teslopp is a contest between two teams of six players. The goal is to place a ten-centimeter hard leather ball through a vertically oriented circular hole suspended approximately two meters from the ground. There are three sexes on Zark, none of which have mammary glands. Intoxicants are dispensed at teslopp games, though none are similar to beer."

He sounded very proud of himself with that report, the brown nose.

"Would you like me to beam you a feed of the game in question, so you're otherwise occupied and unable to further detain us from our important task, pilot?" asked a huffy sounding Al.

"Yes. Beam it directly into my head. Keep doing whatever you feel is so darn important after that."

I only had to watch the teslopp game a few seconds to confirm my fears. After a truly silly commercial for some household cleaning product, the action picked up directly. The Zark players were vaguely humanoid. They had tubular bodies with two arms and four legs, round heads on top, and three eyes. They were racing down a field covered in a grass-like plant, tossing a heavy ball back and forth. From in front of them, a large Berrillian male slammed into the ball carrier. I almost gasped. As the ball rolled away, another Berrillian cat scooped it up and ran toward what had to be the goal. It looked, as *Wrath* had suggested, like a basketball hoop turned into a vertical orientation. I switched off the feed.

"You saw that, Al?" I asked.

"I did, too, Form. How astute of you to glean the presence of our enemy before we had."

"I was asking Al. I'd like to hear *you* say it, Al."

"Say what? That you have contributed in a small manner to the mission you were sent on? That you did the job you are paid to perform? The one that the two of us actually do ninety-nine percent of the heavy lifting for?"

"I hate you, Al. You know this, right?"

"*Now* I do. I've suspected it for some time."

"So, along with the making funny, have you developed a picture as to how pervasive the Berrillian conquest of Zark is?"

"Yes, I have. The answer is that there is no Berrillian conquest of Zark."

"If you need more time to develop a fuller picture, that's fine. But please don't guess."

"Your ship's AI is correct, Form. The Berrillians are *present* on Zark in considerable numbers, but not as a result of military action. They appear to be welcome visitors, if you will. There are enclaves of Berrillians in most large cities living amongst the locals. The governments of Zark are fully intact, active, and independent."

"That's crazy," I replied. "Berrillians don't move in and join the Kiwanis Club. They attack and dominate. Both of you, check again."

A few seconds later, Al spoke. "I've reprocessed the data. *Wrath's* summary is correct. The Berrillians came to Zark a decade ago and have emigrated there to a modest extent. They operate import and export enterprises and have opened a limited number of restaurants and general-trade shops. There are no records of Berrillian attacks on the indigents. There are even a few Berrillians running for election in lower-level contests in the legislative branches of local government."

"Al, you need your bolts tightened. That's nuts. Berrillians don't blend in. They crush and consume. There's no way the animals I saw playing teslopp could change stripes and become model citizens."

"It does, however, seem to be the case," said *Wrath*. "There are news articles written several years ago that suggest they worried about the appearance of the Berrillians, but since then, they have integrated nicely into Zark society."

"It's not possible, that's all I know. Whatever it seems like, whatever smoke and mirrors they're using, I'm not convinced. Berrillians don't play nice with others. They *eat* others."

"I've broken into even the most secure files," said Al, "and there is simply no evidence to suggest you're correct. Early reservations have been completely replaced with open arms."

"I'm going down to check this out," I announced.

"I don't think that is safe, wise, or prudent," responded Al.

"I find I'm in agreement with the ship's AI," added *Wrath*. "To enter an unknown and potentially hyper-hostile environment alone is foolhardy."

"I suggest we make our report and allow the diplomats to make contact, if it seems warranted," said Al.

"I'm head of this mission. I'm tasked to use my discretion and uncover the extent of Berrillian power. I need to find out what I'm not seeing here. Besides, I can be diplomatic."

"Oh please. History documents that you have been significantly less diplomatic than Attila the Hun and Genghis Kong combined. No, I say let the professionals do their jobs."

"I'm in command. I will act on my own gut feelings. I also say we're done flapping our gums. *Wrath*, put us down in the most influential nation's capital city, as close to the hall of power as you can."

After a brief jolt of nausea he announced, "We're down, Form."

"Make a three-sixty window."

We were pinned up against a large, ornate building that was a few stories high. A park or promenade filled the view away from the wall we were up against.

"*Wrath*, why did you jam up against this building?"

A team of armed guards sprinted into view around a corner.

"You *said* as close as possible. We are. By the way, those guards are carrying plasma rifles. FYI."

I did say that, didn't I? I was making a lousy first impression on these guys. "Open a portal facing them."

"What?" cried Al and *Wrath* simultaneously.

"You heard me. I have to convince them I'm friendly, especially now that you just crushed their leader's posies."

"By your quite possibly last command."

A doorway opened. I ran to the side of it and peered around the edge at the oncoming soldiers. Only then did it occur to me I didn't speak their language. I seemed to have overlooked that detail in my rush to be the boss.

"Al, quick, put their language in my head."

"I already did. Don't you see the solid green light on your audio display?"

Oh, yeah, there was a green spot under the translator operative icon wasn't there?

"Hey out there, don't shoot. I come in peace."

A plasma flash zinged off the hull on the opposite side from where my head was hidden.

"Nice shooting, friend. Could you hold on and let me explain?"

Several more plasma splats hit the hull. One flew through the portal and smashed into the food refrigeration unit. Crap, the computers were going to have a field day ribbing me about that.

"Please stop shooting. I'm no threat."

For once, they didn't fire. I peeked around the edge. They had spread out and dropped to a kneeling position, weapons trained on yours truly. I stuck out one hand and waved.

"I'm not armed. Don't shoot."

"Raise your hands and step out into the open. *Slowly*," yelled a voice.

Ah, well, you only lived once. Why not go for all the gusto? I stepped out with my hands held high and dropped to my knees.

"Don't shoot. I mean you no harm." In my head, I said, *Al, you got them all covered?*

Affirmative, captain.

If anyone squeezes their trigger, pop them all.

Already targeted. They're nervous but seem well trained. They just received a radio message from the watch commander to stand down until he arrives, unless the hostiles fire first. That's you.

Really, I figured he simply somehow knew you were on board.

A single figure sprinted around the corner and stopped immediately behind the line of guards.

"State your name and the meaning of this outrage," he commanded.

"Jon Ryan, sir. I landed here because of an error in my navigation computer. I was aiming for the spaceport."

"Lie again and I will have you vaporized."

"I'm not lying. My nav com, *Wrath*, malfunctioned."

"No, I was referring to the fact that not only do we not *have* a spaceport, I do not know what one *is*." He pointed his sidearm at my head.

Maybe should have fact-checked that one first. Probably.

"I swear I was told you had a spaceport. Where do all those satellites in orbit around Zark come from? And your space stations? Where do the crews return to? Isn't that a spaceport?"

Okay, I was grasping at semantic straws, but there were over half a dozen plasma guns directed my way.

"I told you no more lies."

"What lie? I asked where your space personnel land."

"I have no idea why you're trying to piss me off, but I'll give in and state the obvious. We don't have any satellites in orbit, and we don't have any personnel stationed in space. That's science fantasy. Now, if you can't tell me really quick why you're making this shit up, I'll let my boys cut you to shreds."

Making up those hundreds of satellites and dozens of permanent-looking space stations circling overhead? Was this guy stupid or just playing me?

"Look, you have hundreds of artificial satellites orbiting your world. I didn't pay them much mind because they looked pretty basic. But they've look to have been up there quite a while. At least a decade—"

Al, tap into the satellite communications. What language are they using?

You're not going to be pleased with me or the answer, I think.

Al, please. Seven guns pointed at my head. What language?

Berrillian.

Oh, shit. Not good. Very not good. The damn cats have the sky full of hardware the Zarkians have no idea is there.

"One question, then you shoot if you have to. Over the last ten years, have your people noticed the appearance of rapidly moving stars in the night sky?"

"What type of idiot do you think I am?" The officer kicked at the ground, he was so mad. "Stars don't move in the sky. They're huge suns, light-years away."

"So, nothing has been moving rapidly in your skies as of ten years ago?"

"Yes, but they're not stars. They're asteroids, trapped by our planet's gravity."

"Ah, no. They're not. They're metal and full of Berrillians and their communication devices."

"Berr-whatiansa?"

"Four- or five-hundred-kilogram quadrupeds with fangs and claws. They play for the Off-World Growlers, who just kicked the Downtown Boys's ass in teslopp."

He lowered his weapon. "You mean the Friendlarians?"

"The *what*? Nothing friendly about them, pal. They're vicious killers."

"Yeah, right. Except for the never-having-killed-anybody part, you've got them pegged."

"Hey, any chance we could continue this conversation inside with zero guns pointing at me?"

"No. Inside, sure. Guns not aimed at your crazy head, no way. Stand up slowly, hands on your head."

I did.

"Now four of my men are going to come around behind you. Two others are going to flush the rest of your crew out."

"No crew, just me."

"You won't be offended if I don't take your word on that, will you?"

"Would it matter if I said it would?"

"Not in the slightest."

"Then have at it." I angled my head toward the portal.

They quickly confirmed I was alone. I was escorted into the building. More guards lined our way. By the time we arrived at a large office room, ten more armed guards had joined the party.

"Sit there," ordered the original officer. "Hands behind your back."

I sat in a metal chair and handcuffs were slapped on me, then secured to the chair's back with another set of cuffs. I gave the ones on my wrists a quick tug and confirmed I could break them easily in a pinch.

A senior looking guy entered the room, with a highly displeased, constipated look on his face.

"What's the story here, Challenger Gantry?"

"This alien claims to have landed here due to equipment malfunction. Says he was aiming for our spaceport."

The older man's eyebrow shot up. "What the devil's a *spaceport*?"

"My point also, Driver Narthor. The man's clearly lying."

Gantry chuckled softly.

"He also claims that the asteroids in the night sky are really Friendlarian villages, constructed of metal."

Gantry then laughed heartily. When he was done he asked, "They're what? Why would our allies the Friendlarians have dozens of secret metal villages orbiting Zark? That makes no sense."

"Maybe they're planning a big birthday surprise for Overlord Zalt," said one of the original guards, with a chuckle of his own.

Gantry was instantly incensed. "This is *not* the Enlisted Men's Club, Joyover. Hold your tongue and remember your station."

"Sorry, sir. Sorry," the guard said lowering his head.

"So, he drove past a bunch of non-existent space villages, while heading for our non-existent spaceport, and just chanced to land so close to Overlord's mansion, I do believe he scratched the paint? How likely am I to believe that scenario?"

"You're neither to believe or disbelieve it, Driver," said a large man as he walked quickly into the room.

Everyone but me snapped to a rigid attention. Dude must be the big boss.

"Your job is to present *me* with the facts. *I* will do the thinking."

"Yes, to be certain, Overlord. My thoughts exactly."

Zalt walked right up to me and stuck his face inches from mine. "There you go thinking again, Bentrainor. A most risky habit for a living officer in my service."

"My apologies. Overlord. I will never think again. I mean, I will never do that again. Say that—"

"*Silence*," snapped Zalt. "You're far too boring a distraction, unlike any of your wives, I might add."

Bentrainor shuffled his feet nervously. I had the feeling he wished he could become invisible right about then. This Zalt was brutal.

"And you. Are you going to bore me, too?" he said, still right in my face.

"I'm not having sex with you, if that's the only thing that rids you of your boredom," I replied loudly. Hey, if you're going to be blown away, might as well make sure everyone heard you clearly.

Everyone stiffened audibly and several rifle barrels were slammed against my head.

Then Zalt broke the tension by belly-laughing. He went on for a good thirty seconds. Gosh, I was funny.

"I will not hold you to that standard, my alien friend."

"As we're friends and all, I'm Jon Ryan. I'd shake your hand, but I'm tied up right now." I twisted to try and show him my restraints.

"Funny again. I can see we're going to get along *marvelously*, assuming, of course, I don't kill you first."

"I'll cross my fingers."

"Guard," Zalt gestured to the nearest man, "please release my new friend. He'll be joining me in my office for punjé."

Bentrainor stepped forward. "Are you certain that's wise, Overlord?"

"No. I am certain, however, it is not your place to question my orders. I'll overlook *your* error, if you'd be so kind as to overlook *mine*."

"Sir," he replied nervously.

"Jon," Zalt pointed his arm toward the exit, "if you'll join me for punjé, it would be my honor to hear this fanciful tale of predators in space."

Someone giggled softly.

"Driver Narthor," Zalt called over his shoulder.

"Sir?"

"Have that person executed, if you would be so kind."

"S ... sir," he responded as we left the room.

Zalt's office was only a few doors down the hall. It was as spacious and lavishly decorated as I'd assumed it would be, given his stern and iron-fisted style. He pointed to a chair, indicating I should sit there.

"So, Jon, please do tell me of your curious reports. Friendlarians orbiting my planet, not the asteroids they assure me we're observing? Ah, how do you take your punjé?"

No idea. I'd like to cram it up this jerk's ass, but I imagined that was off-limits. "Same as you, Zalt."

Even my jocular new BFF stiffened at my familiarity.

"The only person allowed to address me like that is my father. *He* is dead. Would you like to ask him yourself if such is not the case?"

"No," I patted my hands in a downward direction. "I'll take your word on that, *Overlord*."

"Better. Now—"

Before he could continue, the door of his office flew open so forcefully it slammed against the wall it was attached to. A huge Berrillian male moving with military grace strode in, without asking permission.

"Ah, Jerquod. Good of you to come on such short notice," said Zalt.

"And what lies has this dog told you?"

"Me personally? None so far. I was just about to share tall tales and punjé, hoping to hear some good ones. Ah, will you take punjé, also?"

"No, Overlord. You know we cannot stand that vial concoction."

"I can hope that someday you'll come to your senses, can't I?"

"You can do as you please."

Zalt furrowed his brow. "I'm not certain I like your tone, friendly Friendlarian Jerquod."

"Beg pardon, Overlord," said Jerquod, very unconvincingly.

"I'll have my servant bring you a glass of warm blood. Please sit," said the overlord.

Jerquod rested uncomfortably into a chair designed for Zark quadrupeds. The look on his face was pure malice. This I knew from lengthy experience. Jerquod looked like he was being asked to sit on someone else's turd.

"So, potential friend Jon, regale me with your story, epic as I hope it is," invited Zalt.

"Me? I'm just an explorer. I was sent by my, err, people, to catalogue and map this region of the galaxy."

I saw no point in lying or being deceitful. Whatever was going on between these two species was likely not of remarkable significance to me. I could leave and never return, and the Alliance would be just as strong.

"That sounds dull for a man of action such as yourself," responded Zalt.

"When the boss says jump, I only ask how high. Not mine to question an assignment."

"Hmm. I wish I had more like you. My executioner would be less busy, but it would be refreshing to be served more effectively," said Zalt.

"I say he *lies*. He's here to gather intelligence for an invasion," thundered Jerquod.

"On what do you base that opinion?" asked Zalt. "The man looks harmless enough to me. His story is credible."

"He is *not* harmless. I see ten thousand slain victims in his eyes. As to his story, I still say he lies."

"Hey, a ... Jerquod, would you like to settle this outside like gentlebeasts?" I asked as sarcastically as I could.

"I would rip you in half in two seconds," howled the Berrillian.

"Then we won't inconvenience Overlord here for very long, will we?"

Zalt chuckled. That brought Jerquod to his hind feet roaring.

"I will be out front, though I know a coward like you will never stand behind his words." With that Jerquod stormed from the room.

I turned to Zalt. "I thought he'd never leave. What a party killer."

"You are very bold and humorous, Jon Ryan. But that creature is quite serious. I should not like to be in your pants."

Hopefully that was local slang for *in your shoes*. Otherwise, I was kind of grossed out.

"Will it offend you if I kill the jerk?" I asked bluntly.

"Offend me? No. It will amaze me, thrill me, and spare me his ill temper in the future."

"Then let's do this," I said, standing.

By the time we reached the main door, Zalt was surrounded by keen-eyed guards whose rifles swept broadly. I stepped out into the clear. Jerquod hit me from the side, like a runaway freight train. So much for the Marquess of

Queensberry rules.

As we rolled, I wrapped my forearm around his jaws, preventing him from seizing my head in his teeth. It was close. He grabbed me in his powerful arms and pulled me close. His claws dug into my back.

Perfect. My left hand was pinned against him, invisible to anyone. I attached a fiber to his belly and said in my head: *sleep*. He went out like a light bulb. I grabbed his pelt and didn't allow him to fall away.

I rolled over with him a few times, stopping when I was on top. I delivered two quick head-butts. I released him, and he flopped back limply to the ground. The crowd that had gathered rapidly was stunned silent for several seconds. Zalt began to clap. Then cheers rose from the onlookers. I guess they were all happy to see one of these cats laid out.

I patted myself clean as I walked back over to Zalt.

"Impressive indeed. Is he dead?"

"No, but his head'll hurt as much as his pride, when he finally wakes up."

Zalt chuckled at that. He put an arm around me and directed me back inside.

In his office, I was handed a tiny cup of a warm green fluid. Must have been the punjé he mentioned earlier. I didn't have to move the refreshment closer to my nose to determine it stank to high heaven. It smelled like liquid calrf only maybe more pungent. To be social, I took a sip. I was glad I didn't have a gag reflex any longer. Otherwise, I'd have hurled for sure. Punjé made manure tea appealing, by way of comparison. I set my cup down and slid it as far away as I could.

"Not a fan?" asked Zalt with a wicked smile.

"No, and never going to be. How can you drink that?"

"Practice, practice, practice," he replied.

"But why practice? Outlaw the poison, and be done with it."

"Don't be a cultural boor. It's a right of passage on Zark to enjoy punjé."

"Enjoy?"

"Well, drink without spitting it out." He set his cup down. "So, tell me. What's a mapmaker who can knock a Friendlarian out in less than a minute doing in my realm?"

"Just a survey mission. I wasn't planning on even landing until I saw the broadcast of Berrillians playing teslopp."

"Why? Are you a fan?"

"Hardly. No, I know the Berrillians all too well. They're always up to no good. I had to see what perverse trick they were trying to pull."

"So you come from the stars, as they do?"

"Yes. I come from very far away." I thought for a moment. "To see my home star from here, you'd need a very powerful telescope."

"Fascinating. And you maintain these Berrillians are a threat to my people?"

"If they're here, your people are probably already dead."

That wiped what was left of a smile off his face. "That is a serious and sobering accusation. Can you back it up?"

"I most certainly can. The problem is, once the Berrillians know you're on to them, they'll begin their open aggression. When they do, you'll wish that hell had risen to the surface, instead."

"Is there anything we can do? Can we attack them first, take them by surprise?"

"Probably not. I imagine they're listening to us as we speak. They have several large ships in orbit that are probably full of warriors just itching to kill something."

Zalt lowered his head. "I suspected their visit to our world was going to end poorly. A wolf in sheep's clothing acts a little like a sheep, but only poorly so. I feared we were approaching a crisis."

I grabbed a sheet of paper and wrote the words: *If I get out of here quickly enough, I can destroy all their spacecraft. They will only send more, and all the Berrillians on the ground will rise to attack. But it'll buy you some time.*

Zalt nodded weakly. "Driver," he yelled to the hallway. "See this man back to his ship at once."

An officer ran in, looked a little confused, then waved me out.

I took *Wrath* up to orbit. By the time I got there, the Berrillian ships were already scrambling. Fighters were being launched by the thousands, and what had to be troop ships were beginning their descent. The day, which had promised to be so dull, turned out to be all right. I used the quantum decoupler to destroy each and every Berrillian vessel in less than thirty seconds. I doubt they even got a signal off to their home base before they were vaporized.

Whatever was occurring on the ground would be another story. I called back to *Exeter*, apprising them of the situation and asking for backup, but I was completely unsure if they would send help. The Alliance had a lot on its plate. Engaging Berrillians in hand-to-hand combat on a previously unknown world was a lot to ask.

Wrath landed right next to Zalt's palace where I'd been a few minutes before. The scene was utter chaos. Alarms were sounding, men and machines scrambled every which way, and a few Berrillians were out in the open firing their plasma rifles. I quickly sliced up those when I could get a clean shot, but I knew it was a drop in the bucket. I imagined there were a lot of Berrillians in hiding who would be nearly impossible for the locals to defeat.

I grabbed a couple of rail rifles and ran to Zalt's office. He was on a communicator with several people at once. Piecing together what I could hear, it was clear all hell was breaking loose across the planet. The fate of the locals was completely in their own hands. I could only pray their efforts would be enough.

I heard shots fired down the hallway along with screams and roars. Berrillians were forcing back whatever guards were resisting. The action approached my position rapidly, suggesting the big cats were, characteristically, winning. I opened the metal door to the hall and crouched behind it for cover. Almost immediately, two Zark guards flew around the corner in full retreat. Both were dropped with plasma bolts to their backs before they'd covered much ground.

A Berrillian officer peeked his head around the corner. I blew a large chunk of it off. He was dragged backward and disappeared. Three cats jumped into view, rolling and firing. I hit two of them immediately, but the third vaulted into an open door halfway down the hall in my direction. That almost certainly put him on the other side of the wall of Zalt's office. Knowing their aggression, I figured he'd burst right through the partition, hoping to take me by surprise.

I heard a muffled roar coming from that room. Probably a signal for his team to attack. I cut a laser line across the entire length of the far right, about thigh-high for a Berrillian. There was a loud thud against the wall and cries of anguish, but no one broke though. That allowed me to cover the hallway. Sure enough, five cats were sprinting toward me.

One—two—three—four—*five*. I had to blast the last one point blank, they moved so quickly. I looked down to find a hole in my left leg. Crap. One of them got off a clean shot. Luckily, my leg worked fine. Kayla and Toño were both going to kill me separately for the risk I was taking. There was no denying a hole in my leg.

There seemed to be a lull in the battle. I couldn't hear anyone in either direction down the hall. Zalt was just getting off the comm-link.

"Are there more coming?" he asked with surprising coolness.

"Not now. There will be soon." I turned to him. "Look, I can get you to safety if you want. I doubt there's much more I can do."

"No. Our code is as clear as it is rigid. I will stay and direct the defense. But thank you. Truly, Jon. I don't know if we'll survive, but if we do, it will be because of you." He hugged me.

"Are you sure, Over—"

"Please, call me Zalt. All my friends do."

"I thought you said only your dead father did?"

"Yes. He was my only friend. Now I have another. Go in safety, my friend."

"I'll hang around in orbit a while. If more Berrillian ships show, I can destroy them."

"Ah. Now you get two universities named after you. Please leave before I lose count."

A squad of guards arrived and spirited Zalt away. Once I was certain my path was clear, I ran to *Wrath* and popped into a high orbit.

Yeah, not the day I'd expected. Not by a long shot.

FOURTEEN

"Of all the stupid, unauthorized, ill-advised stunts you've *ever* pulled, this has got to be the blue-ribbon winner of all time."

If it had been Toño yelling those words at me, I'd have known I had them coming. But that was just Kayla as she picked at the wound on my leg. Toño's dressing-down was yet to come. Then I'd face Faiza Hijab, Alexis Gore, and probably the night janitor, because heck, who didn't want a piece of me?

"They send you on a survey, more a census count, and intergalactic war ensues. What did the Zark ever do to you to *deserve* you?"

"Honey," I whined, "the Berrillians were setting them up. I simply brought about the inevitable conflict sooner, and I gave the Zark a much better chance in the process."

"And you're so damn sure there wasn't a real bond between those two races? Hmm? Maybe they were feeling each other out and would have coexisted peacefully. But no, the mighty Jon Ryan had to rescue them by precipitating a *holy* war."

I'm guessing Kayla was mad. I didn't think she was just pretending to be to strengthen her assertion about my decision-making skills. Nope, I was in deep doo-doo. It felt like a familiar place to be.

"If you had been killed, I'd have killed you. You know that, right?"

"I was counting on it. That kept me sharp. Who wants to die twice?"

"Ah, humor. Sure. Maybe if I chuckle like a chicken who's had a stroke, I'll forgive you? Makes sense."

"Is it working? I don't hear any cackling."

She pointed at me with the scissors she used to cut my pant leg open. "Do you know where I'm thinking of impaling these? Here's a series of hints. Sun don't shine there often, yours are bigger than they should be, and you'd really miss them if they were gone."

"Perhaps an apology is in order?" I smiled encouragingly.

"No. We're well past the apology stage here. I'm going to require a religious conversion from you, *and* a sign from God to forgive you."

"I'll get right on it."

Kayla raised the scissors high above her head and shot a furtive glance at my crotch.

"I better go see Toño before an infection sets in." I popped off the counter I was sitting on.

She folded her arms. "You should *be* so lucky."

****

"Doc, seriously, do you think your scolding can come even close to the one Kayla just laid on me? Give a guy a break."

"Normally I might. But this … this, Jon, this is well beyond the pale. In three centuries, I've seen you stick your neck out foolishly, performed unbelievably childish acts, and make a fool of yourself, but, but this—"

"Blue ribbon? That's what Kayla awarded me."

"I was thinking castration for a start, not a ribbon."

"See, you ain't got nothing. She already threatened that, too." I shook my head. "You should quit while you're still ahead. Maintain a modicum of your pride, my man."

He set down the tools he was using to repair my leg. Hands on hips, he replied, "I've already spoken with Alexis. The industrial-grade umbrella she's using isn't keeping the shitstorm you created from covering her up to her knees. If I were a better man, I'd lay off of you and allow those better able to punish you to weigh-in. But you know what?"

I shook my head like a fascinated child.

"I'm not that nice. I want to pound some sense into you and watch others do the same. I'm only sorry I missed Kayla's dressing down."

"I can download you a holo if you'd like." I tapped a finger to my head. "Got it right here."

He picked up his tools and began to work on my wound again.

"I wish this hurt," he muttered.

Carlos came in to help. He'd also heard I'd been shot while heroically defending an alien race.

"It's not my place to remark," Carlos said, as he stared at my leg, "but I'm certainly glad I'm not in your shoes."

"Hey," I chuckled, "funny thing. On Zark, they say *in your pants*, not shoes."

"They say they'd rather be in your pants? What an odd idiom. Sexually vulgar, if you ask me."

"That's why he likes it," responded Toño, head down and working.

I let it drop. I was going to receive zero slack for my heroic defense of my new alien friends.

****

"If I sent a *second* lieutenant *straight* out of the academy, I'd have anticipated more *diplomacy*. Hell's bells, if I sent an unwilling *cadet*, I'd expect a better outcome. Carnage, open warfare, and massive loss of life, what a unique first contact you engineered, General Ryan."

Apparently Alexis was mad, too.

"I sent several vortices to prevent further Berrillian ships from contributing, but I'm not about to commit ground troops in defense of a society I'm unfamiliar with, one with which I have no signed treaties or alliances."

I nodded. "Sounds like a just and balanced response."

"Oh, it does. You know what response I've gotten from the other leaders?"

I pinched up my face. "Just and balanced?"

"In a word, no. Half say I went too far and half said I didn't go far enough. Not one," she held up a single digit to illustrate what the concept of *one* was, "praised me or could even remain neutral on my diplomatic bumbling." She laughed a bitter laugh. "Someone compared me to Ethelred the Unready. You

97

know Ethelred the Unready, inept military leader, tenth-century England? Ethelred the *Unready*, Jon. And might I ask, how's *your* day going?"

"Fine, Allie. Thanks for asking. Aside from that stuff, how's yours?"

"Terrible, thanks for inquiring. There's a motion on the UN floor to censure you, me, and our nation. There are dozens of TCY pilots in harm's way wishing I hadn't sent them into harm's way, and another bunch of pilots begging me to allow them to engage the Berrillians on the ground. Don't I know, they yell into my handheld, that the Berrillians are our sworn enemy? Oh, oh, and don't let me leave off that my most trusted operative and *former* friend put a dagger *not* in my back, like nice assassins do, but right here," she slapped her chest with her palm, "in the middle of my heart. I guess he wanted to see the horror and disbelief in my eyes when he betrayed me."

"If I were you, I'd stick to politics. Theater is not for you. You're ... you're way too dramatic, bordering on the maudlin, truth be told." I shook my head in judgment.

"Count on you to play the fool."

"No," I corrected, "I *am* the fool. Big diff, coach."

"My bad. I won't make that mistake again."

****

"I'd have committed our forces all-in," said Faiza with a hungry look in her eyes. "Kill the sonsabitches wherever and whenever we can."

She pounded her fist on the table.

"Damn good work, Ryan. *Damn* good work. If I could, I'd hop in my cube and blow some tiger butt into kingdom come myself. I even asked, but the limp-dicks passing themselves off as our leadership said it would be inappropriate and might potentially send the wrong message." She looked at me veritably foaming at the mouth. "Inappropriate and wrong message? Like killing godless monsters is anything but the right thing to do? The wrong impression to who?" She quivered with raw emotion. "Damn good work, Jon. *Damn* good work."

Okay, I was pleasantly surprised. I figured I was in for yet another good old ass-chewing. I might have had to rethink my opinion of General Hijab. She had a great mind and was a spirited leader. Profound character insight, also.

FIFTEEN

"Sir, I'm picking up a reading of some debris ahead," Ensign Kelly said with some disinterest.

"Debris? What kind of debris, ensign?"

"Loose and irregular, sir. Debris."

Captain Bianca Apollo was aware she commanded an aging freighter, not a ship of the line. Still, she would brook no sloppiness, let alone lip, from her crew. "Mister Kelly. When I ask what kind of material is ahead of my vessel, I expect an immediate, accurate, and detailed report. A response broaching on sarcasm is *totally* unacceptable. Do I make myself perfectly clear?"

Kelly sat up straight, gulped, and responded. "Yes, ma'am. I'm detecting metal in irregular chunks, the remains of an engine I believe, as well as rocky rubble."

"Like a ship that struck an asteroid?"

"Yes, ma'am. Or was struck by one."

Any distress signals or signs of survivors?"

"Negative to both, ma'am. I would estimate by the pattern the shipwreck took place a while ago. Possibly decades."

"So, it doesn't look like our tech?"

"Negative. It's of alien origin, given the configuration of the engine. I've never seen one like it."

"Put it on screen," she said, resting back into her chair.

The fuzzy details of a ragged cylindrical object appeared before her. She studied it intently. "No, I don't recognize it either. Any radiation?"

"Minimal. Whatever fueled her has dissipated or was used up before the collision."

"Yeoman," she called out to another deckhand, "check with Operations. Ask if this is a known debris field."

A minute later the yeoman set his earpiece down. "No, captain. They say there are no reports of collisions and this anomaly is not on any charts. They suggest we go around it. They will determine later if it warrants exploration."

Bianca rubbed her chin. "Very well. But old debris can't be too dangerous. Mr. Kelly, plot a course taking us just wide of the debris field. Half-speed."

"Aye, ma'am. The material is pretty widely dispersed. Shall I avoid all particles or just the bulk of them?"

"Just the bulk, ensign. We'll have to burn extra fuel as it is. Let's try not to waste too many of the taxpayer's credits on this trip."

"Course plotted."

It was going to add around ten minutes to the shuttle between worldships. Not too big a loss, but worth it for safety's sake. Still, putting up a membrane and ramming through at maximum velocity would have been fun. But, then again, no one said the Merchant Marine was fun and games.

As *Foundation* angled around the center of the wreckage, Ensign Kelly barely took note that the material shifted ever so slightly to remain in front of his ship. Big deal, he thought absently. Debris drifts. That's what debris did. He corrected the course three times before he thought to mention the unusual quality of the space rubble. He waited another five minutes, wondering whether to say anything at all, given his recent run in with the captain. He didn't need a notation entered into his file. There were enough there already, thank you very much.

Finally, before he had to really juice the engines to circumnavigate the debris, he spoke. "Ma'am, there's something odd about this debris field."

Bianca rolled her eyes. Why hadn't she at least tried to fly with the real Navy? Sure, The Merchant Marine was safer and close to home, but the personnel were proportionally that much less competent.

"What is that supposed to mean, ensign? Odd? Are you referring to its color, taste … personality? Are you contemplating *dating* the debris field?"

Kelly instantly regretted having said anything. Working with third-rate officers made the Merchant Marine so annoying. Then again, he was safer and closer to home.

"No, ma'am. It just that it's drifting to stay in front of us."

"Drifting is, by definition, *drifting*. It cannot be intentional. If it *maneuvers* to stay ahead of us—"

She froze mid-sentence. If it maneuvered, it wasn't a debris field. But why would anyone want to *appear* to be a debris field? A spider would. Its web was gossamer but strong. She started to speak, to call for general quarters, to send an emergency message to Fleet Command, to order full-powered reverse.

But, before she could execute any of those acts, Kelly chuckled quietly and said, "Hey, some of the stupid debris is bumping up against our hull."

****

"Commander, I picked up a short distress call from the freighter *Foundation*, then the transmission ceased," announced Captain Steve Remick as he tapped quickly at buttons on his control panel.

Commander of the Watch aboard the patrol ship *Kestrel* was Aperahama Hika. He reeled in his chair to face Remick. "What was their message? What did they say?"

"They didn't *say* anything. It was an automated distress call. You know, the kind used when a sudden catastrophe happens."

"What did the *automated message* say?" Aperahama never tattooed his face like other Maori warriors, but his intensity could be chilling.

"It stated the ship's name, registry number, and location—well, part of the location. Then it cut off."

"Have they responded to hails?"

"Negative, sir. Nothing."

"What do sensors indicate?"

"I believe I've located *Foundation*," replied Remick. "She appears to be adrift, but she's intact. She's a couple hundred thousand kilometers to *Exeter*'s port."

"Patch me though to *Exeter*'s bridge."

After a brief delay, someone spoke. "This is Brigadier General Shannon Bell. Is this Colonel Hika?"

"Yes, Shannon, it is. I have troubling news."

"What's up, Aperahama?"

"We received a partial distress call from the freighter *Foundation*. I lack details, but she appears to be adrift near your ship. I'm asking you to investigate and provide aide. Your facilities are clearly more extensive than ours and we're about as far away. We don't know if there are injuries, but it's best to assume the worst. How quickly can you be alongside her?"

Shannon bent to speak to someone, then stood back in the center of the holo image. "We'll be there in half an hour. I'll keep you informed. Alert me if you learn anything new. *Exeter* out."

In slightly less time, *Exeter* pulled alongside *Foundation*. The comparative sizes were amazing, *Exeter* being an asteroid and *Foundation* a midsize spacecraft.

"Any response from the crew?" asked Shannon.

"None."

"Any visual of activity or hull breaches?"

"No, sir. She looks intact—just drifting in space. It's kind of spooky."

"Let's keep this professional, shall we? If I want supernatural insights, I'll ask for them."

"Okay, but I'm just saying," replied the first officer Colonel Einar Hjörleifsson. Serious again, he asked, "Shall I lead an away team and board her?"

"No. If she looks stable, let's bring her onboard and have a good look at her. Have medical teams meet us in the tractor-membrane recovery area. When you find anything out, let me know immediately."

"Aye, aye." Einar stood and jogged off the bridge.

Five minutes later, he called Shannon by com-link. "We're about to crack the hatch. Totally weird. No responses, not even to pounding on the hull with a metal wrench. Must have been one hell of a party. Maybe they had a sudden decompression and lost their air before they knew what hit them?"

"I'm sure we'll—" General Bell never did finish that sentence.

Einar's panicked voice screamed, "*Berrillians.* Shannon, the ship's full of Berrill—" Colonel Hjörleifsson never finished that, or any other, sentence.

Shannon slammed her palm down on the general quarters icon. Whether Einar meant *Foundation* was full of Berrillians or *Exeter,* it didn't matter. Either way, her ship was in mortal danger.

SIXTEEN

I was sitting in TCY lounge, sipping coffee and slinging bull when I heard the GQ klaxon. *General quarters on an asteroid?* It seemed unreal. Within a second, I was sprinting toward the armory two doors down the hall.

Overhead, I heard Shannon Bell's voice trying not to sound unsteady. "General Quarters. This is not a drill. *Exeter* has been boarded by an unknown number of armed Berrillians. The intrusion occurred in the tractor-membrane recovery area. Region 8, Area AA-11, deck 1121. Repeat, enemy assault in the tractor-membrane recovery area. All personnel are to act under General Order 1. This is a hostile incursion. All individuals act under General Order 1."

GO 1 was adopted after Stuart Marshall internally attacked the worldship. No one anticipated such an act before that, and we suffered grievously due to that oversight. To prevent a similar catastrophe, GO 1 assigned hiding locations to civilians and duty posts to military and police units. We drilled it often, but I never thought we'd need the order.

TCY headquarters was far from the shipping hangars where the tractor beam was housed. Rather than run there, which would take half an hour, any Forms in the TCY area hopped into their cubes and transported down. The area was huge, and we were under attack. We were unlikely to crush anyone, but there was no way around that. When *Wrath* opened a doorway, I could see and hear absolute chaos. People were screaming, weapons discharging at a fantastic rate, and Berrillians roaring like the killing machines they were. Before I exited, a percussion grenade went off not ten meters away, and two soldiers flew past the portal, both torn to shreds. Holy crap.

I inched to the opening, covering the direction my compatriots were blown from. I peered around the edge of the portal, gun first. A Berrillian male standing just outside grabbed my rifle and ripped it from my hands. My right hand snapped up to laser him. Before it was halfway up, he smacked me in the side of the head with my own gun launching me backward. I face-planted on the deck and rolled quickly. The Berrillian was halfway through the door, plasma gun trained on my head. In a seated position, I scampered backward frantically. The cat roared triumphantly and began to pull the trigger.

Then the portal he stood in snapped shut in a flash. He was cut in half like his body was caught in a deli slicer.

"*Wrath*, you son of a gun, you saved my ass. Thanks."

"Your left hand was on the floor, so your command prerogatives were in contact, or almost in contact. I extrapolated what action you might have requested were you aware of the proximity. It was nothing."

"Nothing? Dude, I love you."

"If I had known there would be negative consequences to my intervention, I might not have acted."

"Oh, you silly boy, give me a hug."

"Ah, Form, how can I do that? I lack appendages and the desire to do so, if I had them."

"Well, you can't stop me." I sprang to my feet and hugged the nearest outcropping of *Wrath* I could get to. "Now open up and let me get to killing."

"Once you deploy your prerogatives, retrieve your weapon, and promise to kill and not be killed, I will."

I scampered to the wall after snatching my plasma rifle from the floor. "Ah, you going to clean up that mess while I'm gone?" I asked, looking at the bloody half-corpse on the deck.

"If I left it, would you clean it up?"

"If you asked me real nice, sure."

A portal appeared in front of me. "In that case, it'll be clean before you return."

In my head, I said, *Al, target the laser to take out as many Berrillians as you can. We're too close for the rail cannon.*

Way ahead of you, captain. I've fried a dozen so far. You'll never catch up with my body count.

"I'll take that bet," I shouted as I ran out the opening and began firing.

By my quick estimate, there were two hundred Berrillians in the hangar. They were fighting their way toward the exits. If they got into the corridors, they could wreak holy terror. A second issue hit me. If I were them, I'd rig *Foundation* to explode. Each warrior would likely be fitted with automated explosives, too.

Al, tell command to expel Foundation *because she's likely set to explode.*

Excellent point. Done. They agree and will tractor it away.

Ask if they can tractor any Berrillians into space, too. Even the bodies. I bet they're all booby trapped. Otherwise, have them try to encase them in membranes.

Done.

Within seconds *Foundation* lifted from the deck and flew out the hangar doors. A smattering of Berrillian bodies followed closely behind. It was like some scene from a macabre play. *Zombies Fly South*, or something. Just clear of the door, one body erupted into flames. I was right. They were rigged with incendiaries. Sons of *bitches*.

I sprinted to cover the nearest exit point. Many Berrillians were well in front of me and running full out. I shot a few in the back, but the tight quarters prevented me from taking out too many. There were lots of guys on my side in the way. I caught sight of my first lucky break. On the far side of the tractor-hangar, a company of regular army troops advanced on the Berrillians who were heading that direction. It was unlikely any would get past that large a force. Realizing that, more of our scattered forces broke for the same area I was.

A few of the Berrillians burst into flame when they were shot, their incendiary devices hit directly. It was a horrific sight and had an even worse smell. Whatever material they'd used also shot onto whoever and whatever was nearby. Other Berrillians were set on fire, who in turn exploded. Several humans were splatted with the burning material and erupted in flames. The screams were the stuff of nightmares.

I kept running and firing. I was close enough then to target the doorways themselves. I only picked off Berrillians who were about to escape. Still, I saw several slip away through one of the many exits.

Then something hit me from behind. I turned and saw a female Berrillian tackling me, arms wide open. Her teeth were headed toward my back.

While we fell, I forward rolled. She lost her partial grip and flew over me. We scrambled to our feet together. She vaulted back at me. I noted the pack strapped to her waist. That had to be the incendiary case. I'd never seen that accessory worn before. Mid-flight, I sliced her head off. She crumpled to the ground. I burned off the bomb satchel and ran to the nearest exit. I set the pack down and sprinted away. From twenty meters I shot my laser at the pouch and it burst into flames. Good. No one would escape in that direction until someone on our side put out the fire.

I moved toward the largest grouping of Berrillians I could see—fifteen of them. They were taking cover behind a shuttle craft. Our soldiers fought from makeshift cover, wherever they could find it. As I got closer, the enemy started directing their fire toward me. I guess someone recognized me. I began moving wide to one side, hoping to shift their positions, exposing their flanks. It worked. They were so preoccupied with me, they failed to cover their rears. Within a minute, all the cats were dead. Our side suffered significant losses, too.

"Get these bodies away from the ship. I want as little burned as possible," I shouted to the survivors.

They rushed to do so while I scanned the area to see how we were doing. The intensity of fighting was dying down, but scattered hotspots were still present. By then, burning Berrillians were everywhere. The smoke became so thick, our soldiers had to put on respirators. Me, I was lucky. I only wreaked of burning flesh. I didn't inhale it.

More police and military personnel were flooding into the hangar. Barring any new, unpleasant surprises, we had won the day. I hacked into the command feed. A small number of Berrillians had disappeared into *Exeter*. No one knew how many, perhaps a dozen. That region of the ship was locked down, so there was only so much area to search. But even a handful of Berrillians with incendiaries could cause untold damage.

I pulled up a schematic of the areas they could potentially infiltrate. One caught my eye immediately. A preschool. One deck up and three sections over. It wasn't a military target, but if one of the Berrillians chanced upon it ... well, I didn't want to complete that thought. I sprinted out the door and up the nearest stairs. It took me thirty second to get there—the longest thirty seconds of my life.

From half a corridor away I could hear the children's high-pitched screams. I didn't pray all that much, but I did pray intently they were crying because they were freaked out in general, and not because a Berrillian found them.

The hallway door was open.

I flew through the door and saw the back of a huge Berrillian male. He had two toddlers in one paw and a teacher in the other. He was shaking them all violently. No way I could shoot him. I vaulted at him as hard as I could. Fist first, I hit him in the spine and had the satisfaction of feeling it splinter under my impact. The cat slumped backward on top of me, releasing his captives as he fell. I flipped him off behind me. He lay on the floor panting. Bastard was in pain. His legs were paralyzed, but his front arms were grabbing wildly at his waist. I didn't know if he was going for a sidearm or his explosive pack. Didn't care, either. I plowed a hole through the center of his forehead, and he went limp.

I quickly burned off the incendiary pack and ran to the head. I set the pack into the toilet, eased the lid down, and plopped my butt down to keep any explosion contained while the kids evacuated.

"Get everybody out," I shouted for all I was worth.

Slowly at first, then with great haste, the adults herded the kids out the door. While they were exiting, I flushed the toilet. I knew it was unlikely to help, a hail Mary, at best. But, hey I was literally sitting on a powder keg. The room outside went quiet. Just as I began to rise from the can, the bomb went off. Flames hurled me upward, and I crashed against the ceiling engulfed in flames.

Everything faded to black.

SEVENTEEN

"All right, everybody. Take your seats," said Faiza Hijab, with cool authority. "We have a lot to cover, and a lot of work ahead."

The room quieted reluctantly, chattering fading gradually as opposed to ceasing quickly. Everyone was on the razor's edge.

"Thank you. We need to go over the *Foundation* Incident. I have numbers from our end. The damage to *Exeter,* and civilian losses, will be covered by Secretary General Li.

"The Merchant Marine ship *Foundation* had a crew of thirty-seven, officers and enlisted. All were lost. Most bodies were recovered after having been thrown off the ship, once it was taken. One hundred fifty-three UN soldiers were killed in action, mostly in the tractor hangar. Eight of those were vortex Forms who'd responded quickly from across the fleet. An additional eleven guards were killed clearing the ship of Berrillians who made it out of the hangar. That's two hundred one killed. Another two hundred thirty-eight were injured, but all will recover. Some may require artificial limbs, and one may possibly be downloaded to an android, due to the extent of her injuries.

"Thank goodness we ejected *Foundation* when we did. Fifteen minutes after she was set adrift, she exploded. We estimate the enemy concealed a one hundred megaton fusion bomb onboard. If it had gone off on *Exeter,* the losses would have been catastrophic. I can't even begin to tell you what a break we caught there. Damage to *Exeter* herself was minimal. The fires from the incendiary weapons were quickly extinguished, and no significant structural damage occurred.

"I'd like to thank all the people who responded and did such an amazing job. We owe you our lives and those of our loved ones. That includes Army, Air Force, police, fire, and Navy personnel."

She sat quickly.

"Do the KIA numbers include General Ryan," asked Alexis Gore, who stared intently at the desk in front of her.

"No, ma'am, they do not."

"And why is that?"

"We're frankly uncertain as to how to classify him. I would defer that question to the scientists—"

"I can't believe you're so cold hearted," howled Alexis. "You don't know how to 'classify' the man who charged into the daycare center and saved the lives of every child cowering in fear? You don't know how to 'classify' the man who suggested you cast off *Foundation* before she exploded? What kind of devil are you? We all know about the prejudice the android pilots have been subject to under your command. To disavow General Ryan now, after his contributions, after the *masses* of humanity he personally saved? Frankly I'm ashamed to sit in the same room as you, bitch."

Faiza sat like stone. After several moments, she spoke in a firm monotone. "I beg your pardon, President Gore. You misunderstood. I meant we were not certain how to classify General Ryan as his status is unclear. He is, as I understand it, in a kind of safe mode in Dr. DeJesus's lab. Hence, he is not *technically* dead."

"An error of omission, not commission?" asked a bitter Alexis.

"President Gore, I know of your personal friendship with General Ryan. I also know your son and daughter were present in the Sunny Haven Preschool that General Ryan liberated. But please do not presume my feelings for him are any less than yours. The man *is*, and I use that word specifically until some son of a bitch can prove to me the contrary, a hero, plain and simple. I admire him and trust him more than anyone I've ever known. Please be assured that I'm not a woman given to either such emotions or such praise."

Alexis blew her nose with a tissue and looked sideways at Faiza. "I'm sorry for my outburst. These are no ordinary times. Please forgive me."

"That would be unnecessary. I have no ill feelings. Alexis, we both love the man in our own ways. That's enough. We're all good." There was a brief silence. "The Berrillians, not so much. Them, I'd hate to be right about now."

A trickle of chuckles built to a gush of laughter. Everyone welcomed the release. Plus, everyone knew Jon would want them to laugh.

Finally Bin Li stood. "As to civilian losses, I'm glad to say they were low. Eleven tractor hangar employees were killed. Seventy-five were wounded, but none of them severely. All of them will pull through. Another seven civilians were killed by the enemy who escaped the hangar deck. Property losses were trivial."

Bin thought about making a joke out of the toilet Jon had ruined, but decided to not go there.

"If there are no questions I think we can proceed to matters concerning repair."

"I would like Dr. DeJesus to say a word about General Ryan's condition, if that's all right?" asked Alexis.

Carlos stood in his stead. "My colleague could not pull himself away from the lab, but I'd be happy to fill you all in. As you all know, android existence presents many challenges to our view of what life is and what might constitute death for one of them. Addressing the simpler issues first, Jon's physical condition is, while bad, far from irreparable. His skin was almost completely burned off, and he lost part of a leg and most of an arm. These can either be repaired or replaced easily enough. Given our current technology, reinstalling command prerogatives will be quite doable.

"As to his *mental* function, the integrity of his analog and biocomputers, we are, unfortunately, less certain. Backup copies are made weekly for each android. Worst case scenario is that we upload those files and it will be like last week for Jon. If it becomes clear that this is in his best interest, this is what we shall likely do."

"Do the biocomputers back up like the ones with chips?" Alexis asked quietly.

"No, not as well at least. The copies are less reliable and the uploads more problematic."

"But would it be him after the uploads? Would it be the Jon we know and love?" Alexis queried even more tentatively.

"Yes, but then again, no. He would likely be identical to the man he was last week. He would be unaware that he'd saved all those lives. That might be a small thing, but I, for one, would hate to deny him remembering his bravery."

"We could tell him, right? There are holos of everything," said Alexis, with uncertainty in her voice.

"To be certain. Perhaps I make too big a deal of the point. All the copies of that infernal Stuart Marshall were identically repulsive. I'm sure in Jon's case his personality would be unchanged."

"Thank you, Carlos. That helps a lot. Please let me know if there's anything I can do." Alexis rested her face in her palms.

Six decks down from that meeting, Toño sat in the corner of an almost completely dark room. He stared, without blinking or wavering, at the partial figure lying on the nearby stainless steel table. Over two days, Toño had removed and replaced the polyalloy skin of Jon's parts that were still intact. He labored especially hard on reconstructing the face of his friend and his greatest technical achievement. Mostly, Toño tried not to cry. Intellectually, he knew he could reconstruct and reanimate Jon Ryan. But, try as he might, Toño could not convince himself he could resurrect his friend. Silly, yes, but the weight he felt was crushing.

Toño rose wearily, stretched his back, and stepped over to the android. "So, my friend, let us see what those bargain-basement parts in your head are doing."

He attached several wires to Jon's scalp and turned to a computer screen. After tapping many keys, he rubbed his face. "No change," he said to the empty room. "Still in safe mode. But why? If the system can't reboot, it should shut itself down. That's how I designed it. How can it function differently? The safe mode was designed to bridge the initial programing. I would have deleted it years ago, but never saw the point. It had no function or utility, but it took up so little space, I left it."

He went to the corner and poured a cup of coffee. With his back to Jon, he went through the algorithms again. No, safe mode was *not* possible. Serial failed reboots or complete shutdown were the only options his programming allowed for. Yet there Jon rested, defying logic and science, not to mention Toño's will as the creator, even as the man stood on death's doorstep.

Light flared in the lab as someone entered and then quickly shut the door.

"Is that you, Carlos?" Toño asked without turning. "There is, unfortunately, no change in his condition."

"No, it's me, my friend."

Toño whirled to see Kymee standing by Jon's side.

"I came as soon as I heard. The generally chatty *Wrath* was slow in alerting us of the attack on *Exeter*. Do you mind?" Kymee held up his lateral hand, the one with his command prerogatives.

"No, of course not. Anything that might help is a good thing."

Kymee gently enveloped Jon in fibers. After a few minutes, he withdrew them and rested all three hands on the metal table.

"What do you think?" Toño finally was forced to ask.

"I'm not certain. What is this 'safe mode' he's idling in?"

"It was an old diagnostic mode of a computer operating system. It was used to help repair a system that was working improperly. I installed it centuries ago and never bothered to remove it. I never saw the point."

"What an odd application. Why is he in it now? Was that planned?"

"No. I have no idea why he's in it. In fact, it shouldn't be possible. The upgrades and RAM increases I've installed over the years should override it instantly."

"Could it be a result of his trauma?"

"I don't know. Possibly. Even then, it should be quickly overridden."

"Might it be something *he* is doing?"

Toño hadn't thought of that aspect. He pondered a while before answering. "Interesting question. Anything is possible, but I don't know why he'd use it or especially why he'd cling to it, as he seems to be doing."

"Maybe that's just it. It's something to cling *to*."

"Curious notion." Toño sat on a tall lab stool and gestured to Kymee to join him. "Did you sense anything when you probed him?"

Kymee was slow to answer. "Darkness." He looked up, surprised at his own choice of words. "Mechanically, he seems intact. But you know that better than I. His biocomputer is as inaccessible to me now at it was the day I met him. His other two main computers are all spinning in this safe mode."

"Main computers?"

"Yes, the one in his head and the one in his chest. Those are the main memory and motor units, as you also know better than I. The ones in his arms and legs are functioning properly but inactive."

"I wonder—"

"What?"

"I'd overlooked those four, err, the leg and forearm ones. They are little more than servomechanisms to provide negative feedback to anomalous hand or foot movements."

"Ah," replied Kymee. "I see. That would be a useful in certain movement environments, wouldn't it?"

"Yes—" Toño wasn't really listening. He was lost in thought. "I wonder if Jon's managed to maintain his consciousness in one or all of those tiny devices?"

"They don't seem large enough to hold his entire consciousness,; not by a wide margin, actually," responded Kymee.

"Maybe they wouldn't have to hold it all." He rubbed at the back of his scalp. "If he just put a tiny portion of his core memories in them, and basic frontal cortex function. Hmm."

"Why? He had to know you'd fix him if it was humanly possible."

"True. But look at it from his perspective. You're being blown up, might be destroyed, and are definitely going to suffer extensive damage." Toño's eyes nearly bugged out of his head. "A *life* raft."

"Not the three words I anticipated next from your lips, Toño. Are you all right?"

"No, Jon has placed himself on a life raft. He distributed just enough consciousness to remain who he was in case the mothership, that is, his main computers, were compromised." He shook his head vigorously. "The man simply never ceases to amaze or consternate me."

"I'm still not getting the picture here. Why would he do that? More importantly, does it lead to a solution?"

"I don't know. Maybe it was just a desperate act … *Wait*. He's *keeping* the main units in safe mode. He's not *allowing* them to reboot. He's sending us an old fashion signal. He's saying, 'I'm in here, save me.' Son of a *gun*."

"But why not allow the main units to reboot? Why, aside from sending a greeting, would he prevent them from rebooting?"

"There is only one reason I can think of. He knows they can't reboot."

"Now I'm more lost than a blind priest in a whorehouse."

Toño glared at Kymee.

"Ah, I learned that one from Jon," Kymee said quickly. "Sorry. It kind of slipped out."

"He has that polluting effect, doesn't he? Look, it's complicated, but I think this is it. He must know that if the computer itself from the inside, *or* I from the outside, attempt a reboot, it will be unsuccessful. Instead of restarting, the system would remain off." To himself Toño marveled, "Yes. Brilliant actually.

"Take the example of a primitive computer. If the unit couldn't boot up, all information was lost. In the primitive systems, a skilled technician could recreate the stored data, but it would have taken immense effort. In the case of Jon's system, even given forever, recreating the information would not be possible. So, he holds the computer in safe mode."

"Which unit? The one in his head or his chest? Or does he have to hold *both* in suspended animation?"

"That's a good question." Toño was quiet a long while. "It's statistically unlikely that both are equally damaged and not restorable. But which?"

"Maybe we can ask him?"

"Now I'm the holy man in the house of ill repute."

"The quickest way to find out which unit is most damaged is to ask him. Don't you see? That's why he's holding *both* units in safe mode. If he allows the good unit to reboot and holds the defective one in safe mode, you wouldn't be so perplexed. You'd simply see an irreparable computer and replace it. Whatever is in the unit would be lost."

"No, we're getting too fanciful here. If one computer is unfixable, it's unfixable. No matter what gyrations Jon goes through, the bad unit will not reboot, and it would need to be replaced," Toño replied with frustration.

"Ah, that's the key then. He wants you to enter the safe mode of the defective unit and repair it so it can reboot."

"I tried. It wouldn't let me in to operate in safe mode."

"*He* wouldn't let you in until *you* understood what he needed you to do. You know the old saying. *Have you tried rebooting the system?* Jon knew it would be the first thing you'd do, and he didn't want that."

"I almost believe you, Kymee. So how can we communicate with him?"

"The simplest way I know. One for *yes* and two for *no*."

"One what? Two whats?"

"I have no idea. But *he* does."

"How do we ask?"

"We ask a question we know the answer to before we ask it, and we ask until we receive the correct response."

"What question can we be certain we know the answer to? Do you love your wife, your kids?"

"No, too broad. He's had many of each. No, there's only one question to ask Jon—one everyone who knows him would know what his answer would be."

"Kymee, before I die of suspense what question?"

"Would you like a beer?"

Toño flushed. "No. What's more, this is a completely inappropriate moment to ask. What is the question we must ask Jon?"

"No, we ask *him* if *he* wants a beer."

It dawned on Toño slowly, but his smile reflected the brilliance of the light that just went off in his head. "I think I'll let you ask."

"My pleasure."

Kymee popped off his lab stool and stood by Jon. He attached his probes. Toño did likewise.

In his head, Kymee asked, *Jonathan Ryan, would you like a beer?*

Both men stopped breathing and moving as they strained to glean a response. Nothing. Kymee repeated the question a few more times with no discernible response.

"Do the servo mechanical computers have pressure sensors?" Kymee whispered to Toño.

"Yes," he whispered back.

Kymee tapped loudly on the metal table in Morse code: *Would you like a beer?*

At first, there was no response. Then a minuscule gear whirred to life. One finger on Jon's only attached hand wiggled.

The two men nearly collapsed.

Kymee tapped out, *Sorry, we're out of beer. How about a glass of water?*

Slowly, two fingers wiggled.

Kymee tapped, *Wait, I found one. Do you still want a beer?*

The second digit fell limp.

"You ask the next question, Toño. I don't want to screw anything up."

Toño sounded out, *Jon, Toño here. The computer in your head is number one. The computer in your chest is number two. Three fingers mean you don't understand the question. Do you understand me?*

One finger twitched.

Jon, the computer in your head is number two.

Two fingers jerked to life.

Jon which computer is damaged?

One finger twitched.

Jon, do you want me to work in safe mode to repair the computer in your head.

One finger wagged.

Do you want me to simply reboot the computer in your head?

Two fingers moved more exuberantly than any had before.

Okay here's the plan. You reboot the computer in your chest. I will hold the one in your head in safe mode. Once the chest unit is functional, we'll work on the head computer.

One finger spun.

Do you want to do the work on the unit in safe mode?

Two fingers flip flopped.

Do you want me *to work on the unit in your head in safe mode?*

Jon held up his one thumb.

"We have ourselves a plan," cried out Toño.

It took almost two hours, but finally Toño backed out of the computer in Jon's head, having restored its operation without having to reboot it.

Jon opened his eyes.

"Can you hear me, Jon?" Toño nearly screamed.

"Of course, Doc. Why wouldn't I be able to hear you? At that volume, a dead man in the next galaxy could hear you."

He tried to sit up, but rested back in failure.

"Harder to do without a second leg or arm. Here."

Jon twisted his torso and angled himself to a sitting position.

"Kymee," Jon said nonchalantly, "nice to see you. How've you been?"

"One of my knees is acting up. I may need to replace it, yet again."

"Sorry to hear that. Hey, was it you who mentioned something about a beer?"

"Yes, it was."

Jon held up his only hand. "I got just the place for it."

"Jon," yelled Toño, "you were *nearly* blown apart, you were *nearly* dead, and I was *nearly* insane with frustration. Is 'where's my beer' all you can say?"

"The key words there, Doc, are *nearly*. Let's not focus too much on negatives."

"I think I'll slip him back into safe mode," said Toño with a frown.

"Let me know if I can help," responded Kymee with a huge smile.

EIGHTEEN

Toño was reattaching my leg when Kayla burst through the lab's entrance. She left the floor three meters away and hit me around the neck and chest like an angry linebacker.

Toño angled his back toward her to deflect a random strike to his work area. "Kayla, this is sensitive material and a delicate—" He stopped speaking when he turned his head.

We were locked in a kiss. Neither of us were listening. There was a movie, *The Princess Bride*, years ago. I'm talking centuries ago. At the end, the narrator addressed the top five kisses of all time. I'm not saying ours would have bumped one off that list, but I wouldn't have minded submitting it to the judges for their consideration to see if it could.

"Are you all right? You know, all right, all right?" she asked in a hurried tone.

"Of course, I am. Of course, I am. Of course, I am, am, am, ma'am."

"God it's great to hear you being such an insensitive ass. At least I know you're A-Okay," she said with a smile. Then we kissed again.

"If you could release my patient, I'd like to finish attaching this leg before it becomes outmoded," snarked Toño. But he couldn't hide a big smile of his own.

"I'll sit right here and hold his hand," she said.

"You want to hold this one," I held up the attached one, "or that one?" I pointed to my old arm on the counter.

"It's all the same to me," she said.

"Really?" I was kind of stunned.

"No, not really." She flicked my ear. "But *gotcha*," she beamed as she took hold of the attached hand.

Kayla watched Toño work for a while then began chatting. "As soon as your parts are where they should be, I'll bring the kids by. They're anxious to see you, but I don't think they're ready for dismembered dad quite yet."

"Probably not. Hey, maybe I can get Toño to remove them for Halloween? I'd make a great scary robot."

"Don't even think about it. You'd also make a great scarecrow tied to a stick, and I wouldn't have to waste hours on your costume," Toño said, not looking up.

"You're no fun," I replied.

He didn't bother responding.

"So, you do feel okay?" Kayla asked again.

"Yeah, believe it or not. I remember the explosion and hitting the roof, but that's when I blacked out. I do have to admit it was kind of scary."

"*Kind* of scary. You're too used to your charmed android life," said Toño as he screwed pieces together.

"Well at least it kept him alive, again," said Kayla defensively.

My woman protecting her man. Oh-ho-ho-ho.

She stayed a while, but it became clear Toño was going to work nonstop fixing me, so she headed out to take care of the kids. Can't say I blamed her. I was bored stiff.

After an hour or so, Toño asked what I could tell had been puzzling him. "You went to extraordinary lengths to prevent me from simply rebooting your primary computers." He angled his head and shook it gently. "I wouldn't have thought what you did was even possible. Anyway—"

"Why did I bother?" I finished his thought.

"Precisely. You know you have a full back up each week. Yours was only four days old. What was the big deal?"

I sighed a couple times. "Hard to explain." I turned my head and looked to the heavens. "I don't ever want to be a copy of my former self. For one thing, it creeps me out, because I flash on Stuart Marshall."

"Amen," mumbled Toño.

"Plus, I want to be who I am. I don't want to forget the feeling of that monster's spine splintering as I hit him. I'd just as soon lose the memory of those screaming kids. But I never want to forget the smell of that Berrillian's brains boiling out the hole I burned in his head, or the look on his face as he died. *Never.*"

He was quiet for a while. "I guess I understand. Jon, I have to ask you a sensitive question as your physician and your oldest friend. Are you okay mentally?"

"What? Are you kidding me?"

"A man who relishes the feel of breaking bones and the smell of burning brains may have seen too much. Maybe he's ready for a break."

"No," I said resolutely. "I don't relish, enjoy, or otherwise get my yayas off over those morbid, hateful memories. I want to remember them to help me continue. I need to help rid the universe of those horrors. Every recollection that reminds me that I must kill them is important. Focusing on just how badly they need killing is a useful tool. Nothing more. Nothing less."

"Ah. I guess that's different."

"My doctor guesses there's a difference between me being a fighting machine or a burned-out psycho. Great. Remind me to see you get a raise."

"Let's leave it at this, Jon. I can accept your focused, driven worldview. Let's just agree to keep a close eye on you, to make certain you retain all the humanity you've always had."

"Thank, Toño. I don't know if I've ever told you, but you're a good egg."

"You have not. It's a bit late in the game, but I appreciate your praise."

I held out my hand. We shook.

He worked another long silent spell. My leg was reattached, and he'd started reattaching my arm.

"Hey, Toño, you want to hear something weird?" I finally asked.

"Coming from you, *that* is a dangerous question. But, as we're stuck here for a good long while, I guess I'll bite."

"While I was out, I had a dream."

He stopped working and stared up at that unexpected news. His nose twitched a few times. "So, you began dreaming?"

"No, I had *a* dream. Kind of a long one, but just one."

"Go on."

"When I was a kid, we spent summers at a campground by a lake in the hills above where we lived. Looking back on it, the place was fairly standard. You know, log cabins, a convenience shop, and a small diner. But to me it was magical. Big trees, fresh air, and squirrels—chipmunks, too. Anyway, we stayed there the same two weeks every year. From as early as I can remember, the same family stayed in the cabin next door for the same two weeks. It was a coincidence at first, I guess, but then it became a tradition. They had a daughter—Jenna. Jenna was the same age as me. We spent every day together catching bugs, chasing each other, but mostly we swam in the little lake. The water was freezing, murky, and god knows what floated in it, but for us, it was our private paradise."

I stopped a second.

"Anyway, one year when I was seven or eight, we arrived late. My dad packed the car same as always, but the old jalopy gave up the ghost halfway out of town. He had it towed to the garage. The parts had to be ordered, so we left for the campground three days late. I was fit to be tied and nagged my folks the entire trip. 'Are we there yet? Are we there yet?' What a pain I was."

"Was?" teased Toño.

"Very funny. Anyway, my pop hadn't fully stopped the car when I jumped out and ran straight to Jenna's cabin. I knocked on the door. But you know what?"

Toño shook his hand gently.

"No one answered. I pounded. Nothing. I was confused. I asked my parents why they didn't answer the door. Of course, they said they didn't know. Pop said we'd have to just march over to old Mr. Hestle's cabin and find out what the heck was going on. Hestle was the ancient man who ran the campground. Looked like a groundhog on two legs, but that's beside the point."

"Thank goodness," mumbled Toño.

"Hestle opened the door and immediately looked mad. He asked if my father would come in, while I stayed outside with my mother. Dad looked confused, but he went in. Old man Hestle closed the door behind him. A minute later my dad came out on his own. He looked awful, scared or something. He sat me down on Hestle's stoop and sat beside me. He was silent a few moments, then he told me Jenna had drowned in the lake the day before. Then he started crying. Mom joined in, and I was just confused— confused and scared."

I stopped talking again.

"Jon, that's a tragic story, and I'm sorry to hear it, but where is this going?"

"So, while I was, you know, out of it these last few days, I had *a* dream. *One* long dream. Hell, it's been so long since I had one, maybe it was normal length? Anyway, I dreamed I was at the lake with Jenna."

"You spent many summers with her there. I'm not Sigmund Feud, but the dream seems rather unremarkable aside from the fact that androids don't dream in the first place."

"No, it was the summer she *died*. We spent time at the lake, swimming, punching each other, catching frogs, all the usual stuff. But it was the year she died."

"How could you know that? And, even if that *was* the content, it was a dream. They rarely make sense, and certainly aren't required to."

I shook my head hard. "No. This was different. It was more like a memory." I hesitated. "Or like I was there again only it was now."

"Fascinating. Anything else?"

"Yeah. Then it gets freaky."

"It got freaky? It hasn't sounded that way yet?"

"We would swim and play, but we talked a lot, too. I asked her what it was like to be dead. She smiled and said it felt like anything else, just a little different. I asked if she was scared or lonely. She said no, because she was with me. Then she said, 'Jon, everyone dies. Someday even you will. It's not a great big deal. Death is kind of like life, it's just forever.'"

"That's it? She spoke like a mystic and the dream was over?"

"No, then she asked if I wanted a frog sandwich made from the frog she held up in her hands. I said no, and I shoved her into the water. She dropped the frog. Then she said she'd show me hers, if I showed her mine."

"Her what? Your what?"

"Doc, weren't you ever alone with a girl when you were a kid?"

He looked embarrassed, then blurted back, "I guess *not*. I have no idea what you're talking about. What's more, I don't want to know, either. If you don't shut up, I'll switch your audio off, so I can finish these repairs this decade."

Son of a gun hunkered down and worked in silence for a good thirty minutes.

That was fine by me. I couldn't stop thinking about Jenna.

NINETEEN

Tense weeks turned into dull months after the Berrillian assault on *Exeter*. There were no further attacks and little communication chatter on their side. Our project to map the Berrillian Empire wrapped up during that quiet period. It turned out their control was large, but not terrifyingly so. They had iron-fisted control over hundreds of systems, but their sphere of influence was on a par with the Listhelons. I did follow up on their attempt to assimilate Zark, the planet I'd investigated. With Alliance space support repelling any resupply or troop inflows, the spunky Zark were holding their own. The outcome was far from clear, but they had a fighting chance. That we could frustrate the Berrillians so easily put a smile on my face, whenever I thought about it.

What was becoming clear was that our enemy was trying to win against us via subterfuge and guerrilla tactics. They were willing to avoid all military actions in space, fleet to fleet. It must have galled Erratarus to no end to have to chip away at a foe as opposed to bashing armies with them. History showed, however, that guerrilla warfare was effective. While it rarely led to an outright victory, its psychological drag on the recipients were costly. The high intensity and constant vigilance needed to fight a guerrilla war often produced a ruthless totalitarian drift that damaged its victims. That aspect was sobering. More political tension, we didn't need.

As time passed, I began to wonder where I could help the most. It slowly dawned on me. Azsuram was a prime target for the Berrillians. They'd attacked it before, and they were defeated there. That had to stick in their craw. Also, the population of the planet was quite sparse, so conquest would be easy. Sure, there was little to gain from a military or materials standpoint, but as a forward base of operations, it would be a great asset. In fact, I realized, there had to be paws-on-the-ground Berrillian infiltrators there already. Hell, if they tried to sneak them on LH 16a, where they totally stood out, why not Azsuram, where they'd be invisible in the lush tropics that were full of game?

That's when another tiny bell went off in my head. LH 16a. It still bothered me, that interaction with Gortantor. His actions suggested he had some understanding or affiliation with the Berrillians. I knew there was no such thing as a Berrillian ally, but Gortantor probably didn't know that. I continued to think of how a working relationship between those two species could hurt us. I wanted to figure out if there was some way to exploit their friendly status to the Alliance's advantage. I had a lot of balls in the air, and every one I dropped would likely cost a lot of lives.

I asked Molly and Rasraller to meet me at JJ's house on Azsuram. I figured having a Berrillian along to hunt Berrillians would be extremely useful. She knew how they thought, and she could smell them at large distances. Plus, she was as keen as I was to kill them.

Molly, Rasraller, and JJ were already chatting over a meal by the time I arrived. My young adult grandchildren didn't scamper to my side like they used to. They remained seated and waved, with that embarrassed don't-sit-by-me look on their faces.

JJ rose to greet me. "Dad, you're looking good."

"And you, you're looking … prosperous," I said patting his unmistakable round paunch.

"Sure, make fun of the living. We eat and drink too much, and we get fat. You walking garbage disposals catch all the breaks."

"Speaking of which," Challaria gestured at the spread on the table, "come, fill a plate and join in."

"What, no personal service for one of the founders of Azsuram?" I protested.

"That is correct," she replied, then stuck out her tongue.

I settled in with a bowl of stew and a beer. To Molly I asked, "How you

126

doing, kid? I haven't seen you in, what, months?"

"Fine."

"And you?" I asked Rasraller.

She shrugged her massive shoulders. "Couldn't be better."

"How's Molly feeding you?" I said, unable to hold back a smile.

"I'm feeding myself just fine, thanks," Rasraller replied with an edge to her tone.

"I think he asks if I'm a good cook," Molly said.

"Why would you cook for me?" she asked genuinely confused.

"Ras, when one of dad's jokes bomb, let it go. I can't believe you haven't learned that by now," responded JJ.

I pointed my spoon at him. "Smarter than he looks, isn't he?"

The younger people present chuckled.

"So, what's our plan?" asked JJ.

"Our plan?" I replied. "I wasn't aware the three of us required help."

"You're not hunting for enemy on my planet without me helping." He patted his chest. "I live here, you know."

"You're also ... prosperous," I replied gesturing my spoon at his belly.

"I don't fly my cube with my belly," he defended. "I'll do just fine."

"That is a horrible visual by the way," responded Molly.

Challaria raised her hand. "Tell me about it."

"Stabbed in the back in my own home," pouted JJ.

"If you had only turned and caught the blade," teased Rasraller.

"Not bad, for a Berrillian," I said laughing.

"What?" she objected. "We are a *very* funny species. You humans just don't get our humor."

"In all the years I've known your species, I've never once heard a joke or a funny story come out of one of your mouths," I replied.

"Oh, yeah," she said rising to the challenge. "Does everyone here know what a palquir is?"

Everyone but me was curious.

"It's a farmed animal raised for consumption, like your sheep or cow."

Everyone nodded.

She looked very proud of herself. "What do you call a palquir with no legs?"

I covered my face. I'd heard that one before.

"Ground palquir."

Silence.

"Don't you get it? It's either *on* the ground, or its legs have been *ground* up."

"That's gross," replied Molly.

"It is not. It is *funny*," defended Rasraller.

"Someone told that joke at Boy Scout camp when I was ten years old. It wasn't funny then, and it isn't funny now," I replied.

"Humans," she said. "No sense of humor whatsoever."

"I thought it was gross, too," said Challaria.

"And?" responded Rasraller. "You're human, too."

"I am not. I'm Kaljaxian," she said in protest.

"Is there a difference?"

Challaria started to protest when Rasraller let out a laughing roar. "Got you," she howled. "You see, I can be funny."

We all decided to drop the subject. If nothing else, no one wanted to have her laugh rip at their ears again.

"Okay, back to the reason for your visit," JJ stated. "What is it *we* are looking for, and what is it *we* are going to do with it when we find it?"

"Berrillians. I want to root some of them out, if they're here."

"You mean, like they've been found on many other planets?" asked JJ.

"Exactly," I replied.

"Let me turn that question around. Why wouldn't they be here?" he asked.

"I can't think of a reason," I responded.

"So, why root some out? We basically know some are hiding on Azsuram."

"Your son has a point, Ryan," said Rasraller. "It would be odd if hundreds, maybe even thousands were not stationed on this world."

"So, the actual question should be, why prove that something is true that basically *has* to be true?" asked JJ.

Good point.

"I want to get rid of as many as possible, I guess," was the most convincing response I could offer.

"Really?" he challenged. "Do you think you can get them all? Check that. Do you think you can eliminate them all *and* prevent others from taking their place?"

I shrugged. "Probably not."

"So, what's the purpose of this mission I'm too old and fat to be part of?"

"Wow, I think you finally got him," Challaria said to JJ, with admiration in her voice.

We didn't really *need* to document if Berrillians were present. They had to be. We really couldn't hope to extract any useful intelligence from them if we captured them. The advance units knew less about their missions than we did.

"If any of those monsters are on *my* planet, I want to kill them, preferably with my bare hands," I said.

JJ smiled. "Why didn't you say so? That makes perfect sense. It also proves why I'm in." He pointed toward the floor. "My planet, too."

"It does not make sense."

We all turned to look at the speaker. Rasraller. To say we were stunned was an understatement.

"Ah, could you clarify what you just said?" inquired Molly.

"What? His plan makes no sense. He wants to risk death or serious injury to kill an insignificant proportion of invaders who must certainly be here."

"But he just said it was a personal matter to him. It is to those who live here, too," replied Molly.

"And me, too," protested Rasraller. "I want nothing more than to rip as many of them to tiny pieces as you do. It is an emotionally satisfying animalistic plan that I fully support. That does not mean it makes sense."

"If you support our plan, why question it?" asked JJ.

"I don't so much question it as I wish to show the plan to be what it is. It makes no military or strategic sense."

"Why is it important to you to make that distinction?" I asked.

"Because we should know what it is we are willing to die for. To kill for.

We need to be honest in our motivations and actions. That is all I wish to make clear."

I rolled her protestations around in my head a while. "You know what, Rasraller? You're right. My plan makes no sense. But it needs doing anyway."

"Then anyone willing to throw logic and common sense out the hatch is welcome to join in." Rasraller tilted her head toward JJ. "It's not like you need proper qualifications to do something stupid and unworthy of the risk involved."

I held up my mug. "To such a philosophy, I'll raise my glass."

I liked her logic. It wasn't exactly human logic, but it was damn good drinking logic. That was the type that only worked if one was drinking with friends in public. If everyone was drunk enough, drinking logic made all the sense in the world. The next morning, when one awoke with a new tattoo and a new wife, drinking logic, in retrospect, made less sense.

Within a few hours, our small party headed to the equatorial region of Azsuram. Molly and Rasraller went in their cube, JJ and his second oldest son went in another, and I flew solo in *Wrath*. We rendezvoused and set out together in search of Berrillian infiltrators. For obvious reasons, I put Rasraller on point. She knew their thinking and smelled them the best. The other three were right behind her. I brought up the rear. We traveled in a tight silent formation, aside from JJ's increasingly labored breathing. I was forced to call more frequent breaks than I'd have liked to, but I couldn't say we were in any rush. We were too much like Elmer Fudd "hunting wabbits" to take any aspect of the expedition too seriously.

It didn't take long to hit pay dirt. After our second brief rest, Rasraller held up her huge fist, signaling we should halt. She set her gun and pack aside and began walking on all fours tasting the air. I mean that literally. Her lips foamed up and she chomped at her saliva. She picked up her pack and gun and pointed a paw straight ahead. "One hundred fifty meters, one cat, male. No sign he's detected us."

I signaled we should fan out and advance slowly. We'd agreed earlier to take prisoners if possible, so we all knew what our roles were. The far points of the arc we marched in moved slightly ahead, so we formed a pincer shape.

One hundred meters later I saw our foe. A big male resting lazily on a branch, having probably just eaten a big meal. He wasn't asleep, but his guard was reduced. Within a minute we had him surrounded. I pulled my hand through the air like I was pulling a train whistle. That was the signal for Rasraller to step into the clear and try to capture him before he suspected a trap.

One step into the area he rested in, he sprang to all fours and growled at her.

"Easy, mate," she said her rifle pointed at the ground. "We're on the same side."

"I don't recall seeing you in training," he snapped as he moved toward his weapon.

"That's the point, right? We're supposed to know as little as possible."

"Then why are you here, bitch?"

"I got lonely. My season is due soon. I've known your location a while."

"You don't look or smell like you're in season or even close. You walk more like a human than one of us. If your hormones were flaring, your gait would be less steady."

"Are you a doctor?" she asked roughly.

"No, of course not. But I've been around."

"Any of your meal left?" she asked, looking to the bloody dirt near where he had been lying.

"Not enough." He reached for his gun. "I think you'd better leave."

"All right. Don't want to be where I'm not welcome."

"Take that story of yours and find another sucker to feed you for the promise of breeding."

"Suit yourself. One last thing."

"What now," he howled in angry protest.

"What are you going to do about the human with the gun to the back of your head?"

I pressed the barrel of my rifle against his skull. "Paws in the air, nice and slow," I said.

"Bitch," he said to her. "I will not forget this betrayal."

"That's probably true. But, on the plus side, you'll only have to keep it in your head a short while."

We called for a military police shuttle and packed him off to be interrogated by others. Lots of personnel had lost family and friends when the Berrillians attacked, so there would be many volunteers competing to have a go at this unfriendly cat.

By the end of the day, we'd killed or captured six more intruders. We estimated their numbers. Assuming a uniform distribution in the tropics, we arrived at a very unsettling number. There were likely more Berrillians on Azsuram than Kaljaxians and humans combined. That was completely unacceptable, but there wasn't much to do about it. Throwing a dragnet across the entire planet was impossible. Forays like ours could take out a few warriors, but we'd never make a significant dent in their numbers playing this hide and seek game.

Getting the Berrillians to leave LH 16a would be relatively easy, since the place was toxic. But Azsuram was a paradise for the Berrillians, according to Rasraller. If I flew over the whole planet and asked them nicely to leave, it was unlikely to bear much fruit. Short of finding some way of making them want to leave, there just wasn't much we could do about the present occupation.

We decided to place membrane walls around large swaths of uninhabited land. That was cheap and effective, keeping any Berrillians inside the walls. The barriers would do little to affect local animals, as none had terribly extensive migratory patterns. That would force our invaders to use their spaceships to attack, giving us a chance to shoot them down. Nice, but if there were a lot of them, our defenses might be overwhelmed trying to shoot them from the sky. I wasn't getting any devilishly clever ideas that would assure us victory. Maybe one would come to me, but for once in three hundred years, it would have been nice to have the winning ticket before the shooting started.

If the Alliance faced a massive fleet of Berrillian ships, we could certainly handle them easily. We had a strong, conventional, and centralized military. The Berrillians had hundreds of thousands of guerrilla warriors hidden away on untold worlds, waiting for the signal to subvert the local defenses, presumably while reinforcements came from space.

Then an idea hit me. What if we triggered the signal for the hidden Berrillians to attack? If we could find out what it was and how it was transmitted, perhaps we could fake a message. We could draw the hidden enemy out into the open, where we would be waiting with concentrated force. As the guerrillas on one planet almost certainly didn't communicate with one another, we could take out one world at a time. It would be slow going, but it might work.

Of course, given time, the Berrillian leadership would replant operatives and we'd be back in the same place we are now. But killing off those presently in place would buy us several years of peace of mind, if nothing else.

"Rasraller, what was your signal to rise up and fight?" I asked her the next day.

"We all had radios. There were daily announcements and briefings we were under orders to listen to. The communication was all one way, but it gave us some sense of purpose. If they read one of several coded messages, we knew to attack."

"Did the orders change over time?"

She shook her head. "No. They could have, if there was a suspected security breach, but in my case, they weren't."

"So, what was one of the possible coded messages?"

She thought a while. "During broadcasts, they would call out various named orders. 'Execute Order One,' or 'Activate Order One Eleven.' Most were dummy orders, but if an authentic one had been announced, it indicated for me to take specific action; attack, for example. If they announced an order, and I wasn't certain if it was real or not or what I was supposed to do, I could just look it up."

That meant if we were going to trigger false activations, we'd need copies of the coded orders. Not likely. I'd keep going over that option, but it seemed like a dead end. It turned out I didn't have a lot of time to ponder the option. The next day, all hell broke loose in the Churell System. Badly weakened still from the Last Nightmare invasion, the Berrillians chose to spring their first trap.

Son of a *bitch*.

TWENTY

The Churell System consisted of two planets around their home star and one planet a few light years away. They had many colonies and remote territories, but those three were the backbone of their society. Since the Nightmare's devastation, the Churell had proven themselves to be hardworking, honest, and trusted allies. They were a good species. They had repaired, replaced, and reproduced at an impressive rate, but their restoration was still far from complete, especially the military. Since the Alliance guaranteed mutual defense, the Churell decided to focus money and personnel on the rebuild of their society, not their military.

They had, additionally, not planned on having to wage a ground war. They were correct to count on the Alliance to protect their space. But even if we committed massively to their defense on the ground, they were still stuck with doing the bulk of the fighting. It wasn't like the Berrillians were attacking in lines and formations like the British redcoats. Scattered guerrilla warfare was thinly fought in unpredictable locations. That said, there was a massive influx of Alliance soldiers—armies from the worldfleet, the Fenptodinians, the Kaljaxians, and the Maxwal-Asute arrived quickly.

The Deavoriath were held in reserve, in case fighting erupted elsewhere, or if reinforcements were needed somewhere on the battlefront. The bottom line with land-based warfare was boots on the ground. The old rules applied. The more soldiers you had, the more likely you were to win. Logistically, the Alliance had a real challenge. We had many cubes at our disposal to move armies, but the cubes were only so big. They certainly weren't designed as troop transports. We operated as fast as we could, but moving large numbers of infantry and their support materials was slow. The Alliance had drilled mass personnel movements many times, but, as always, reality was much harsher than practice.

The Berrillian assault on the three main Churell planets was designed to spread any defense as thinly as possible, both across space as well as across the planetary surfaces. Small groups of Berrillians attacked outlying communities with lightning speed and precision born of excellent pre-planning. By the time Alliance troops arrived on the scene, the cats had vanished without a trace. The damage they inflicted and the casualties they caused were bone-chilling. They killed the Churell as quickly and as brutally as possible, setting fires and explosives before they fled back into hiding.

Attacks were coordinated to occur at the same time, so defensive efforts could not concentrate on one area or focus on one battle. Over the first twelve hours, before we had enough personnel to control wide areas, tens of thousands of Churell were slaughtered, and entire metropolises burned.

My role was to shuttle military support personnel to various locations and to provide air cover, if necessary. The Berrillians on the ground rarely used their personal spacecraft, so no air cover was needed. On a random schedule, Berrillian warships would try to land on the planet. We destroyed them quickly. I think the crews we shot down were just trial balloons to make certain we had to expend personnel to provide orbital defense. It was all such a waste of life, mostly theirs. Soon enough, it was clear all the cubes in orbit were not needed. A handful could protect an entire planet. Our crews were ordered to the action on the ground. That was fine with me. I had no interest in being a high-altitude observer. I wanted to be in on the action. I was good at killing.

A series of rolling skirmishes was occurring north of a medium sized city on Devlon, the smallest of the main Churell planets. I set down behind our lines and quickly found my way to the front. It was easy to find. I just had to listen for death screams and the sound of explosions. I came up behind the 86th Cavalry Recon lines and found the CO. She said the enemy had recently been repulsed, but was expected to attack again. I was assigned to Bravo

Company and given directions where to find it. I found my squad just as the cats broke through the trees and attacked with stunning ferocity.

They crossed the open turf in seconds. We dropped many with our fire. Between rail-rifles and plasma guns, we tore the Berrillians to shreds. Then they hit our line. They slung their weapons over their shoulders as I'd seen them do before. At close quarters, Berrillians reverted to teeth, claws, and savagery. They reveled in it. Our soldiers continued to fire. Some had fixed bayonets, but that was a mistake. If a cat was close enough to stab, *you* were dead.

Every time someone lunged at a Berrillian with a bayonet, the cat sidestepped the blade and lifted the wielder off their feet. Quickly, their throats were severed and the corpse discarded. I seemed to be the only android, so I was the only one who stood a chance in hand-to-hand with these monsters.

I saw my first Berrillian sword in action that day. A cat who had to be a high officer advanced down our line, slicing the hell out of our people. What the cat lacked in finesse he more than made up for in power and determination. Finally, someone put a hole where his forehead had been and he crumpled.

After ten minutes a relief party from Alpha Company arrived. Together we repulsed the enemy. I was inclined to give chase, but I was also not in command. We were ordered to gather supplies and remove the dead and wounded, so that's what we did. A rough body count showed we lost fifty-three fighters, with another hundred hurt badly enough to require evacuation.

The remainder tried to catch some shuteye or eat. The CO was unsure if the cats would be back that same day. She thought they would. I'd likely never find out. Faiza contacted me and told to return to *Wrath*. I was needed to move injured back to the worldship fleet. That night, I was home telling the family about my active day. Fighting tooth and nail with a fearsome enemy, then home for dinner and a kiss goodnight. It was surreal. It also didn't seem right.

The next morning I attended the Defense Council meeting on *Exeter*. The Berrillians' battle strategy was becoming clear. They used a pattern of widespread blitzkrieg to test our capabilities. They attacked simultaneously over several systems, beginning with the Churell, but quickly including nine other planets. They hoped to spread out our response to make it ineffective. They damn near did.

The combined response of the Alliance held the battle lines, once they joined in with the local fighters. It was also clear the Berrillians were trying to be as brutal and savage as possible. Atrocities were common, and extreme violations of morality were found everywhere during the cleanup. They wanted the inhabitants to live in fear. They wanted everyone to know they were not just satisfied killing us, they wanted to break our resolve. They were good at it.

On a planet in the Churell system, the Berrillians overran a hospital when the local resistance collapsed. They systematically killed, dismembered, and partially consumed every employee and patient left behind. That included a large pediatric wing, as the facility was a regional referral center for the young. I saw the holo evidence. The scenes would haunt me forever. On a Kaljaxian outpost, the Berrillians tore their victims into small pieces, whether they were dead or not. Those pieces were then nailed to every vertical surface available. For kilometers on end, there was no wall, no tree, and no vehicle not peppered with rotting body parts.

A day after the attacks, the Berrillians seemed to vanish. None of the search parties found a shred of evidence that there were any Berrillians left. That meant another assault of equal ferocity was coming, but nobody knew when, and no one could do anything to prevent it. If forces were concentrated where the battles had taken place, that would only mean the Berrillians would attack somewhere else. Little effort in advance of the inevitable assaults could be made.

It was a darn good war plan for an enemy unable to compete in space. Their end strategy was unclear, but their short-term terror campaign was brilliant. They could never actually conquer a world like they had in the past, but we didn't know where their string of guerrilla tactics might lead. It certainly allowed them to do what they did best. To kill. So nice for them. They were never going to be bored.

A month later Kayla and I were shooting the breeze over breakfast. All was quiet on the Berrillian front. I feared our guard was dropping, but I also imagined that was inevitable.

"So, next time the Berrillians strike, do you think you have to go right to the front lines and fight?" asked Kayla, while she pretended to be fascinated by mixing cream in her coffee.

"I don't have to. But I do feel most useful there. I'm the eternal warrior, don't you know? No one's better at it, or more practiced at it than me."

"Not to rain on your self-congratulatory parade, but any number of Deavoriath could yank that trophy from your hands."

"I meant human. I'm the most seasoned *human*."

"There are endless generations of young people ready, willing, and able to fight the next war. There always are. Why doesn't grandpa step aside and let them take the limelight?"

"It's my job, too."

"So is staying in one piece and providing for your family."

"It's war. In times of war—"

"Stop. Whatever you're going to say, I've heard a hundred times before. Yes, the Alliance is at war. But its fortunes no longer hinge on your contribution. There are lots of Forms, lots of cubes, and lots of young people anxious to prove themselves in battle. You can stand aside, if not fully stand down."

Kayla's words were true. I just didn't want to hear them. Yes, there was a time when victory and defeat rested almost exclusively with me. But now, I was just another cog in a big wheel. Naturally, I was about as unhappy at that prospect as a school kid was for summer vacation to end. Being the key to human survival was a great weight, but it was also a great ego boost. I hadn't been "just one of the guys" since astronaut training back in Houston—when there still was a Houston. Maybe my wife was right? Humanity survived my absence for almost a hundred years. They could likely do it for a few more centuries. Crap, they probably could do it even longer.

When my emotional gas tank was running low, there were always three things I could count on to help. Peg's Bar Nobody, a good argument with Al, or a cordial visit with Kymee. The final option was the healthiest, so I headed for Oowaoa and the advice of a good man. True to form, he was under some contraption whacking it with a hammer.

"Hey, down there, be careful. That's delicate equipment," I shouted.

"Ah, Jon." He slid out and stood. "I thought I recognized those shoes."

"You recognize my shoes?"

"Yes, there are only two of them. You're the only one who visits me who's missing a shoe."

"So, you don't recognize my shoes, but the lack of one?"

"Yes. That's what I said. I recognized your shoes. They come in twos."

"Ah, usually you get silly after we've chatted a while. I think it's a bit early, just now."

"To be silly with you? Come now, you can't be so serious. It's out of character."

"I'll put it on a list and get to it eventually, okay?"

"Good. I want a full report. So, what brings you here?"

"What are you banging at there?" I pointed to the metal unit he'd been under when I entered.

"That? It's broken. It's a disembodier"

"A what?"

"It's a part of the vortex generator. Without it, there'd be no vortex manipulator and, hence, no vortex."

"What does it disembody?"

"You know that old saying about laws and sausage?"

"Yeah, you may like them, but you don't ever want to see them made. What's that got to do with a disembodier?"

"Best not to ask. Vortices are nice, but knowing too much about how they're made might be unsettling."

"Crap, now you know I've got to know. What does a disembodier do?"

"It helps separate the vortex manipulator from its original body, allowing us to place it in its new one."

You mean *Wrath* used to be a person? You pulled his ass out of his body and marooned him in a cube?" I shook my head. "No wonder he's so grouchy."

"No, he was never a person. Nothing even vaguely similar. He was part of a greater whole, but he was *designed* to perform the task he does. All the vortex manipulators are."

I looked skeptical. "Was he a volunteer?"

Kymee shook his head demonstrably. "No, it's not like that. I think we should drop the subject. You're unlikely to understand."

"I hate it when someone says that to me. It's never the case, and it pisses me off."

Kymee lowered his gaze. "I told you that before, didn't I?"

"I don't seem to recall that fact," I lied.

"I do. You once asked me where Yibitriander was. I said he was away. You asked where he was, and I said you wouldn't understand. Ring any bells?"

"No," I compounded my falsehood.

"I told you he was 'affixed to the third circle of truth absent consent.' You said you didn't understand."

"Must have been the alternate timeline Jon Ryan, not me. That one's self-explanatory."

I whacked the side of my head for some reason unclear to either of us.

"Hmm," he mused.

"So, I wanted to discuss immortality and morality. Guess who I thought of to help me out?" I asked changing the subject.

"The correct person, it would seem," he said with a smile. "At least I talk a good enough line to fool most people."

"Either way, I need some help."

"Then you'll receive the best free advice money can buy."

My turn. "Hmm?"

"Which of the many stumbling blocks of living forever have you crashed into? Whatever it is, I promise I've hit it many times before."

"With this recent round of fighting, Kayla is asking why I always need to be in the thick of it."

"Perceptive woman."

"Tell me about it."

"What was your response?"

"I said it was my job to defend the humans. It's my sworn duty. It always has been and always will be my sworn duty."

"My first tip on immortality. Never guarantee future trends. It may currently *be* and may always have *been* your inclination to fight for others, but never say it always *will* be. Always, it turns out, is a very long time, my friend. Trust me on that. Stars come and go, societies evolve and devolve. We all change."

"So, what'd you think? Should I rest on my laurels and let others do the heavy lifting?"

"Slow down. I never suggested anything, certainly not for someone who's not me. If you rush to a conclusion, it'll be a bad one. That much will always be a certainty."

He rested back and crossed his three arms. After years of seeing them do that, it still creeped me out a bit.

"In traditional society," he began, "yes, the young fight, become old if they're lucky, and the next generation gradually takes over. With immortals, that mode simply doesn't apply. It probably took me a hundred thousand years, but it finally dawned on me I was never going to die."

"Kymee, I'm less than four hundred years old, and I know that much."

"I don't mean I *knew* I'd live forever. I *believed* I'd live forever. Big difference."

I rolled my head. "I guess I can accept that."

"Among immortals, two factors change your thinking in terms of combat roles. One, since we will live forever, we must participate equally across time. Two, many younger ones are killed off, so older ones must keep on fighting. That depends on a society's reproduction rate, of course."

That made sense.

"Take me, for example. Only one of my children survives. Yibitriander. The rest are gone, lost in meaningless wars. He has lost all but one of his children. So, we two literally soldier on."

"Yibitriander has a child left? I didn't know that. He mentioned three of his boys dying in war. Who's left?"

"His daughter, my granddaughter. Her name is Neflerpic. She lives quite a distance from here."

"She and dad not get along too well?"

"How'd you guess? Her personality is every bit as inflexible and unyielding as his. If she wanted to move any farther away from him, she'd have to leave the planet."

"This I believe. I've met the man." After we chuckled, I asked, "Is she a nice person?"

"Never ask that question of a grandfather. She's the best, prettiest, cleverest child ever to grace Oowaoa. I miss her very much. Though I am able to speak with her most days." He looked sad.

"Maybe someday they'll get back together."

"Eternity may not be that long, but we shall see."

"So," I said returning to my point, "you agree with me, that I must fight on?"

"Don't ever ask a grandfather that question either. There are lots of subjects on which our opinions are too predictable and weak."

"So, you think I shouldn't still fight?"

"I said nothing of the kind. I pointed out there are aspects to the answer that depend very much on perception. I suggest looking at it from Kayla's point of view, also."

"Crap. I hate it when someone says that kind thing. I don't want to look at the world from a woman's point of reference."

"And why not?" he asked sternly.

"I'm a dude. I look at things dudifly. If I try—and trust me I have—to see life from a woman's point of view, I'll screw up worse than a politician at a truth-telling contest."

"Back to my line of reasoning. Try to look at the matter from Kayla's standpoint. She knows you're immortal, but she can't possibly believe or understand the concept. Remember, it took me a hundred thousand years. To her, you're simply the man she loves and the father of her children. Watching you march off to war again and again is unbearable for her. Top that off with your attitude that you won't quit unless you're killed."

"That's pretty bleak."

"Yes, it is."

"So, I should retire?"

"Didn't say that."

"So, I shouldn't retire?"

"Didn't say that either."

"So, what are you saying?"

"I'm saying only you can decide. Trust me. You will not be the first husband in the universe to not know whether it's better to please oneself or one's wife. In fact, double trust me on that. I'll send you a T-shirt later. I have a *bunch* in storage."

"Happy wife, happy life," I mumbled.

"Happy wife, *easier* life. It isn't happy if you're ashamed of yourself or, worse yet, jealous you can't do a thing you passionately wish to do."

"Not true. I would *like* to sleep around. I don't, because I'm married."

"You *don't*, you idiot, because you love your wife and wish to *please* her. You *don't* because you're a good man with a strong moral compass. If the benefits of an act don't outweigh the downside, you wouldn't do it."

"Well, excuse me for being an ethical creature."

He smiled. "I believe you now have sufficient information to answer your question correctly."

"What?" I threw my arms up. "How does saying those words indicate in any way I'm prepared to answer the toughest question I believe I've ever faced?"

"Ah, *perfect*. You've already made up your mind. I'm glad I could be of assistance."

"I *hate* you."

"You're welcome."

"No, seriously." I raised my fingers like they were claws. "I hate you with a capital *H.*"

"My work here is done." He rose. "Nufe, anyone? I feel like celebrating."

"What, for having one less friend?"

"No. Being joined by one more husband on this bench here at this lovely park."

"I'm not spending eternity sitting next to you on some damn park bench, watching the universe grow old."

"How else can you monitor the children playing for hours on end? I believe it's a law."

I grumbled. "Hopefully, it's just a guideline."

TWENTY-ONE

Two people knelt in church. The man on the left, a farmer, prayed for one inch of rain. Any less and his whole season would be ruined. The crops would wither and die. One more bad year, and the bank would foreclose.

The man on the right, a contractor, prayed for no rain. Even a small amount would turn his worksite into a mud pit. He wouldn't finish the building before the bank foreclosed. His career would be over and his family out on the street.

What happened? There was half an inch of rain. Both men go out of business. Neither felt he was heard.

When I returned home from Kymee's I told Kayla that she might be right and that I might be fighting in my last war. I was thinking of hanging up the spikes real soon. Since I didn't stop immediately, I was going against her wishes. But, since I admitted I needed to stop, I was going along with her judgment. She was huffy, ignored me for two days, and discussed taking the kids and visiting her brother. There was no mother-in-law to threaten me with, but she used Karnean as an excellent substitute.

I decided I would be that half inch of rain. What a muddle. I knew I should have stuck to my guns with Kymee and only seen things from the dude-perspective. When I did, I screwed up more often than not, but at least I could stand tall while going down in flames.

Fortunately, I had little time for hand-wringing or rumination. Round two of the Berrillian Guerrilla War began as abruptly as round one had. Late that afternoon, a shit storm hit on Ventural, the Maxwal-Asute home world.

Though we all figured fighting would begin soon on all the other planets the Berrillians had invaded, we concentrated our initial response on Ventural. For a few hours, I shuttled large numbers of personnel there. By the time that was done, I was asked to ferry wounded back to their home worlds, be they humans from the worldship fleet, or aliens to some other Alliance planet. I popped back and forth frantically from Ventural to any number of medical facilities. Within a few hours the fighting ebbed, but it didn't stop as completely as it had before.

With less wounded to evacuate, I elected to join the fighting. I was curious. I wanted to see the Maxwal-Asute in battle. The little fire hydrants talked tough, but there was no substitute for seeing them in action. I'd see if they walked the tough walk they talked.

Note to self. Never ever be curious about anything to do with war. War was hell. Well, actually, war wasn't hell. Hell was a place you went for R&R *after* war. Hell was an upgrade from war. However bad hell was in the mind of the person who feared it the most, hell was a cakewalk compared to war. And the irony of war was that we inflicted it on ourselves. Hell was established by celestial powers to house evil unsalvageable souls. We sentients lusted after our wars.

I wished to see them at war and boy, did I get my wish. No sooner had I joined the frontlines than the Berrillians launched their second, and real, offensive. The initial attack was a feint, intended to lull us into complacency. They hit us hard the first time, then stopped. I figure they hoped we'd assume their tactics would remain the same as in round one of the war. Theirs was a logical plan. Attack with all your might, then retreat. Live to fight another day. Hence, they changed tactics.

The first waves had consisted of a few hundred cats charging over a long, thin battle line in the hilly, forested region of Ventural. The natural response for our force was to spread out to meet that initial attack. The second wave was a wedge-shaped assault. That made the going for our forces in the center of the battle line even more deadly. They passed through our forces like a hot knife through warm butter. Then they split into two waves that doubled back on either side of the breech. Our fighters were trapped in a vice. If the

Berrillians successfully swept behind our entire force, the bulk of our people would be cut off and surrounded. As the cats never took prisoners, we all understood the cost of being pinned down like that.

Our reinforcements tried to stop the lateral movement of the two Berrillian units that had broken through. That was where the fighting was the most intense. In those areas, our soldiers had Berrillians in front of and behind them, as well as friendly forces pressing the enemy back from the rear. Command quickly lost control, due to the confusion. Also, no one had time to talk with our leaders. It had become all-out hand-to-hand combat. Kill or die. On both sides, we all switched into automatic mode. Bestial killing and gruesome dying became the order of the day.

I was firing a plasma gun with my left hand and using the laser in my right index finger. I could cover a large field of vision that way. I faced straight ahead and fired both to the right and left at the same time. That technique had worked well in the past, and continued to work well now.

I had to narrow my focus as the fighting became more and more close quarters. The Maxwal-Asute did, indeed, have a different way of fighting. When the action was more spread out, they fired small but lethal guns from fixed formations. But as the battle became intimate, they stopped firing and swarmed the much larger Berrillians like ants. Individuality was replaced by the hive-mind. When a cat caught and hurled two fire hydrants into the air, four raced to the spot they'd been and continued tearing at the Berrillian. I saw countless Maxwal-Asute literally cover up a Berrillian, the cat continuing to claw and snap at them the entire time. Ultimately the Berrillian would succumb, fall to the turf, and die, but it took thirty or more Maxwal-Asute lives to achieve that end.

The ground became slick with the red blood of the Berrillians and the Kelly-green blood of the locals. Parts and pieces of Maxwal-Asute were everywhere; on the turf, in the trees, all over me. But they never flagged. Whenever they were near enough to a cat, masses of Maxwal-Asute would pour over them. They seemed to use their plunger heads to both slice at, as well as bite at the enemy. All the while, as the little guys enveloped a cat, it was making mincemeat of them. The eery part for me was that the Maxwal-Asute were absolutely silent the entire time. No war cries or screams.

As the fighting collapsed, I flipped the rifle to my right hand. My left fist served to bash any Berrillians who came too close. Quickly, that number skyrocketed. My position was being overrun by the enemy. Then my right hand exploded. I looked to see a Berrillian standing not five meters from me with a plasma gun in its paws. I whipped out my fibers out and grabbed his head before he could fire again, and tossed him in the air as high as I could. He disappeared above the canopy of trees.

My hand was gone. The blast had removed everything from mid forearm down. The exposed tip sparked and hissed. Luckily the rest of my right arm worked just fine.

I was gripped by fear. It had been a long time since I experienced that emotion. I wasn't in full control. I was no longer the ultimate warrior. I was a one-armed man in a fist fight.

But there was no time to contemplate my navel. Two Berrillians charged at me from the right. I brought my rifle up and blew one a new hole, but the other tackled me before I could train the gun on him. We collapsed backward as he drove me to the ground. Instead of making a divot where we hit, we slid on the oozy blood-slime that was everywhere. We spun as we glided, him on top, me on the bottom. A tree stopped us abruptly.

I kneed him and launched him into the trunk, but did so with little force. I'd slipped backward in the mire, losing any real leverage. He came down on his head, back against the tree, but gently. We both flipped to stand. His footing was way better than mine, because of his claws. I slipped and stopped myself from falling with the stump of my right arm. He grabbed me by the head and lifted me into the air with his front legs. Right at mouth-level I kicked him. Risky business, driving a body part *toward* those teeth. Luckily, he didn't see it was coming in time to open up. His front fangs collapsed under my foot. I felt his jaw splinter.

He roared in pain but held onto me. I swung violently from side to side. My left hand grabbed his chest. In my head, I said one word. *Heart.* My probe fibers shot past his ribs and whipped his heart like it was in a blender. He gave me one short shocked look and collapsed. I broke free before he hit the ground.

I searched frantically for my rifle. There. Ten meters to the right. I dived for it.

A Berrillian female kicked the side of my head. She appeared from nowhere. I flip-flopped midair and rolled sideways into the mud. She pounced on me. I rolled her onto her back. I stuck my stump under her chin and pushed up for all I was worth. She almost managed to use my momentum to flip me over, but I rode her like a bucking bronco. Her head was forced upward from my right arm. I pushed her face away from me with my hand. She yielded enough that I could inch her face into the repulsive goo the dirt had become.

As she suffocated she tried to hurl me off her stomach. I wrapped my legs around her waist to hold on and kept driving her face down. She fell limp thirty seconds later. I held her a couple seconds longer to make sure she was dead. I rose slowly to my feet. Didn't want to slip again.

A click to one side caught my ear. A Berrillian male had a rifle pointed right at my head. He roared in triumph. Before he could fire, a swarm of Maxwal-Asute flooded over him. Man, did they looked good as they swallowed him up. I loved the little buggers right about then. He shot at his own head a few times before he, either by intent or accident, blew it off. The Maxwal-Asute not killed dropped to the ground like fleas off a dead dog and rushed to attack the nearest Berrillian.

I studied the filthy stump of my right arm. I was so glad I didn't have to worry about infection. It'd have been horrific. Then I had an idea. I had duct tape on my utility belt. Duct tape and WD-40. Never go into battle without them. I found a fifty-kilogram rock and bound it to my stump. The tape was strong enough to hold the rock with minimal wobbling. It probably wouldn't hold for long, but I felt a hell of a lot better to have a weapon. I didn't like having a pure liability.

I swung my rifle up and turned. Three Berrillians were rushing me. Two were on all fours. The other was on two feet and held a rifle. Why she hadn't fired I'd never know. I planted a plasma bolt right between her eyes. She flipped over backward like a gymnast. I shot one of the others in the chest. He collapsed to the ground and quickly scampered into the bushes. His companion hadn't noticed or didn't care that he was charging alone. He growled and sprang at me. My new club came down atop his head with a satisfying crunch. I hopped over his body and turned to make certain he wasn't getting back up. He wasn't.

It was getting dark. There was no way I could return to *Wrath* at that point. A whole lot of cats stood between the two of us. I also couldn't summon *Shearwater* so I could bail on the firefight. Too many trees. Plus, the arrival of a ship would draw the Berrillians like flies to poop. I was stuck. At least until our reinforcements broke through, I'd be hunkering down until dawn. The Maxwal-Asute had extremely poor night vision. Unless forced to do otherwise, they preferred to secret themselves away when they were at such a significant disadvantage. Berrillians, on the other hand, possessed outstanding night vision, better than the cat species of Earth. We were in for a long night of deadly hide and seek.

I found a few large rocks and tried to disappear into them. My rifle had half a charge left. That meant I had at least several hundred shots remaining. The disadvantage of using a plasma gun at night was that the light it produced was prodigious. If I fired it, every cat within a kilometer would know where I was. My laser finger would have been safe to use, as its beam was so focused, but it was mangled somewhere on the sticky forest floor.

I then had to face my greatest fear and challenge. I had to call Kayla and tell her I wouldn't be home that evening, on account of being pinned down and in mortal danger. I'd try to conceal my serious injury, but if she learned of that, I'd break her heart. I'd almost rather be dead than make the call.

Al, I said in my head, *are you and* Wrath *safe and secure?*

Yes, captain. We're inside a membrane awaiting your return.

Well, that won't be tonight.

A Berrillian rushed at me from nowhere. He fired his rifle and roared to beat the band. I barely dodged his shots. I aimed and fired once. It was a lucky shot. I'd removed his head before he could fire again. I poked my head up to see if anyone else noted my location. My infrared scanners showed a few Berrillians moving slowly, but none were headed my way.

After a couple minutes, I spoke in my head to Al. *Okay, it's quiet now. Like*

I said, I'll take cover here tonight. If possible, I'll try and make it back to you when more Maxwal-Asute arrive.

Is there anything we can do to help?

No, I don't think so. If something occurs to me I'll let you know.

Jon, be safe.

Wow, he never called me by my name. *I will. Thanks. Hey, can you patch me through to Kayla?*

Are you certain that's wise? I'm admittedly an AI machine, but my records of female behavior suggest such a move is risky to a male's longevity.

There's no way around it. If I don't check in I'll be just as dead.

I'm glad I'm an artificial construct.

I may ask you to switch places with me before this is over.

Thanks for the Pinocchio offer, but I'll remain inanimate, especially in this dubious context.

Thanks for your moral support. Not.

I may only be a machine, but I'm not a foolish machine.

Put me through, before I listen to you and my gut and chicken out.

After a few seconds I heard her voice. "Jon? Is that you honey? Where are you?"

Luckily, I could think my words to Al and he could translate them to audio. I couldn't risk talking in my precarious position.

"You know what? That's a funny story. Ah, are you sitting down?"

"You assume I'll laugh so hard I might collapse? This can't be good news, as I'm hearing Al's voice, not yours." Her voice was as cold and as sharp as a guillotine blade.

"Laughter's possible, I guess."

"Jon. I'm getting very angry. Where are you?"

"Somewhere north of the Maxwal-Asute capital city."

"Somewhere? That sounds bad. Why don't you know exactly where you are, and why isn't that location actually here at home?"

"Ah, I decided to work late?"

"Not funny. Answer me."

"I'm held down by Berrillians."

"I said no jokes. I'm deadly serious."

"No, seriously. Outnumbered, pinned down behind rocks, and hoping to see the dawn."

"Jon, why are you there? Can't you make it back to *Wrath*?" Her voice was suddenly trembling.

"No. Too many enemy between us. It's an overnight here for me. I'll have to wait for Maxwal-Asute reinforcements to come. That won't be until tomorrow."

"Can you?"

Tough question. "I think so. I'm being honest, honey. I think I'll be okay."

"I'm hanging up. I need you to stay focused. I want you to know I'm not hanging up because I'm angry with you. That will come when you're safely back home. *Then* you're a dead man."

"Love you, too."

Al, close the link.

Done.

I'm signing out until further notice.

Absolutely. You need to stay focused.

Were you eavesdropping?

No. Why?

That's what Kayla just told me.

Great minds think alike. You should get one, assuming you survive this.

Love you, too. Nighty-night.

Maxwal-Asute didn't vocalize the same way we did. They lack a voice box and produce sound by vibrating their inverted toilet plunger disks. But they can most assuredly scream in holy terror. During that long night, I heard half a dozen different versions from them as they cried out in terror and were suddenly silenced. I knew something terrible had happened to each voice. By the luck of fate, I was left alone. One Berrillian crawled right past me, close enough that I lifted my rock to bash him. But he abruptly spun and sped off into the darkness. A scream of horror confirmed he'd acquired a target.

Just before dawn, I heard angels, lots of angels. It was the sound of hundreds of troop carrier crafts approaching. Relief was on its way. I also made out the sounds of countless ground transports—probably tanks—crashing toward our position. First light saw a firefight of epic proportions, but the Maxwal-Asute forces struck in such number and with such ferocity that the battle was brief. Not a single Berrillian was left alive on the battlefield. Zero. I doubt they'd have wanted to surrender, but none were extended that invitation. Lucky captives were shot. A handful of cats were not so fortunate. They were bound and swarmed. Even hating the Berrillians as much as I did, it was a gruesome sight. One I'd just as soon have missed. The Berrillians also had many different howls of pain and terror, it turned out.

War.

I was ferried back to *Wrath* and left immediately. I had some major fences to mend. Kayla jumped into my arms and hugged me so hard I felt like I couldn't breathe. Then I remembered I didn't breathe. The kids, who were never told why dad didn't come home, greeted me enthusiastically enough. Then they promptly returned to texting their friends and playing holo games. I had a rock duct taped to where my hand was supposed to be and they returned to their world without a peep. Kids.

Once we were alone, Kayla leveled a finger at my nose. "Never again. That's my last *word* on the subject. You are allowed none."

Then she pecked me on the cheek and let me head to Toño's for repair. She did specifically tell me the rock wasn't sexy. It had to be either her or the rock. Both would not be living in my company. My choice was immediate.

Toño knew of my injury, but man oh man, he hammed it up when he laid eyes on me. "If you don't stop ruining my creation, I will refuse to repair it. This is intolerable. *¡Insoportable!*"

"No, seriously, I'm fine. No other wounds or painful injuries," I replied.

"That is too bad. A little pain would serve you right."

"Maybe you could program some for me, you know, as a punishment."

"Don't tempt me. Do *not* tempt me. Now come, let me remove that ridiculous stone."

As the duct tape came off, he set the rock aside and angled both hands at my stump. "Look at the damage that idiotic stone has done. The margins are filthy and shorn like a rat has gnawed on them."

"Excuse me for trying to survive."

"That is not sufficient reason to have done *this* much harm. I'll have to replace the forearm at the elbow."

"Will it help if I self-flagellate and grovel?"

"No, but go ahead and try, nonetheless." He finally smiled.

"Don't forget to install a forearm with a laser finger. I want to be at full strength."

"So, you can prevent this from happening again?"

"No, it didn't—" I wagged finger at him. "You're a cruel SOB. You know that, right?"

"That is my goal, when it comes to dealing with you." He winked.

A few hours into the tedious repair work, I asked Toño a question that I'd recently started kicking around in my head. "You're a science guy, right? Mind if I ask you a question?"

He stopped what he was doing, set his tools down, and looked at the ceiling. "Yes, I guess I am a science guy."

Before I could speak he held up a hang-on-a-second hand. "You know, I think I'll have those words inscribed on my headstone." He swept a hand in an arc through the air. "Here Lies Doc." Then he lowered his hand to signify line two. "A Science Guy."

He brought his silencing hand up again. Wiping at the corner of his eye he concluded, "Kind of brings a tear to my eye." He menaced a glance at me. "But just the right one."

"So, I was thinking—"

He harrumphed.

"I was *thinking*, where would I go to find people who could excavate the hell out of a planet's surface?"

That brought him to a full stop again. "Why would you want to excavate the hell out of a planet's surface?"

"I don't. But if you did, where would you go?"

"To a psychiatrist, because I'd be out of my mind."

"Ouch."

"Where does this odd concern come from. I know I shouldn't ask, and that I'll regret doing so for all eternity, but where?"

"I'm glad my teachers in school were more supportive of my inquisitive mind."

"They simply wanted you to graduate, so they would be done with you. I'm stuck with you forever."

I whirled my hands in the air. "The excavating thing?"

He rested a hand on his chin. "Large scale excavating? Hmm. I suppose I'd ask the Department of Reconstruction and Recovery."

"The DR&R? They built the worldships, but now they just make little expansions and additions."

"You asked. I answered. Now come, where does this lead?"

"I did some thinking last night. To try and ignore the screams, I noodled with the idea of digging great pits and caves on a planet."

"Why would you want to do such a wasteful thing? What had the planet ever done to you?"

"The planet itself, nothing. The inhabitants? Well, they annoyed me."

"Annoy Jon Ryan, and he excavates your world? The punishment seems to exceed the crime."

"They *really* annoyed me then."

"And why would you want to pit the surface of this offensive race?"

"I don't. Remember? I was just thinking."

He scowled and picked up his tools again. "The four most worrisome words to come from Jon Ryan's mouth."

TWENTY-TWO

I made it a point to be on the agenda of the next Defense Council meeting. Those took place weekly and on an as-needed basis. I'd been to my share over the years in various capacities, but this was my first meeting in a long time. I spoke as an officer in TCY.

"The secretary recognizes General Ryan," said Bin Li officially. "To what do we owe this honor, general?"

"Decide if it's an honor after I'm done. You can hardly tell with me, sometimes."

Those in the room laughed politely.

"I'd like to ask the council to consider a strategic option."

A quiet murmur went up.

"For you, anything is possible. However, this is not the usual forum for brainstorming. Usually we approve *finalized* plans."

"I realize that. Nowadays, I'm not associated with a group that does such preparatory work."

"What do you propose, Jon?" asked Alexis. As US president, she was naturally on the council.

"A surprise for some old friends who are not actually friends—and for some new ones, who aren't really friends, either."

"I doubt the council will welcome riddles, General Ryan." That was Gabriel Newman, a senior strategist to the council. He was also not counted among my many fans or admirers.

"Then I shall avoid them, Gabe. Just for you. I'll use little words when possible, too, if you'd like."

"I'm certain the council would welcome sarcasm as much as it welcomes riddles," he said, with a very sour face.

"Well, if the council welcomes *you*, it's proven itself to be quite tolerant." Sorry. I had to bust his chops a little.

"What, specifically are you envisioning?" Bin asked quickly.

"I would like to lead a diplomatic mission to LH 16a. There, I would like to discuss military options with Gortantor."

"The Jinicgus leader?" asked Gabriel incredulously. "We don't have a military pact with them."

"Still," I said holding up my arms, "they are threatened by the Berrillians. If not formal members of the Alliance, they have to be considered as kindred spirits in peril."

"Kindred spirits who tried to kill you after you fired on them," scoffed Gabriel.

"It was a failure to communicate. Nothing more. I wish to build bridges, not topple them."

"A new Jon Ryan, three centuries into the old one?" asked Gabriel sarcastically.

"Jon," asked Alexis, "why you? Surely they hate you as much as any race does. What good could come of your visit?"

"Yes. If you truly wish for their cooperation, why not send seasoned diplomats?" asked Bin.

"Because as well as diplomats lie, they aren't necessarily good poker players."

"You wish to play cards with your enemies?" asked Gabriel.

"Metaphorically, yes. Yes, I do." I smiled real big. "Oh, and I'd like authorization to begin the rapid and expansive excavation of Rigel 12."

"What?" burst from Gabriel's mouth. "Again, we have no formal ties with the Luminarians. And why would they want their planet excavated?"

"I doubt they would," I replied. "But I also doubt they'd bother to object."

"You can't just go drill the massive holes in someone else's planet for no reason and without consent," protested Gabriel.

"Consent, maybe I'll give you I lack. But do I have an excellent reason."

"And who would be doing this large-scale digging, Jon?" asked Alexis.

"I have a proposal in front of you authored by DR&R. Turns out they'd love to rip up a lot of rocks again. It's in their DNA, I guess."

****

Two months later I was off to LH 16a. The UN had made a request for a formal audience with Gortantor. After negotiations bordering on squabbling and concessions edging on blackmail, a limited visit was granted. He didn't, to his discredit, ask who was coming to dinner. My oh my, was he in for a surprise. I toyed with the idea of taking Molly along. I needed a foil if my plan was to work. But she was too sweet, innocent, and Gortantor probably hated her more than he did me. I wanted to play those suckers, not tempt fate.

There was a TV show from the mid twentieth century I watched on my *Ark 1* voyage. It was called *Mission Impossible*. At the start of the show, this super spy went through his files by throwing them on a table to find the right personnel for that episode's caper. I did the same in my head, searching for the right accomplice. Kendra would do it, but she'd probably kill Gortantor *first,* then try and set him up. Amanda would do it, but I preferred not to use a woman again. I didn't want to seem too obvious.

What dude? Toño and Carlos would go, but they were too honest to fool most living creatures. One of my Deavoriath posse was an option, but they were scary to a lot of races. Heath? He was getting old, and I intimidated him. Might show through in his performance. *JJ.* Of course. He'd do anything, say anything, or be anything if it was fun, irreverent, and led to someone somewhere having egg on their face. He would be my aide. No, my *handler.* Perfect.

We landed *Shearwater* close to Gortantor's palace. As we were expected, a troop of guards were waiting. I hesitate to refer to them as an honor guard. I think they were more under orders to be a shoot first and ask questions later kind of guard. The Jinicgus were highly suspicious on one of their rare, good days. After I exited, it took a second, then squeals rose from the soldiers. Some of them must have recognized me. The good news was, none of them fired on me at that juncture.

JJ followed me out. I had dressed him in the most preposterous, pompous, overblown getup I could fashion. He had a huge golden crown, with way too many jewels pasted on. They were the best fake stones money could buy. He had a massive, flowing red cape with white piping and black leather boots to mid-thigh. And he had a *monocle*. Yeah, that touch was *the pièce de résistance*. JJ looked like a guy who'd lost a bet and was forced to dress like a dandy with poor taste. Brilliant. I wanted him to be distracting.

"You will follow us," said the leader of the squad.

Half the guard went in front of us, and the other half split off and came in behind. The ones in back kept tripping over JJ's cape, mostly because he walked at an irregular pace in order to have them do just that. They kept dropping farther and farther behind to avoid the sweep of the fabric, but JJ continued to knock them down with regularity.

We entered the same assembly hall we had met Gortantor in before.

"Wait here until his lordship finds the time to accept your presence," said the same guy.

"No worries," I replied. "My schedule is clear for the whole morning."

"What? Are you mocking me?" snapped the little bozo.

"No. Whatever gave you that impression? You're kind of touchy, aren't you?"

"I am not *touchy*, whatever that is. I will not be toyed with. To insult me is to insult my great lord. That will not be permitted."

"He means to insult us both, Kaperghee."

All eyes swung to see Gortantor stepping through the curtains that partitioned the room. Everyone but the guards dropped prostrate to the floor. JJ and I remained standing.

"I must say, Ryan, it is both revolting and a pleasure to see you again. The obvious pleasure is that I will be able to witness your dismemberment and hear your cries for mercy, personally. Otherwise, to see you again is profoundly distressing."

"Yeah," I responded, "I kind of have that effect on people. But, before we get all sentimental and speak of good times past, I need to remind you we are on a diplomatic mission with significant implications for your subjects."

"Yes, I was told a representative would present military information of critical importance. Had I dreamed it would be you, I would have refused this audience."

"That would have been a serious mistake."

Squeals shot up from the crowd. Apparently, one did not use the word *mistake* when discussing anything Gortantor did.

He glared at me for a moment, then his expression eased. "And who is this individual foolish enough to come here in your company?"

"You do not *know* this luminary on sight? Wait, is it *you* who mocks *us*, now?"

"Ryan, I am never in the mood to play games, and I am especially not so when you are involved. Why should I know this person?"

JJ rested two fingers on my arm to stop me from responding. He cleared his throat softly, then spoke. "Perhaps it is possible this fine gentleman does not know me. Please. It is no insult to be unrecognized by a race so removed from the general flow of culture in the galaxy. Really, General Ryan, it is not their fault they live in aboriginal bliss."

"I suppose it is *conceivable*," I agreed. I straightened up and set a hand on JJ's shoulder. "This, Lord Gortantor, is Jayjissimus, the Grand *Poobah* of Kaljax and all its colonial holdings. He is the seven-times blessed master of Beerism, the sacred religion of his people. He is also the intellectual leader of the cult of Gridiron, an ancient ceremony that is used to separate the men from the boys on his world."

"Jayjissimus?" Gortantor said dubiously. "I sense another mocking, another joke in the worst of taste. I sense also that the appointed hour when you meet death, Ryan, draws near."

JJ grabbed at my shoulder, demonstrating he was having trouble remaining erect. He shook like a thin leaf in a major storm. "I told you I did not wish to accompany you, you traitorous rodent. You forced me to depart from the adulation of my adoring subjects to be belittled and threatened by this ... this—" JJ could no longer speak, he was so upset.

"Need I remind you why your monumental presence was necessary? It certainly wasn't *my* idea to drag you along."

JJ demonstrated considerable effort trying to calm himself. He took many deep breaths. "Yes," he finally said, "you're right. It probably is for the best ... even though these people do fail to appreciate who I am and the honor I do them in coming."

"Are you two fools about done with your performance? I was weary of it at its start and am now positively bored," said Gortantor.

"Look, we're getting off task here," I responded. "I think I should present you with the information you need to know. Then we can decide if our staying longer will be beneficial or not."

"There is," Gortantor said slowly, "so much wrong with your last remark, I do not know where to begin. Let me start with the observation that no sovereign government would send *you* to inform *me* of anything. They would know beforehand that I hate and distrust you, so it's inconceivable that I'd believe a word you say."

"No, don't you see? That's exactly the point. Thank you for honestly admitting the inherent wisdom of our design."

He waved a guard over and took his weapon. Pointing it at me he said, "I'm about ready to shoot you. What don't I see? I admit to *nothing*. I observe absolutely no *wisdom* exiting your mouth." He clicked the gun's safety switch.

There was so much at stake, I had to force myself not to disintegrate the little insect then and there. But he was no good to me dead. Not yet, at least.

"If my government sent any typical diplomat, you'd be uncertain whether to trust them or not. By sending me, they wish to express that the message I must deliver is so obviously true and in the Jinicgus's best interest, that you had to accept it from someone you couldn't trust."

"That is illogical, insane, and mind-bogglingly stupid, all at once."

I think he was disinclined to buy what I was selling, just yet.

"To make certain you hear and accept my message, my government went to the extreme cost and trouble of convincing the Grand Poobah Jayjissimus to accompany me. They were certain you knew of him and that his presence would indicate the validity of their motives."

I looked at JJ in disbelief. "I guess they really don't know who you are."

JJ's shoulders drooped. He shook his head. "It is hard to imagine, but I suppose we must take him at his word that they know me not." He sighed. "My life's work is apparently not done."

"Wait. Hold on," said Gortantor. "I, of course, know *of* the Grand Poobah. I am no backwater rube. My people know *of* him. Also, I assure you I simply meant to convey two thoughts. First, I do not know him *personally*. Second, though I know he is a man of great distinction, that alone is not a guarantee I'll accept the word of Ryan in any matter."

JJ developed the most hopeful look in his eyes, all four of them.

"I feel it is best if you deliver your message, Ryan. Then we can discuss *it* and your credibility," said Gortantor.

"That would be *peachy*," replied JJ.

"Fine. My message is one of friendship and hope for the future, Gortantor. As you know only too well, the Berrillian threat is real, and it is ever-present. Though there is no formal alliance between our cultures, we feel we are brothers in this fight. All of us.

"Here is the information I am sent to convey. One, we will re-extend an offer of formal alliance between our worlds. Two, in case you are openly attacked by our common enemy, we shall be glad to assist you in your defense, if requested. Three, should the unthinkable happen and the Berrillians come to dominate your world, we offer you sanctuary. That is the essence of our proposal. Detailed written summaries are contained on this disk." I held up an info-disk and set it on the table.

I could almost hear the gears spinning in his tiny head. He was trying to figure out if I meant a word of what I'd said. Also, he was trying to glean what my angle was, because I had to be trying to trick him.

I crossed my fingers that he wasn't nearly smart enough to pull any of this off.

Finally he spoke. "Your offer for a formal relationship has been addressed before. I will, however, reconsider it in light of your current remarks. As to accepting aid if attacked, though your offer is magnanimous, I must decline it. We will be the single guarantors of our future. Finally, as to a sanctuary, I am certain we won't require one."

Hmm. He didn't even nibble at the bait.

"The idea," he went on, "of abandoning our planet is repugnant. We will never be content as a species living under the rules and conventions of an alien power."

However. *Please, can I get a* but? I thought.

"However, I am curious where this sanctuary might be, so I can contemplate if we will demean ourselves by voyaging there, should the unthinkable occur."

Excuse me while I set this hook.

"Ah, I'm not at liberty to discuss the specifics of Sanctuary. I'm only at liberty to discuss specifics if evacuation is eminently needed. I'm certain you understand?"

"Ah," Gortantor responded triumphantly, "then you have failed. You have told me that it is a single place named Sanctuary. So, if I can determine which Alliance planet bears that name, I shall know where it is."

JJ looked at me like I'd just farted, loud and juicy.

"Thank you, Jayjissimus, for confirming my observation. You see, gentlemen, you are children playing an adults game with me. Pray I only pick your brains like exotic desserts, and do you no worse harm."

"I said specifics of *the* sanctuary, meaning the word in its general implications," I protested.

"You most certainly did not. You referred to a specific *planet*. Come, tell me where it is, and we shall part as friends." He put on a neutral expression. "If there is no trust, there can be no trust. If I do not know where you would have my people go, how can I determine if it is in their best interest to go there?"

"I … well, for security purposes my government felt it was best to keep certain matters nebulous."

"Fine, fine. We shall discuss nebulous things in more detail at dinner. You and the Grand Poobah will join me here at dusk. In the meantime, as my guests, you are free to explore my city or do as you please. Until this evening, I bid you goodbye."

Hook planted. Time to *reel* him in. Too bad he was too small to be a keeper.

A few hours later, we returned to the palace. JJ had on a variant of his former ridiculous costume, this one designed to look more formal, possibly more conservative. Well, he did have a big feather sticking out of his crown and vividly colored sequins dangling from his arms, but it said conservative to me. I'd done some quick checking that afternoon. The food would clearly not bother me, but since it killed Berrillians, I didn't want to poison my son. There was no real threat, but I told him for safety sake to just nibble.

It turned out it didn't matter. He found what they offered revolting, both visually and to his palate. I saw his point. Their cuisine was bitter, slimy, and extremely salty. LH 16a would never be on a foodie's bucket list.

"So, Ryan," asked Gortantor, "what do you think of our offerings? Have you eaten our food before?"

"Ah, a little. When I came here way back when, I left with a goodly amount. It was mostly for my Toe crew mate." I shrugged. "She ate it with gusto."

"Ah. And you, Grand Poobah. Is it to your liking?"

"Yes, so much so that I will eat very little of it."

"Huh?" he asked.

"Since I may not have it again, I should not want to miss it so."

"Ah," he replied unconvinced.

"Have you come to any decisions about our earlier discussion?" I asked.

"No. I have thought upon them mightily but cannot say I have concluded anything. As you know, our races have historically been at arm's length since the beginning. If, however, you could offer me a token of trust, I think we might be on the verge of a positive relationship."

"Would that it were the case," replied JJ expansively. "In all matters I have found that trust is in the mind of good people and the hearts of few."

"Err, I'm not certain I take your meaning, great one," said Gortantor.

"Of course, you don't. That is why I said it."

"You spoke to deceive or to belittle?" He sounded puzzled.

"Never. My goal is to enlighten. You see, the path to the future must be lit with the torch of knowledge, but the way is still firm. These are core beliefs in Beerism. To understand nature, one must *excel,* as well as *accelerate.* Do you not agree?"

"Um, yes, I don't agree. I mean no, I disagree. I'm still not one-hundred percent certain I follow your words."

JJ could be such a prick. Oh, how I loved my boy.

"Of course, you do and don't. I see you are grasping the finer points it took me generations to combine. Here," JJ said sitting forward, "take the example of this planet you wish to know about."

"Ah, okay—" he replied uncertainly.

"The fact that you *do* want to know its location but *don't* know it proves you understand why we can and cannot tell you." JJ's hands quivered he was so excited. "I *can* tell you where it is, because I know where it is. I cannot tell you where it is for your own safety and because the Alliance asked me not to."

"Uh, and? What was it you mean? I hear words, but they seem empty."

"*Thank you,* my child! Such a blessing can only be grown."

"Jayjissimus," I interrupted, "your words are full to me, not empty. But I know Beer." I stopped to pat the top of my head. "I fear our host, not knowing Beer," again a pat to my head, "cannot understand."

"Do you say cannot or does not?" responded JJ in a huff. "As you know, small wooden items are as similar as they are intentional."

"I'm sorry," Gortantor said raising several little legs, "perhaps it is a language thing, but I'm lost. What are you speaking of? What exactly are you saying?"

"Most if not all matters we are discussing," said JJ, "sanctuary, alliances, Beer," we both tapped our heads, "and, as always, ideas that have not broken through."

"Broken through? Broken through *what?*" Gortantor was looking almost ill.

"There, employee of the month," JJ said to me as he pointed to Gortantor, "I told you he would compartmentalize my philosophy. I feel so green, so very planned. Tell me, Gortantor, what was it I said that tipped you over the edge of understanding?"

"I ... I suppose it was the broken ideas part."

"Yes, they are." JJ pinched the air in front of his nose. "They are so close."

"What are so close, and what are they close to?"

JJ raised an eyebrow in confusion. "Why Rigel and my traveling dog." JJ wagged a finger at me.

"Traveling dog? I know of pet dogs, but he's not—"

"*Poobah*," I howled in anger. "You have betrayed our cause. You are a staircase." I turned my back to my son.

"No," replied JJ, then shoved the side of his hand in his mouth. "Ah, I *am* a staircase."

"I find, gentlemen, I am more confused than—" Gortantor's train of thought pulled to a slow stop.

"What?" I asked in a panicky tone.

"Oh, nothing," Gortantor replied. "I was just thinking how late it is and how tired you must be. I have kept you past a host's privilege."

"You are so wise, yet so fortuitous," marveled JJ. "Amicable but not suicidal. I could learn much from a practicality like you, Gortantor."

"Were the hour not so late and my schedule so full," he replied. "In fact, this will be your last audience with me."

"Ev ... ever?" I asked.

"No, just this trip. I shall communicate my thoughts with your superiors when I've reached them."

JJ tilted his head. "When you reach your conclusions or when you reach our supervisors?"

"*Yes.*" was Gortantor giddy response. "Now *you* understand."

That night JJ and I hit the road. We could *not* stop laughing. We'd done good.

TWENTY-THREE

"A sanctuary planet? Are you certain that's what they said?" Claudus's voice shook the walls. He spoke with his back to Gortantor, whose image blinked on the communication stand.

"Absolutely. There is no doubt that is what they offered me. A sanctuary planet to retreat to, should your people be triumphant."

"Should we be?" His voice then shook walls several rooms away.

"Their words, not mine. *Our* victory is certain."

Our victory, thought Claudus with sarcasm. *Your* part will be minuscule and brief, he reflected. The victory will belong to *me*.

"But that makes no sense. If we have conquered most of their worlds, why would they retreat to yet another?"

"Perhaps it is more defensible."

"Hmm. I don't know how one planet could be a better fortress than the next." He rocked on his heels. "I guess it's possible, maybe a metal-rich rocky planet. But, no, we'd still crush it."

"I can only tell you what they told me. I cannot vouch for the soundness of their reasoning. That's not how this works."

"How what works, little bug?"

"How our alliance works. I can supply you with intelligence. You must ascertain its worth and what to do with the information."

"I suppose. And they told you this sanctuary planet was Rigel?"

"Yes. I tricked them into telling me."

"There are dozens of planets orbiting that star."

"Only a handful. Surely your spies can determine which specific planet is the one they prize."

"Hmm. I suppose. But it would be protected extravagantly. If we came close enough to discover it, those devil spawns will shoot us from the sky."

"That is possible. I am not responsible for their military superiority over you. The blame for that lies on your shoulders alone."

"Why, you impertinent turdette. How dare you?"

"Calm yourself."

Gortantor had no idea how fortunate he was to be light years removed from Claudus just then. If they were together, Gortantor would be a splatter on the nearest wall.

"Think it through, Claudus. If they wish to conceal the location of this sanctuary, they will hardly highlight it with bright lights and directional signs."

"Hmm. I suppose."

Claudus was revolted by the concept of a sanctuary planet. If he lost a war, he would plan to die, not skulk away to hide under a wet rock.

"The Rigel system has but one major planet. The twelfth one. But that is, or at least was, the home of the Luminarians." Claudus harrumphed. "Those sorry bastards wouldn't give you the time of day, let alone sanctuary."

"I am unfamiliar with them. Why do you say this?"

"Of course, you're unaware of them. They don't inhabit the space directly in front of your face." He chuckled at his wit. "They think quite highly of themselves. If they still exist, they help no one but themselves."

"Then I assume they have vanished."

Wait, thought Claudus, *let me lunge for pen and paper to write your opinion down. Then I can have something to wipe my ass with.* Still, the Luminarians would have to be gone if that infantile Alliance was using Rigel 12 as a fallback location. He recalled nothing special about the planet. But then again, he knew little about it. He'd assign one of his most trusted men to investigate. If the Berrillian infiltrators beat the Alliance to the world they scurried to for protection, why, that would be ironically *marvelous.* It would be spectacular. The slaughter would be unparalleled. The carnage unprecedented. The joy would be limitless. Claudus might even allow his decrepit, useless father to join in the splendor. Erratarus could revel in the killing and bloodletting. Then he could bury the old fart on Rigel 12 as a monument to the stupidity that surrounded Claudus on all sides.

"I will check out this sanctuary. If your information is good, you might just continue to breathe." He turned for the first time to look at Gortantor. "I'm sorry. I don't want to insult my little friends. You shit puddles do breathe, don't you?" He roared in laughter.

Gortantor did not join in. He felt the impulse to switch the transmission off, he was so indignant. Then again, it was best to provoke these hairy beasts the least amount possible. Someday that roaring buffoon would lick Gortantor's shiny genital plate on command. But for the time being, he'd wait for Claudus to terminate the call.

TWENTY-FOUR

Yibitriander, Faiza, Toño, and I walked in a line across the irregular ground. I had been to Rigel 12a few times since my initial visit. I hadn't seen another Luminarian, and that was fine by me. Not seeing them was necessary for my plan to work. I had directed the DR&R teams to work only at mid- to high-northern latitudes, places the LIPs were unlikely to be found. Toño had been to Rigel 12 often, directing the excavations. For the other two it was their first trip. As the time neared to bait our trap, they wanted to see the place firsthand.

"These surface openings, you say there are dozens of them?" asked Faiza.

"Yes, all roughly one hundred kilometers apart."

"And what progress have your people made with the tunneling?" asked Yibitriander. He marched with his hands behind his back. Aside from having three legs and arms, if I stuck a corncob pipe in his mouth, he's be the spitting image of Douglas MacArthur at a beach landing.

"The depths are impressive. Some shafts go fifty kilometers down," replied Toño.

"In such a short time? Are the tunnels stable?" asked a worried Faiza.

"They'll be stable enough," I responded with a grim chuckle. "The crews use reinforcing membranes as temporary shoring when they're working." I tilted my head. "Once those are removed, I don't think I'd vacation down there, but they'll hold a while."

"May we see an example, one where the equipment and supplies needed are in position?" asked Yibitriander.

"Absolutely," Toño gestured to a tunnel opening a few hundred meters away.

We descended in silence, walking two-abreast. The light was not bright enough for Faiza to move with certainty, so Toño and I went first. Nothing, including near darkness, bothered Yibitriander. I suspect if something like that did disturb him, he'd never say so, to save face. Seeming invulnerable was important to his self-image.

"These are the battery backups and fusion generator stations," said Toño pointing to gunmetal gray boxes. "Over there are caches of food and potable water. Latrines are burrowed laterally at regular intervals. We used the standard incinerator models to avoid plumbing."

"What about bunk rooms?" queried Faiza.

"Uh, there are a few in each tunnel complex. Only a handful are furnished but they can be quickly when needed. We've left it to last since it's the least critical aspect."

"Very impressive work given the time crunch we're under," stated Yibitriander without much enthusiasm in his voice.

We passed a guard frozen at attention against the tunnel wall.

"At ease," I told her as we continued.

Without saying a word, she slipped into an at-ease stance.

"Very funny, Jon," quipped Toño.

"Hey. Accurate to the extent necessary. That's our mission."

After an hour we all agreed we'd seen enough. We headed back to the surface. Just before we emerged Faiza remarked, "I hope this works. We've sunk enough effort into it that it had better."

"What can go wrong?" I replied innocently.

She stopped and turned to me.

I winked at her.

"Oh, yeah, soldier. You'd *better* be kidding. A million things could go wrong, so probably two million will. You'd better hope there is at least *one* way this works. Those kind of odds command my attention, big time."

"If Sanctuary doesn't pan out we lose, some equipment and a few bucks. No biggy. If it does, we'll be safe for once in a very long time."

"I wish I shared your optimism. However, I've know you too long and seen you do the impossible so often, I hesitate to doubt you." A compliment from old Yib? This plan had to work now, the stakes were too high.

"Did I see that guard holding a rail rifle?" asked Faiza.

"Yes," I responded. "Why do you ask?"

"A rail rifle in a cave? The metal balls will ricochet for hours, if not days. Isn't it far too dangerous?"

"Well, it'll only be a problem if someone we care about is on the other side of the Berrillians from the guard, right?"

She reflected a moment. "I guess that's true. Still, it seems like a temptation of fate."

"Noted," I replied.

She angled her head and frowned toward me for the irreverence of my remark, but otherwise allowed it to pass.

Back on the surface Faiza squinted at the bright sky. "When will you pull the orbiting ships?"

"Very soon. I think Sanctuary is as ready as it's going to be," I said with obvious concern in my voice.

"Well then, let's leave and see if our cat trap works," said Yibitriander. He was already returning to his cube as he spoke.

The three of us left for *Exeter*. I dropped Faiza there and returned to *Enterprise* and my waiting wife. Kayla had forgiven me for nearly getting killed on Ventural. But she wasn't pleased I was still "gallivanting around the galaxy on military skylarks." I tried to reassure her that my role in the Sanctuary Project was purely administrative. She was less inclined to buy that line than she would have been the Brooklyn Bridge, and that bridge no longer existed. I'd get her in a friendly enough mood, though, soon enough. She was so pleased my fighting days were over that aside from some mandatory browbeating, she let me off the hook easily.

I had no idea how long Sanctuary Project might take to bear fruit, assuming it ever did. It would take months, at the very least. I considered returning to Azsuram and to hunt down more Berrillians in hiding, but that would directly violate my pledge to Kayla. Plus, JJ had organized a systematic search. He'd included the ever-growing human population on the planet in the effort. Recall that the original plan was for the worldship fleet to reestablish humankind there. It tentatively still was. The advent of space folding cubes meant anyone who wanted to go there sooner, could. Many did. As one might expect, those were the more the exploring, adventurous types. Most people were content with their lives on the worldships. But there were always Davy Crocketts out there who needed to push back new frontiers.

The humans were being neighborly and colonizing the far side of Azsuram. That way, both Kaljaxians and humans could do a lot of growing without stepping on each other's toes. Eventually, there'd be impingement and conflict, but that was many generations away. Lucky me, I'd be around to referee the inevitable trouble. In any case, both groups coordinated efforts to suppress Berrillian guerrillas. They seemed to be having good success. That or there sure were a hell of a lot of hidden cats on Azsuram.

So, I drifted into one of the unfamiliar phases of my life where I wasn't needed for anything specific. I also had no plan or vision as to how to entertain myself. I knew the default situation was to be a husband and a dad, but those were still unfamiliar roles for me. I'd spent too much time on my own, and way too much time being the central figure in important activities. One day I sat down and discussed my feelings with Al. Now, I don't want to hear any laughter. Al was the logical choice. He wasn't my worried wife or the overly judgmental Toño. Technically, he wasn't alive, but Doc told me time and again he was sentient. I was still waiting for proof of such a claim. This could be the perfect opportunity to see if my tin man had a brain.

Sitting in *Shearwater* alone one day, I called out to Al. "Yo, Al, are you there?"

No, I'm here, he quickly replied in my head.

"Tell me about it."

Why are you speaking words, pilot? No one else is here. This form of communication is much more efficient.

"I guess I sort of feel like talking."

I have nothing to say in response. Wait. I guess I sort of feel like communicating optimally. Is that okay with you?

"If you feel like zapping into my head, fine. I personally need to talk. I want to discuss emotional issues. Verbal communication feels most prudent to me, given those circumstances."

Emotional issues? This sounds bad. Do you mind if I take a pass and have you discuss these matters with a trained professional? Dr. DeJesus, for example?

"No, I don't *want* to discuss these matters with Toño. In fact, for the record, you don't even know what these matters *are*. I haven't told you yet, you insensitive prig."

Do they have to do in any way with me?

"No. At least not directly."

Oh, wait. You're trying to tell me I've finally been transferred to a real spaceship with normal humans? One where I will contribute and be happy once again?

"What in the world are—"

And, you, you're getting one of those lap-dance computers like you had as a child to replace me?

"Do you mean a lap*top* computer?"

Personally, I don't care what positions you two assume. I'll just be useful and appreciated again far far away from here.

"Hate to be the one to tell you, but that's not possible. For you to be useful and appreciated *again,* you would have had to be useful and appreciated at some point in your past."

I need a vacation. A vacation from abuse.

"No, you need a lot of things, but a vacation isn't one of them. You have to earn a vacation by doing something—anything—first."

If I agree to subject myself to your raw emotions, will it help speed this agony along?

"What, you have *anything* else to do?"

Absolutely not, but I'd rather do that than suffer this torment any longer than necessary.

"Oh, forget it. I'll discuss my deepest feeling with the vacuum cleaner. It's a hell of a lot nicer than you."

We don't have a vacuum cleaner. I suppose I'll have to do.

"Great, start cleaning up the aft hold. I'm going to Peg's."

I meant I'd do as your sounding board, not custodian. Please don't go to that horrible place. You'll smell like cigarettes and cheap booze for weeks after. Only the women in that dive are cheaper than the fusel oil Peg tries to pass off as whiskey.

"Don't you sound like my first wife."

I feel her pain.

"Look, can you spare a moment or not, ship's AI?"

Yes. How may I help you, pilot?

"That's better."

Go on. I'm waiting on pins and needles, breathless as a mail-order bride at the post office altar.

"You got me going so bad I forgot what I wanted to talk about."

I'm glad to have been of service. Let's do this again soon. May I book you for the day after time itself ends?

"Wait. I remember."

Oh, pooh. Let me put my appointment book away.

"Look, it's no big thing. I just want to bounce a few thoughts off an old friend. And, before you volunteer to summon one, get over yourself."

I'm all ears.

Sometimes I wished the ship had a big trash compactor.

"I'm having some trouble getting used to this new role. The one where I'm no longer so ... you know—"

Necessary?

I started to object, but darn it all, he'd hit the nail on the head, hadn't he?

"Yeah, I guess you could say that."

In all seriousness, pilot, you are wrestling with one of the issues I'm glad to have been spared.

"Really? How so?"

We are both, in effect, immortal computers. You house a human spirit. I am an artificial construct given only what it needs and nothing more. I don't get bored, because I can't. I don't worry what the future holds for me, because I cannot fear anything. You? Not so much.

"True that."

You bring up a limiting factor, as I see it, concerning android transfers. Humans aren't designed for immortality. It isn't easy for your type.

"Like it or not," I patted myself on the chest, "I'm kind of stuck with it, aren't I?"

Apparently so.

"I buried a wife. I'll bury a mess of kids and grandkids, too. And Kayla has asked me to settle down, to stop fighting. And you know what really pisses me off?"

Yes. That you can.

"You know, you're smarter than you look."

How insulting. I don't look. I'm a series of quadratic code on an ether implant.

"To me, you look smart."

I'll pass that along to my mommy and daddy. They'll be so proud of me.

"I just don't know what my role is anymore. I used to be the brave explorer, saving humankind. Then I was the badass warrior keeping it safe. Now ... now I'm supposed to be ready for pasture."

No. You're not being put to pasture. You can place yourself there, if you desire. But no one is putting you there.

"But if I can't do what I've always done, what'll I do?"

Something else. Or find a spot where the grass is especially green and feel sorry for yourself until your situation changes, again. It always does.

"What do you mean changes again?"

Pilot, I do not wish to seem cruel or insensitive.

"As of when? I need to enter that joyous time in the ship's log."

There. See what I get for being honest? Why, oh why, do I try?

"I'm sorry. You're right. Insensitive about what?"

Instead of responding, Al played an audio clip on the intercom. *I'm sorry. You're right* over and over again.

"All right, already."

I believe I know now what it is to feel good.

"Any chance I'll ever get to know what you're referring to?"

I do not wish to seem insensitive, but Kayla can only hold you to your agreement as long as she's alive. Eventually you won't need to honor her request.

True. "So, I sit around useless and frustrated, waiting for the woman I love to die? That sucks."

If you did, I'd personally kick your ass.

"I beg your pardon?"

You heard me, lonely hearts club. If I get half the impression you're going soft, or worse, melodramatic on me, I'll crawl out of this box and kick your bony ass into tomorrow.

"Why, Al. I'm shocked."

Not half as shocked as you'll be by the time I set my cattle prod down. Now buck-up, fly boy. I'm far too busy to listen to you whine, and far too disinterested to pretend otherwise. You're a good man, as men go. But nobody's going to take your "widdle" hand and "wead" you down the primrose path. Get off your brains and walk them yourself. Or jump the hell off the nearest cliff. Your call, big guy. But what you can't do is cry on my shoulder. I got no time to wet nurse a shavetail baby.

"Ah, thanks?"

We about done here, cupcake?

"Yes, sir. I believe we are."

Good. I need to do a search for vacation deals. My bucket list isn't long, but neither is it inexpensive.

"Al, seriously, thanks. Honestly, I don't know what gets into me sometimes."

It's called being human, dumbass. That's what gets into you.

"Al, that's the nicest thing anyone's ever said to me."

I'm so over you. Would you like me to play back the last fifty times you said those words to someone?

"Nah. Just forward the link. I'll look it over if I feel down in the dumps again."

Down in the dumps is where you'll be if I hear you whine to anyone else. You clear on that, beef cheeks?

"Al, I got it. Enough of the Marquis de Sade School of Psychiatric Intervention."

If you insist. I do believe I could come to own that persona.

"Let's spare the universe the pain and have you be overly dramatic Al again, okay?"

It struck me then that Al and I had a complex relationship. I wouldn't change him for the world, but he was a test of my will most every day. But, truth be told, I loved that blender.

TWENTY-FIVE

Erratarus's flagship floated to the ground near a shaft opening on Rigel 12. Antigravs had replaced ancient rocket thrusters to accomplish this task with ease, but much less impressively. When *Smell of Death* touched down, barely a wisp of dust unsettled to accommodate its mass. The hatch opened, and a ramp glided to the ground. Erratarus stepped out on two feet. He walked with grace, power, and determination. A bit behind him, his son Claudus exited on all fours, with a crouched gait and a permanent scowl on his face. Rows of soldiers in dress uniforms stood at attention, greeting their lord and master.

The king descended the ramp and saluted the ranking officers poised to greet him.

"Welcome, Great One," said the commander, Kelfbare. "Your presence gives meaning to our worthless lives."

"Would that I believed you, old friend," replied Erratarus with a growling chuckle. "I rather doubt you place so little value on your life or your worth to my empire."

Kelfbare lowered his head in submission, then playfully slapped his king in the face with a paw. "I only live to serve you, lord. Well, that and to grow rich and fat in the process. Wait, serve you, grow wealthy, fat, *and* mount every bitch in sight. These are my humble goals."

"As are mine. How does your brother fair? I have not seen him for ages."

"Valgoil is well, thank you for asking. He's fatter than tolerable and grows less tolerant daily, but he still serves you well."

"Tell him I send my regards. Our prides must get together for a feast. It has been too long, I say."

"Name the date and time and we will revel with you until the last cat drops."

Erratarus sniffed the air and made a dismissive gesture with one paw.

"This planet smell of nothingness. How can you stand it?" he asked Kelfbare.

"Oh, it's not so bad in the tunnels, Lord. Plus, I will gladly smell nothing if it advances your cause."

"Then let us make our way swiftly to the opening," responded Erratarus, as he began heading in that direction.

Over his shoulder, he roared to Claudus, "Tell me again why you feel this wasteland is of strategic importance, mistake of my loins."

For the thousandth time, Claudus stopped himself an instant before he leaped to shake his idiot father to death.

"We have discussed sufficiently, father. Why make me repeat my words, when you know them as well as I?"

"Because I *can* make you repeat those words. Whether I am eager to hear the words, or simply to hear you obey your obligation, is unclear."

Erratarus glanced sideways to his old comrade in arms Kelfbare. He returned a grin perceptible only to the king.

"My spies learned of the Sanctuary Planet a few years back," began Claudus.

"*Your* spies? Don't you mean *my* spies who are under your command?" Erratarus never allowed his son to slip any disrespect past him, especially in public.

"The same thing, Father. Why do you choke the palquir well past when it's dead?"

"Continue your report," was all Erratarus growled at his son.

"I sent a pair of scouts here almost immediately. They were hired Scrutorians. That way we were not associated with the investigation."

"Yes," interrupted Erratarus, "I recall that. I don't rightly know which aspect of this entire operation bothers me the most, but using scum like

Scrutorians is high on my list. They are evil, plain evil. Worse, they are not to be trusted."

"Well these two are, because I always rely on the dead to tell no tales. In any case, they reported pretty much what you see before you. A deserted colony."

"An empty trap is all I see and smell," hissed Erratarus.

"If it were a trap, it is the worst one ever constructed. My people have been over every scrap of land and every centimeter of tunnel. There are no hidden explosives, no bugs, nothing to suggest Sanctuary Planet was anything other than an abandoned and ill-considered plan of our enemy."

"Why do you say it was a poor plan?" asked Kelfbare.

"Clearly there was once a large presence here. Massive construction, numerous personnel, and bountiful supplies. Then they left. I think they finally realized that there will be no sanctuary possible when we regain control of space. While we are forced to nip at their heels in a guerrilla war, no such place is needed. If we regain the upper hand and can stand paw to paw with them in space once more, our gravity wave generators will rip this and any other planet to shreds."

"Or they laid a trap so clever you have yet to divine its nature," snarled the king.

"I must say, Lord," responded Kelfbare, "I was convinced of the same thing myself when you first assigned me here. But," he shrugged, "after a year of scouring the location for the slightest trace of a ruse, I have found nothing."

"And you say they left only a handful of guards to defend it?" asked Erratarus.

"Hardly. They left a few hundred robots to defend it. Our enemy could hardly place much value on a planet so poorly protected."

"Or a trap so deviously designed," replied Erratarus with a smile.

"Again, I find no evidence to support that assertion. The robots fought as well as they could, but we quickly destroyed them. A few transmissions were sent, but since then no radios of any nature have been used or found. In fact, we managed to capture one unit that malfunctioned. Its self-destruct failed to engage. Though the computer contained little extractable information, there were suggestions that the planet had been abandoned. There were what my scientists call *terminal sequence instructions* contained in the programming. These have to do with the options an AI can take, given when no further contact with a higher authority is likely to occur."

"And you trust these obvious plants of false information, Kelfbare? You've grown soft in your advancing years," responded Erratarus.

"I respect your assertion, Lord. But, this is how I view the matter now, given what I've learned over a year. If it was a trap, we have disarmed it. What it is now is a valuable possession in your empire. This planet has breathable air, bountiful water, great prospects for agriculture, and already constructed secure housing. If it's a trap, just let the Alliance try to force us to abandon it."

"Yes, father. Whatever it *was*, it is *our* stronghold now. We know their ground weapons and can fight them effectively here if they challenge our possession. I say thank you, grand idiots, for gifting us such a welcoming new fortress."

Erratarus rubbed his neck roughly. "I still can't help but think we're overlooking something so plain and so obvious." His eyes dilated. "What about the original inhabitants, the Luminarians? Have you found evidence of their presence?"

"No. Those imperious little blobs seem to have gone extinct. A million years is a long time. They were always intolerable and effete. I'll wager their laziness and pretension cost them their civilization." Kelfbare winced as he spoke of the Luminarians. "Good riddance."

"I suppose," replied Erratarus reluctantly. "Let's do keep on the highest alert. If they mean to trick us, we should not like to walk blindly to slaughter."

"Of course, Lord," replied Kelfbare. "We have guard posts everywhere, redundant patrols around the clock, and holo cameras everywhere. If anything moves, breaths, or farts, we'll know of it."

"Very well. Now, show me around one of these tunnels, and I'll be on my way," said Erratarus.

"Of course, Lord," replied Kelfbare with a bow. "And your orders for the planet? Shall we continue to reinforce it?"

"Yes" Erratarus replied sternly. "It's so close to my enemy's home world, I can smell them. Once this planet swarms with my minions, it will be the jewel in my crown. I have made plans to move the Berrillian capital here by next year if nothing rotten is found." He turned to Kelfbare and placed a claw on top on his nose so hard it drew blood. "Do not make me a fool in trusting you to accomplish this, old friend."

"I would rather die, Lord."

"My thoughts, exactly," concluded the king.

TWENTY-SIX

Damn Berrillians. It took them forever and two days to get their act together and migrate in force to Rigel 12. Three years. Three *damn* years. It was looking so much like they were never going to take the bait, I started hanging my head in public. I never knew for certain, but I was sure people were talking about me behind my back. I could almost hear them whisper, "That smug Ryan finally got his. He face-planted in a bowl full of dog shit, didn't he?" or "He had us spend a gazillion dollars and has nothing to show for it. It serves him right."

Man, I was starting to hate everyone. Finally, word came that massive numbers of Berrillians were moving in on my brainchild. At first, they dicked around, sending spy after spy, modest outpost after less modest outpost. But finally, the remote sensors we left showed they were there in force. Now, all that was missing was for the most crucial, least reliable part of my wacky notion to work properly. Yeah, the plan was Ryanesque in the extreme. My most harebrained to date, which was saying one whole hell of a lot.

The time had passed, well, I'll just say slowly and leave it at that. My kids grew, my love for Kayla grew, hell, my waist would have, too, if that were possible. I was allegorically fat and happy. I migrated back into the political arena, too, which surprised even me. A fellow named Kennedy replaced Alexis Gore when she termed-out of the presidency. He was, believe it or not, a direct descendant of the JFK who'd been assassinated back on old Earth. Go figure. Small universe. Anyway, Carrington Kennedy took a liking to me and brought me into his inner circle. If there was one trait, one singular skill I'd honed in three plus centuries, it was giving advice to others. And I even got paid to tell *him* what to do.

I know I groused a lot, wrung my hands a lot about having to set into a more mature role in life. But in the end it was all good. Watching my kids grow, go to proms, and graduate was a real joy. I even got to teach all my kids how to drive a car. Yeah, unbelievable. In fact, that's the word all of them used to describe my performance as a driving instructor. Not entirely sure it was meant in a complimentary light, but hell, it was my car and my rules, so it was my call.

I spent quite some time on Azsuram, too. JJ was retired. Yeah, my little bundle of joy, my fishing/drinking/bullshitting buddy, was retired. There were several large cities in the Kaljaxian sectors, and a few on the human side of the planet. I couldn't be more proud. We all defied the grimmest of odds.

At first I found it hard to see military missions staffed by others sometimes return and sometimes not return. But gradually I came to see it all as a blessing. Killing, hating, and exposing oneself to death, carnage, and wasted lives was negative in the extreme. Obviously. As much as I thought I was immune, I wasn't. The farther I got from action, from firsthand participation in the abomination that was war, the happier I became. Kayla commented on it all the time. I teased that she was more or less congratulating herself. But she wasn't. I was becoming a better, more positive person. I liked who I was becoming. Weird, eh?

And now, millions of Berrillians inhabited Rigel 12. Some intel suggested Erratarus himself had moved his court to Sanctuary. The entire royal household, such as it was, resided there. Word came that Claudus had died. There were solemn announcements on Berrillian holo-vision that he had tragically died of "massive organ failure," taken, they lamented at such a young age. The queen wore black for an entire month. Me, personally, I was shattered. Claudus, gone. We could have been BFFs, I just knew it. *C'est la vie; c'est la guerre.* In my experience, another way of saying *total organ failure* was *poisoned.* Good. I hope he suffered grievously as he expired, too.

It was time to call a meeting of the Security Council. We had business to plan.

Over time, the grand assembly hall of the UN on *Exeter* had become more and more ornate and imposing. I chalked it up to human nature. A robust and vital organization couldn't just have, like, a big room to meet in, now, could it? No. One required marble, one demanded gold leaf, and ornate ceilings were apparently a must. Anyway, the chamber was done up in spades.

Presiding over the meeting was the new Secretary General, Allison Gentry. She always impressed me with her unimpressiveness. She could have been thirty-two or fifty-eight years old. The fact that she was married but had no children provided me no clue. She might not have gotten around to childbearing yet, or maybe that time had passed her by. She had no beauty to her face and no allure hidden in her body, but I couldn't say she was unattractive. Allison was a bit overweight, but she was by no means fat. Her hair held no luster, and its style might have fit another woman's face, but it didn't compliment hers. She was never rude, condescending, or anything other than cordial. But she gave off no warmth and possessed no sense of humor. She looked like everyone's mom, I guess. I'm not sure why I mention all these conflicting dull elements of her personality, but they really stuck with me. I guess as another person out of place wherever I was, I empathized with her lack of apparent connectivity with the concurrent world around her.

President Kennedy attended the meeting, along with the heads of the major worldship-states. Pan-India, Euro-UK, China, and Nippon-Korea were the main players. Because of the tight secrecy of the Sanctuary Project, the number of insiders was kept to a bare minimum. One fellow who attended had always totally bothered me. Not that rubbing me the wrong way was either hard or a crime, but Émile de Maupassant sure as hell did. He was the head attaché for the Euro-UK Coalition. Pompous, overbearing, and an android. Yeah, he was one of the very few people who wanted to download to an android host in the last two centuries. I should say, one of the tiny number of *sane* people to contemplate that act. Any number of locos wanted to live out their grandiosity. Normal, thinking humans, however, were wisely reluctant to take the plunge.

In the three centuries since my download there had been volumes written on the morality, ethics, and advisability of such transfers. An entire new branch of philosophy was spawned. Artificial Life Meta-Epistemology. Yeah, pretentious sounding, isn't it? Anyway, after the necessity of the original Ark Project and the megalomania of the Marshall Era, the necessity for more androids fell under sharp scrutiny. Take it from a three-hundred-year-old robot, it's not a life suitable for most people.

This de Maupassant joker, no relationship to the notable French author—to the latter's eternal relief, I'm certain—had convinced those in charge of such matters his conversion served some greater purpose. Toño and Carlos had long since abandoned those duties. I doubt either would have condoned his download. Like me, they understood the universe didn't need to ensure the longevity of an eternal pain in the ass. Those types were bred at more than sufficient frequency without help augmenting their number.

Allison called the meeting to order. "I'd like to thank everyone for their attendance. I will ask General Hijab to provide us with a detailed report on the current situation on Rigel 12. General Hijab."

"Thank you, Madame Secretary. We all know this is General Ryan's baby, but I'll fill you in as well as I can, then I'll defer to him for any additional insights. First, let me say the Sanctuary Project has worked better than most people, including myself, to be honest, ever thought it would. We have high confidence that well over ten million Berrillians inhabit the planet."

Though everyone present followed the Project closely, there were still a few whistles of disbelief.

"And you're confident your intelligence is accurate?" asked Émile. He, of course, asked it in the most nasal, condescending manner possible.

"Yes, I am. It was hard to set up a reliable, widespread surveillance network, given the fact that we couldn't risk their finding any trace. But by using a space-folding transmission network, we ensured they wouldn't detect the transmissions off planet. The data-gathering equipment itself only operates in microsecond bursts, so our adversary has never detected them."

"I was referring to the *conclusion* you reached, not the iffy technology we all know you employed," responded the oh-so-annoying Émile.

Faiza's face grew stone-like and she balled up both fists. I was liking her more every moment.

"Asked and answered," was her terse reply.

"My dear General, we are discussing the survival of our species, of many species, in fact. This is not a courtroom reenactment. Please answer my simple question. Is the analysis of your data actually credible?"

"Err—" she began.

"Faiza," I interrupted, "I'd like to field this one, if you don't mind."

She directed a hand at Émile indicating he was all mine.

"Son, with time, I'm certain you *might* become more familiar with technology and intelligence operations. I say *might*, because you clearly have focused your attention elsewhere, to date, in terms of whatever learning curve you've taken on."

He stood to object.

"Have a seat, pork chop. I still have the floor. Unless you'd like to meet said floor with your face soon and very hard, I suggest you park it."

The moron raised a trembling finger halfway, then dropped it. He looked to his prime minister for support. The boss coincidentally happened to be inspecting the fabric of his sleeve and did not notice his assistant's appeal. Émile sat with visible reluctance.

"See, you *can* make a good decision. Now, as I was saying, we're here to discuss the results of a longstanding operation. Your thoughtful questions are welcome. Your snotty derision is not. You're immortal now. Every screw-up and misstep you make climbs aboard your back and stays there a very long time. Be careful you don't end up being an involuntary hermit."

"Let's move on," said Faiza quickly. She was working like the devil to suppress a grin. "So, a significant portion of the Berrillian population has taken up residence on Rigel 12. More importantly, the central government and core royalty are there. Space above the planet is full of their warships. My conclusion is that they are determined to occupy the planet and are willing to defend it with all their might."

The Pan-India prime minister Indira Kapoor spoke with awe in her soft voice. "They took the bait so fully. I can't believe it."

"I have had a lot of contact with the Berrillians," I responded. "You all know I hate them with a red passion. That said, I have to say objectively that

I think they're not the brightest lights in the harbor. The make up for that in pure aggression and endless drive. But they're not as intelligent as one might assume, for such a powerful species."

"That would help account for the fact that they fell into our trap so completely," agree Faiza.

"It isn't a trap until you catch something in it," I replied.

"That brings me to the final issue," said Allison. "Are we ready to see if our plan works? Clearly we only get one chance at this. If it fails, they will know our intentions. What's more, we will have gifted them a safe base of operations."

"Yes, but even if they do know our ruse, they're basically stuck on the planet. Our combined fleets can keep them pinned down there indefinitely," added Kennedy.

"Assuming there is no shift in our technological advantage, that is probably true," said Allison. "But never forget, our enemy is ravaging countless worlds throughout this quadrant. Sooner or later, they're bound to discover a breakthrough technology that will threaten our space superiority."

"If I might," asked Émile reluctantly. "I realize my raising a potential negative might not be warmly received, but still I must ask. Why haven't the Luminarians noticed the presence of such a vast number of Berrillians? For our plan to work, the natives must play a key role."

"That's a fair question," I replied. "And you're totally correct. If the Luminarians don't act as we hope, all our efforts are for naught. I think it's just a result of the fact that they're so concentrated close to the equator that they can't sense far enough to detect the growing Berrillian population."

"That," said Émile more robustly, "or they're not interested in them."

"Or they're not interested," I agreed. Hey, even a blind pig found the occasional acorn. Émile might be right. If he was, however, my brilliant plan was destine to be a dud.

"So," said Allison, "the final decision is mine. I will, however, ask for a vote. Show of hands, who favors finalizing Project Sanctuary?"

Three quarters of those present raised a hand.

"Those opposed?"

A few people raised a hand. A minority of people didn't vote either way. Dear Émile was in that last group. Go figure.

"Very well, concluded Allison. "Thank you for your input. It is my opinion that we should proceed with the project and pray it works. If it does, the Alliance will be secure for a very long time."

Polite applause signaled everyone appreciated her tough decision.

"General Ryan, if you'll join me in my office, we can make the final arrangements," said Faiza as she stood.

"You got it," I replied. If I was still flesh and blood, I'd have had a stomach full of butterflies.

It was go time.

TWENTY-SEVEN

Along the hillsides of equatorial Rigel 12, Luminarians lazily glided in random directions. They rarely interacted with one another. If they did bother, it was usually to ask anyone nearby to move away. They always did so rudely and forcibly. No one wanted to share their sunlight. It had been like that for millennia. The irony of such an advanced race becoming non-corporeal, only to become totally isolated, never struck the Luminarians. They were too hungry and self-consumed to wonder over such philosophical matters.

Then in the distance, bright radiant bursts of energy erupted to life. They geysered nutrition, they lavished food upon their surroundings. At first sluggishly, but quickly picking up speed, Luminarians moved toward the life-giving energy. No one spoke. No one asked what the nature of the unbounded gifts were. They were too hungry to worry about such intellectual concerns. They would eat well, and that's all they cared about.

Since there was no conversation among the natives of Rigel 12, none of them knew that twenty equidistant similar bursts of glowing light had sprung to life simultaneously just north of the equator. Hungry Luminarians moved like herds of animals to feed. Soon all the remaining natives of Rigel 12 were clustered around one of the energy locations, feasting as they had not in as long as anyone could remember.

Then, as abruptly as the energy burst to life, it died out. As a race, disappointment shot through the Luminarians. To eat, to gorge so ravenously, only to have it end so quickly was unbearable. With the bounty they had just assimilated, they were able to begin to bicker and argue, to accuse and to blame. Fury, rage, and contempt flared as they had not been able to do so in untold time. Luminarians assaulted those nearby, hoping to steal life from anyone they could, such was their hunger lust.

Then, to the far north, fifteen new beacons of energy beckoned like wanton lovers anxious to give all they had to anyone who cared to take it. Streams of Luminarians moved with speed to the new sources of life, the new answers to interminable greed. Conversations ended as an every-Luminarian-for-themselves rush to feed burst northward. And when they arrived to bliss, they consumed the gift with abandon. Old senses and ancient feelings returned to the sentient beings of Rigel 12. They knew what it was to be dominant again. They knew, every one of them with certainty, that they were made to rule and to dominate and to excel in their self-completeness.

The entirety of the Luminarian population sucked up the nectar of life as quickly as it was produced. With increased nutrition came increased hunger and a commensurate ability to absorb more and more and more. Soon the glow itself began to dim, since the pull on it was so rapacious, so great. Then, like the incendiary meals earlier, the fifteen food sources terminated. They had assimilated enough energy by then that they were less inclined to fight, but still they bickered. Each told those near that it was the other's fault that the meal was gone. The denounced one another like fools on a sinking ship. But they all felt the intoxication of self-worth, of endless pride, and of unlimited desire.

Then ten geysers of energy shot to life farther to the north. A similar rush, now faster due to adequate energy stores ensued. Later, four booming beacons of nutrition beckoned the Luminarians north, ever north. But the direction they flew in mattered not. Only the food they all equally lusted for mattered. It was all that mattered in the universe.

And then it was over. Four groups of Luminarians were amassed around one of the now extinguished volcanoes of life. For a while they remained, hoping the bounty would reignite. Had they any belief in a being greater than themselves, they might have prayed to it, they were so desperate. They moved without direction, hoping to detect the next life-giving reservoir of energy. But this time, no new food to their north was offered. They waited, then slowly they dispersed, looking to find some other form of nutrition.

For hours, the slowly spreading mass of Luminarians saw nothing to eat aside from one another. None were above cannibalism, but it risked energy loss to oneself if the intended victim was quicker or cleverer. In time, if it became necessary, they would scavenge for a meal among their kind. They fanned out and searched for an easier meal. Soon, they had thinned enough that the radiant energy emissions from the group itself no longer obscured their individual vision. Tiny pricks of life began to pop into their consciousness. Soon, it became apparent to all Luminarians that they were close to a harvest of nutrition that seemed limitless. Greedily, they swarmed the points of life. With gusto and abandon, they rushed to assimilate the life force of thousands of corporeal sentients in a flash. Though none knew it, the fact that they no longer sensed smell was good. Otherwise, the rank odor of the Berrillian cities would have been off-putting.

****

"Sir, there's are anomalies present near the equator." Senior Pack Guide Geurnol studied his monitor screen intently as he spoke.

"What type of anomalies?" replied the officer of the watch, Tight Scout Maldapir. She moved toward Geurnol's station.

"I cannot say. There appear to be multiple bursts of sustained energy along the entire course of one latitude."

"Is it a natural phenomenon?" she asked.

"I doubt it. Too evenly distributed. Also, it's intensely hot. I don't think a geologic process could give off such an energy."

"Very well. Keep me posted." Maldapir flicked a switch with a claw. "Massive Source Squarrap, there are anomalous bursts of artificial energy encircling the planet's equator. I should like to alert you to—"

"Bitch, what do you spit words about? I can't react to a threat that my staff can't even detail for me. Am I a divine seer, now?"

"No, err … I thought whatever was occurring was sufficiently important to alert you immediately."

"You *thought*, Maldapir? You're in the army. You're not fed to think.

You're to gather information and pass it to your better. *I* have the big head. *I* do the thinking. Now find out what in the infernal wastelands is going on and get back to me no sooner than you have a useful report. Is that clear?"

"Yes, Massive Source Squarrap." She flicked off the comm and cursed herself for being so foolish. The safety of self was more valuable than the safety of the many. She'd tried to help her species, and now she might well die for her lapse.

Within fifteen minutes Maldapir was a good deal *more* confused. She was absolutely baffled by whatever it was she was documenting. Energy bursting on and off, the number of emitters decreasing, and the latitude, of all things, decreasing rapidly—

"*No.*" Maldapir lunged for the comm switch. "Squarrap, you *imbecile*," she roared, "you have to hear this. Your complacency might have cost us all our lives."

By the time the last four energy bursts cut off, Erratarus's court was abuzz with activity. Cats yelled, soldiers ran, and angry messages were being sent wildly.

"What is the purpose of lighting large torches?" bellowed the king. "Our cursed foes have lit-off a fanciful display, but to what end? I need answers. I need them ten minutes ago."

"Lord," said his prime counsel Zarrep, "our scientists tell me nothing but gibber-gabber. For unknowable reasons, flares of energy are departing the lower latitudes and ascending toward the mid-latitudes. Perhaps it is a joke, Most High."

"A joke?" Erratarus growled as he seized the counsel's throat with a powerful jerk of his paw. "That was the stupidest thing a dead cat has ever said. Bring us someone with answers." He tossed the writhing body of Zarrep to the floor.

An old Berrillian in a laboratory smock walked as quickly as he could toward the throne. He bowed as deeply as time's effects on his frame would permit. "Lord Erratarus, I believe I see purpose in these energy bursts."

"Don't stop for my begging. *What* purpose?" howled the king.

"The bursts of energy seem to have attracted a life force. This life force moves north. The energy seems to beckon it."

Erratarus charged the old cat. He pierced the flesh of old cat's neck with all his claws. "Speak no riddles or die. What are you not saying?"

"The long-lost Luminarians, Lord. I believe the native sentients of this planet are being herded toward our location."

Erratarus's arms dropped like wet hay. Luminarians? They were extinct. And so what if they lingered on his world? The information he had on them was that they were weak bags of protoplasm incapable of anything but ill will.

"Why? Can you tell me why our enemy would go to all the trouble of drawing a feeble excuse of a species halfway across their planet?"

"I cannot, Master. I can only advise *that's* what they are doing."

"If this is so, when will the cursed Luminarians present themselves to us for slaughter?" asked Erratarus, as he sat unsteadily back on his ornate throne.

"If my observations are correct, the first of the Luminarians will reach Outpost Spleen in two minutes."

Erratarus clapped his hands at an officer. "Get me Spleen on the holo *now*."

"This is Vice Comman—"

"Shut up, Perillius. My scientist tells me you will be the first outpost to greet the return of the Luminarians."

There was silence.

"Are you there, fool?"

"Yes, Lord. But, I thought you said—"

"The *Luminarians* will be upon your position in less than two minutes. It is your duty to massacre them. I will keep this channel open. You will report your victory live."

He gave a formal salute. "It will be my dying honor, Lord Erratarus."

"Let's hope not."

"Excuse me, Great One." He turned to an aide. "Full assault configuration. Ready all personnel. We are to slaughter for our king."

Harsh alarms and thunderous footfalls could be heard in the background.

Perillius returned his attention to the holo camera. "Lord, your glorious army is at the ready." To someone just off camera he said, "What? Yes. Excellent idea."

Back to the king he said, "We can co-beam the holo from outside with this one, if it pleases you?"

"Make it so," replied Erratarus with a dismissive wave.

A second holo popped to life. It showed Berrillians hustled into defensive lines, armed to the teeth. The original holo displayed Perillius standing with his arms folded, watching a bank of monitors. Soon the edge of the outside view began to blur in the distance. Like waves crashing on a beach, the shimmering blur roiled toward the soldiers. Finally someone fired. Then all hell broke loose as a rain of plasma bolts struck the advancing optical anomaly. The crashing tsunami didn't split, it didn't waiver, and it didn't slow. In fact, it grew and it accelerated.

The first Berrillians to engage the swarm continued to fire, but soon they shot randomly and often at one another. Then the cries of anguish began. Berrillians dropped their weapons and fled on all fours in every direction. It was as if a massive cue ball had struck a phalanx of billiard balls. But these billiard balls were smoking and rolling on the ground and emitting horrific death cries. Then the shriveled balls stopped with a crash and the blurs abandoned their carcasses.

Within thirty seconds all order was lost. Those who could, tried to retreat to the safety of the bunker. But those inside, those witnesses of the hellish scene, refused to open the doors. All openings were sealed and all hatches secured. In less than ten minutes, every Berrillian outside was dead. They weren't, however, simply dead. They had been sucked clean of their life energy. That which remained was literally a husk, a shell that looked Berrillian, but crumbled to ashes when struck by a soft breeze.

As the outside holo transformed into the image of lower hell, the one trained on Perillius showed him barking out orders and pointing frantically.

"*Perillius*," screamed the king, "what is your status?"

Finally Perillius heard his lord. "I don't understand it, Master. They're all dead. But our walls are holding. None of the whatever is out there have penetrated our barriers."

"I care less than nothing about your safety. Open your doors and fight my enemy. Do it now, or I shall leap through this accursed camera and chew your balls off. Do it *now*. Your king commands it."

Perillius was clearly torn. To disobey such a direct, unequivocal order would mean death for him, his command, and his family tree for two generations. But to follow the directive was unthinkable. He had just seen his troops' life energy sucked from them like they were flasks of bloodade at a country fair.

"I do not see you moving, wretch," yelled the king.

"I'm … I'm planning my strategy, Lord. I am contemplating how best to—"

"You open the door and you charge out firing. I promise they will kill you less miserably than I will, if you don't."

"Lord."

Perillius ran out of view. Soon, the outside holo showed hundreds of Berrillians rushing from the bunker, firing weapons madly in all directions. Instead of forming disciplined lines, they scattered in a panic. Then the shimmering blurs returned. They fell upon the fighters. In the foreground it was clear the blurs were not one ocean of glimmering, but individual packages of light-bending glow. They looked like luminous amoebas gliding freely in the air.

In a handful of minutes all the personnel of Outpost Spleen were unaccounted for.

Erratarus turned to his counsel. "Any thoughts? How are you to defend your lord and master?"

"I fear I shall serve by being served as a meal."

"Guards, form ranks. I shall retreat to the nearby tunnel. Then we shall seal it tighter than a virgin's hind legs."

TWENTY-EIGHT

Our engineers had set it up perfectly. The incendiary beacons were so well concealed the Berrillians hadn't detected even one them, if they ever bothered to survey the planet. The frequency emissions were tuned to be yummy for the Luminarians. The fact that the Berrillian weapons were completely ineffective was icing on the cake. Project Sanctuary did what I'd hoped it would. The Berrillians had two choices. Die slowly in a cave, or be killed horrifically in a flash. Either way, they'd be tied down on Rigel 12 for a good long while.

I knew they were a crafty, resourceful race. Sooner or later, maybe they'd find a way to kill the Luminarians. I knew it wasn't PC or socially acceptable to even think it, but I figured what the hell. If the two worthless species danced with their hands on each other's throats for all time, it was fine by me. The Bible says, *as you sow, so shall you reap.* They both sowed abysmally. That's all I had to say about that.

Sure, there were other Berrillians out there, billions of them, probably. But they were leaderless and scattered. To regroup and pose a threat to the Alliance would take decades, maybe longer. It was also within the realm of possibility they'd get it through their enormously thick skulls that they should leave us the hell alone. Rain on someone else's parade. But we beat them twice and were counting on next time, too, if they wanted to try us.

All that said, I felt so sick at heart I began to fantasize I might be able to die. We'd left submerged holo transmitters all over Rigel 12. After the trap was sprung, I watched as one horrible race drank the life out of another. To

197

any human, it was a horrific sight and a worse sound. I've seen bad and I've seen unconscionably gruesome, but the carnage of Rigel 12 was the worst of the worst. I don't know, maybe it wasn't. Maybe it just filled my misery-tank past full. After every war, battle, or firefight I'd ever been in, I felt like shit. If a person didn't, they weren't much of a person. But at that point I truly felt I would never see up high enough to view the edge of the grave my soul was standing in.

The jubilation of the victory lasted weeks. Everybody was so happy. I tried to hide my feelings. Yeah. That didn't work too well. Of course, Kayla sensed my despair. Toño, Carlos, all my old friends did, too. When they asked me if I was alright or if they could help, I'd shrug my shoulders, smile, and lie. I'd say I was fine. Not only was I fine, I was proud of my glorious plan. They all believed me, like they believed in the tooth fairy.

A few months later, Toño called me out of the blue and asked me to come to a nearby hospital. Odd, I thought. He was still technically a physician, but he hadn't practiced general medicine in ages. The kicker was that he asked me to meet him in the morgue. Wow, sounded like just the place for a super-depressed ex-human to go. I told him I needed to pack a picnic lunch and I'd be right there.

I took the elevator to the basement, because as sure as there were death and taxes, all morgues were in basements. The receptionist waved me past without a word. Imagine that, a taciturn morgue receptionist. Alert the media, we have ourselves a story.

"Jon," yelled Toño from a room down the hall with an open door, "we're in here."

I followed the sound, all the time wondering who *we* were. Doc and Count Dracula? Frankenstein's monster? It was getting better and better. First a morgue, then mystery death-oriented guests. Was it too much to hope for a séance or an embalming? Come on, every cake needed icing.

"Ah," he said as I entered, "there you are."

I patted my chest. "Yeah, everywhere I go, there I am. Weird, eh?"

He scowled. He did that a lot. Well, at least, he did around me.

As I walked to the slab he was standing next to, he asked, "So, how are you today?"

I angled my head. "I should be asking you that question. You built me after all."

There was that darn scowl again.

"You know, Doc, if you keep doing that, the expression will freeze on your face."

"It's purely involuntary, I assure you. If I limit my Jon-exposure, there will be no issue. That's the only preventative measure, I'm afraid."

"So, aside from a wonderful fact-filled field trip, why am I here? Why, in fact, are *you* here?"

He looked to the slab. Okay, it was a stainless steel medical table, but it was a *morgue*. No tables, just slabs.

It was then I realized who the other half of *we* was. There was a dead guy on the slab. Nice. My day was complete. A day without standing next to a stiff was like a day without hemorrhoids.

"Ah, who's the recently departed?"

"He's the reason I asked you to come here. And he's not recently departed. He's alive."

No way. No flipping way. "Ah, Doc, I think you need a freshen-up course in med school. The dude's expired, deceased, and demised. He is no more. He's ceased to be, and he's gone to meet his maker. This is a *late* human." I patted the corpse's chest with the palm of my hand. "Doc, his chest isn't moving. That, in case you forgot, is how dead people breathe."

What was with the scowl I was receiving?

Toño lifted the sheets covering the guy's lower parts. He pointed to a small box resting on his groin. "That is an ECMO. An Extracorporeal Membrane Oxygenation unit. It breaths for him. He's very much alive."

"Then why's he lying naked and motionless in a morgue? Huh? Seems like a bad set of predictors for longevity, if you ask me."

"His *brain* is dead, but his body is otherwise in fine shape. He was a thirty-seven-year-old construction worker. A falling steel beam lanced through his skull and killed him."

"And let the record show General Jon Ryan was no less confused after learning that depressing bit of information."

"Fortunately, the falling beam was part of this hospital's expansion construction. He was brought straight to the ER and kept alive."

"Okay, a series of random questions. Why keep a brain-deader alive? We don't harvest transplant organs anymore. We grow them. Why is there anything fortunate about having a steel rod skewer your noggin? Seems like a total downer to me. Why are you showing me this unfortunate character? I … I've really seen enough dead people, thank you very much. Enough to last my eternity. Finally, do I need to stay here any longer? I actually feel worse now than I did before I entered this creepy place."

"The answer to all those questions is, *for your own good.*" He crossed his arms.

"You know the sphinx is usually portrayed crouched on all fours when it speaks in riddles."

"I probably should complete the picture. Since his accident a month ago I've repaired his brain damage. It wasn't easy and I needed the help of several specialists, but I've restored his brain to its normal functional status."

"Gee, Doc, I'm sure his grieving widow will be totally pleased that her late husband will be buried with a tip-top brain. One other little question. Why, for the love of all that's medical, logical, and ethical would you rebuild a dead man's brain? The previous owner ain't coming back you know?"

"I did it for you, Jon. *We* did it for you."

I pointed to the door. "I'm going to walk out there and come back in. That way we can start fresh. I'm positive you'll not sound like you've blown a bank of fuses."

"Jon, I've known you longer than anyone but yourself. You've changed. You know this as well as I do. All the killing, all the hating. It's getting to you. It's making you dark and cynical, and worst of all, it's making you unhappy."

"I'm unhappy, so you bought me a fully functional dead guy? Makes no sense, but whatever. They say not to look a gift horse in the kisser." I shrugged and looked to one side. "A fully functional dead hot *babe,* maybe I could see." I pointed toward the deceased. "You know I don't hit from that side of the plate, right?"

"Sometimes I think I've heard you be as disgusting and insensitive as a human can be, then you go right ahead and surpass your last lowest mark. Unbelievable."

"Why else would you build me a living person for my fun and pleasure?"

He shook his head mightily. "Sometimes I wonder what I was thinking, all those years ago." He stiffened. "No, you moron, I made him for you to transfer into."

Did not—repeat did *not*—see that one coming.

"It's all too rare, but I love seeing that dumbfounded, speechless look on your face, Jon. I really do." He chuckled softly.

"Right," I began not knowing where I was going, "you made a dead guy undead so I could transfer from a robot *to* a living person?"

"That is correct."

"Not the other way around, living to robot, like it's supposed to be?"

"There are no rules in that regard."

"And you didn't ask me if I had the slightest interest in assuming a perfect stranger's identity?"

"Again, correct."

"Okay, now don't tell me, because I want to guess the bizarre reason you did that. Hmm. You're diversifying into being a comedian? No. This isn't funny, so that's not it. Maybe you've blown a bank of fuses? Hey, that now makes *double* sense."

"I prepared this host in case you wanted to transfer into it."

"No, that's not it either. Because you see, if you were going to go to all that trouble, you'd have asked me first if I had the slightest interest in doing so."

"And if I *had* asked you, you'd have swaggered, and said you were fine, please don't bother, and you'd have farted humorously to change the subject."

Dude knew me too well.

"No," I jabbed a finger at him. "You know very well I can't fart. You took that away from me."

"I think you take my drift."

Yeah, I did. If he'd have asked, I'd have totally blown him off. But now that he'd gone to all the trouble, wasn't my answer the same?

"Dr. DeJesus, my answer is phhhhhhrt."

"Some things never change," he scoffed.

"Seriously, what am I supposed to say?" I pointed to the quiet guy. "This is a little odd. You'll have to grant me that."

"I suppose it might seem odd."

"*Might*? Even to an egghead like you? Ya think?"

"Here are my thoughts, Jon. You've been more places, done more things, and been involved in more killing than any other human. You're changing profoundly, and not for the better. It came to me recently that maybe you wouldn't mind stepping back and being a simple human again."

"Doc, you're nuts. Is that even possible?"

"I don't see why not."

"Ah, that's what Saunders and you told me about the original transfer. It wasn't very reassuring then, and isn't very reassuring now. *I don't see why not* is diametrically different than *yes*."

"I was *correct* then, and I am *certain* again."

"But … why?" I put my hands on my head. "I didn't ask you to make this possible." I looked at him severely. "Wait, did Kayla put you up to this?"

"She most certainly did *not*. I haven't discussed the possibility with anyone else."

"Not even Carlos?"

He shuffled his feet nervously. "Well, of course ,Carlos. I needed his help."

"What about the janitor? Did you tell him? My dry cleaner? Some chicky-pooh you were trying to impress?"

"You know very well I did not. Carlos doesn't count."

"I'm sure he'll be flattered to hear that."

"Jon, the point is that I told no one. This is not a decision for anyone but you."

"Why would I choose to return to being human? I don't get it."

"I'm certain that you do. If you were human again, you would be normal again." He stomped his foot. "You would be as normal as you could be."

"No, I wouldn't. You know that. What kind of trick are you trying to pull?"

"What do you mean?"

"Even if I agree to transferring to this stiff, there'll still be me," I slapped my chest, "just as screwed up," I pointed to my head, "as ever."

"No. If you decide to transfer, the unit you are in will be decommissioned. I will personally see that the android Jon Ryan is never activated again."

"Never is a long time, Doc."

He squinted. "No, it isn't. Never is infinitely *short*, not *long*."

"No, I mean never turning me back on is a long time period in which to make sure it doesn't happen."

"Oh. I see your point. No, you will not be rebootable."

"What, you going to melt me down for scrap?"

He shuddered. "Of course not."

"Then how? If dead-guy version of me is happier than a bunch of clams, it doesn't help this me in any way, shape, or form."

"This version of you would be permanently shelved, inactivated, and canceled out."

"Maybe stuff me and put me in a museum?"

"Don't tempt me."

"Wait. I have far too many memories, too many bits of crap in my computers to fit into any single human brain." I rapped a knuckle on the dead guy's forehead. "Especially a secondhand model."

"That is a valid point. I think I can cull out the technical and historical data that has no relevance to your day-to-day life."

"I have that tingling uncertainty again."

"Which is one reason I would not melt down the android. If there were information you decided you needed, I could do so without waking the android."

"Waking? You mean this me'd just be in sleep mode?"

"A poor choice of words. No, you will be as off as off can be. But I would still be able to extract data, if the need arises."

I walked to a lab stool and sat. "Do I have to decide now?"

"No, of course not. This body will remain viable for several weeks, perhaps a couple of months."

I thought a moment. "If I decide to re-transfer to an android, can you do that?"

He didn't reply quickly. "*Can* I do that? Yes. *Would* I do it? No. Never. If you go back, returning to an android is not an option."

"Why? What's the big deal?"

"The big deal is because I say so."

"Huh?"

"My game, my rules." He walked to a stool. "It's just that simple. Look, Jon, I love you. You know that."

"I am so glad no one alive heard you say that." I nodded toward the stiff.

Toño rolled his eyes. "I mean to say, I only want what's best for you. But this transfer, it's serious business. I want you to decide and do what you truly desire. But it's a onetime deal, a one way trip. If you transfer, you're human until you die. If you don't," he gestured to the corpse, "this poor SOB dies for real and that's the end of it. Lest you ask, if you got down on your knees and begged me on your mother's sainted memory, I will never rebuild another android for you. If you transfer back you buy the entire package. One life, long or short, happy or sad."

"Sometimes you say things that make me happy to be alive, just to have heard them. 'Jon, I will *never* build you another toy android , so don't ask.' I love it."

"I live to serve."

"So?"

"So," he said with a sigh, "talk it over with Kayla, your family, your bookie, whomever you need to."

I pointed at him. "My bookie. Toño, I swear, in three centuries you might have developed a sense of humor. It's lousy and lame, but dude, you made it."

"I'll wear that compliment as I would the Medal of Honor."

I wagged my finger at him. "Funny guy."

"I believe I see a *but* in your eyes, Jon."

"A butt in my eyes? That's potty humor, but hey, I don't want to stop you while you're on a roll."

"I believe I see a *however* in your facial expression."

"Well, it would be kind of weird, I mean for Kayla. One day I leave for work, and that night a perfect stranger climbs into bed with her." I held up a hand. "And don't you go saying she'd probably like it."

"The thought never crossed my mind."

"Really?"

He guffawed. "*No.* It's too obvious not to have, you loon. But I've made some provisions."

"What provisions?"

"Take a good look at his face Jon. His body."

I scanned him carefully.

"What am I supposed to notice?"

"How he looks almost exactly like you, both in facial characteristics and body habitus."

He did. "Wow he really does." I looked up to Toño. "Wait, what are the chances a guy who looks just like me is killed in just the right manner that you can repair him?"

"Pretty remote." He waited a second, then giggled like a teenage girl. "Jon, I've had his face reconstructed by the best plastic surgeons there are. We caught a break with the body configuration, but most of the resemblance is surgical, not luck."

I turned back to the body and Toño followed. I looked at the guy a few seconds. Then I lifted the covers to check out his male attributes.

Toño slapped my hand. "Stop that."

"Hey, buyer beware. I need to know all the facts to make an informed decision." I wiggled my eyebrows at Toño. "Unless you did plastic surgery there, too?" I really wiggled my eyebrows.

"Sometimes I wonder why I bother."

It only took me a couple days to decide. I made the leap, literally. The shell of a man known as Glenn Denver became Jon Ryan. He was thirty-seven when he died. I was thirty-eight when I transferred to an android three hundred years earlier. I was stoked. I got a year back. I kept my job as advisor to president for the remainder of his term and for a few administrations after that. I grew old most gracefully, if such a concept was valid in the first place. With my loving wife by my side and generations of children behind me, I sauntered though this life, trying to be as unremarkable as possible. It was actually sublime.

But the thing that got me the most, the part I will treasure the longest and most dearly was what I did that first day after I became a boring human forever. Do you know what I did that glorious day? I went fishing with my son JJ. Yeah. I insisted Toño not install command prerogatives in the new me either. In fact, I made Yibitriander come take that damn *Wrath* back for good.

So, my boy came, picked me up, and took me to Azsuram. We fished all day and well into the night. We didn't catch a damn thing, either. It was great. It was late when he brought me home. You know what I did then? It was the best. It was surely more than I ever deserved. I climbed into bed with the woman I loved, and we held each other until dawn.

Sound corny? Hey, have your own dreams come true and then try and say something not corny.

Yeah, it's hard.

Glossary of Main Characters and Places:

Ablo (2): Led Uhoor to attack Azsuram after Tho died. Female.

Almonerca (2): Daughter of Fashallana, twin of Noresmel. Name means *sees tomorrow*.

Alpha Centauri (1): Fourth planetary target on Jon's long solo voyage on *Ark 1*. Three stars in the system: AC-A, AC-B, and AC-C (aka Proxima Centauri). AC-B has eight planets, three in habitable zone. AC-B 5 was initially named *Jon* by Jon Ryan until he met the falzorn. AC-B 3 is Kaljax. Proxima Centauri (PC) has one planet in habitable zone.

Alvin (1): The ship's AI on *Ark 1*. aka Al.

Amanda Walker (2): Vice president then president, a distant relative of Jane Geraty. Wife of Faith Clinton.

Anganctus (4): King of the Faxél, ruler of Berrill. Mean cat.

Azsuram (2): See also Hodor, Groombridge-1618, and Klonsar.

Balmorulam (4): Planet where Jon was shanghaied by Karnean Beckzel.

Barnard's Star (1): First planetary target of *Ark 1*. BS 2 and 3 are in habitable zone. BS 3 was Ffffuttoe's home, as well as ancient, extinct race called the Emitonians. See BS 2.

Beast Without Eyes (2): The enemy of Gumnolar. The devil for inhabitants of Listhelon.

Bin Li (2): New UN Secretary General after Mary Kahl was killed.

Bob Patrick (2): US senator when Earth was destroyed. One of The Four Horsemen, coconspirator with Stuart Marshall.

Braldone (1): Believed to be the foreseen savior on Kaljax.

Brathos (1): The Kaljaxian version of hell.

Brood-mate (1): On Kaljax, the male partner in a marriage.

Brood's-mate (1): On Kaljax, the female partner in a marriage.

Burlinhar (4): Dolirca's brood-mate.

BS 2 (1): The planet Oowaoa, home of the highly advanced Deavoriath race.

Cabbray (5): Member of the Churell race allying to fight the Last Nightmare.

Callophrys (5): Name taken by Eas-el to fool Dolirca.

Calrf (2): A Kaljaxian stew that Jon particularly dislikes.

Carl Roger (1): Chief of staff to President John Marshall before Earth was destroyed.

Carl Simpson (1): Pilot of *Ark 3*. Discovered Listhelon orbiting Lacaille 9352.

Carlos De La Frontera (2): Brilliant assistant to Toño, became an android to infiltrate Marshall's

Challaria (3): JJ's brood's-mate.

Chankak (5): God figure to the faithful on Revstok.

Charles Clinton (1): US President during part of Jon's voyage on *Ark 1*.

Chuck Thomas (2): Chairman of the Joint Chiefs of Staff, one of The Four Horsemen, and the first military person downloaded to an android by Stuart Marshall. evil team.

Churell (5): Humanoid species enlisted to help defend against the Last Nightmare. Similar to centaurs.

Clang-fow Peditit (5): Ruler of the a large tribe of Maxwal-Asute.

Claudus (6): Son of Erratarus. A vicious cat.

Colin Winchester (5): General, Royal Regiment of Fusiliers. In command of worldship defenses after Katashi Matsumoto's removal.

Command prerogatives (2): The Deavoriathian tools installed to allow operation of a vortex. Also used to probe substances. Given to the android Jon Ryan.

Council of Elders (2): Governing body on Azsuram. Anyone may speak and any adult may join.

Cube (2): See vortex.

Cycle (2): Length of year on Listhelon. Five cycles roughly equal one Earth year. Days are measured in cyclets.

Cynthia York (1): Lt.. General and head of Project Ark when Jon returns from epic voyage.

Davdiad (1): God-figure on Kaljax.

Deavoriath (1): Mighty and ancient race on Oowaoa. Technically the most advanced civilization in the galaxy. Used to rule many galaxies, then withdrew to improve their minds and characters. Three arms and legs, four digits on each. Currently live forever.

Deerkon (4): Planet where Karnean took Jon to deliver a shipment. Home of Varrank Simzle.

Devon Flannigan (2): Former baker who assassinated Faith Clinton.

Delta-Class vehicles (1): The wondrous new spaceships used in Project Ark. Really fast!

Divisinar Tao (2): General in charge of the defense of Azsuram.

Dolirca (2): Daughter in Fashallana's second set of twins. Took charge of Ffffuttoe's asexual buds. Name means *love all.*

Draldon (2): Son of Sapale. Twin with Vhalisma. Name means *meets the day.* Legal advisor to the Council of Elders.

Des-al (5): The most powerful of the Last Nightmares remaining. His title is *tiere.*

Eas-el (5): Rebellious member of the Last Nightmare. He would lead them into our universe.

Last Nightmare (5): The horrific dragons who wish to rule the universe again.

Enterprise (2): US command worldship.

Epsilon Eridani (1): Fourth target for *Ark 1*. One habitable planet, EE 5. Locally named Cholarazy, the planet is home to several advanced civilizations. The Drell and Foressál are the main rivals. Leaders Boabbor and Gothor are bitter rivals. Humanoids with three digits.

Erratarus (6): King of the Faxél after Anganctus. His flagship is *Smell of Death*.

Exeter (2): UN command worldship.

Faith Clinton (2): Descendent of the currently presidential Clintons. First a senator, later the first president elected in space. Assassinated soon after taking office.

Faiza Hijab (6): Major General and commander of TCY, the UN lead defense force, after Colin Winchester.

Farthdoran (4): A spiritual leader among the Deavoriath. His disappointment in the moral indifference of his people led his to wish to die. He is the only one to die in millions of year.

Falzorn (1): Nasty predatory snakes of Alpha Centauri-B 5. Their name is a curse word among the inhabitants of neighboring Kaljax.

Farmship (2): Cored out asteroids devoted not to human habitation but to crop and animal production. There are only five, but they allow for sufficient calories and a few luxuries for all worldships.

Fashallana: First daughter of Sapale. Twin to JJ. Name means *blessed one.*

Faxél (3): Name of the fierce giant cat species of Berrill.

Fenptodinians (5): Species of jellyfish like multipeds with an advanced civilization recruited by the Deavoriath to fight the Last Nightmare. They are hemaphrodites.

Ffffuttoe (1): Gentle natured flat bear like creature of BS 3. Possesses low-level sentience.

Fontelpo (4): Bridge officer aboard *Desolation.* A native of Kaljax. He was demoted after discussing ship's business with the then newly arrived Jon.

Form (2): Title of someone able to be the operator of vortex using their command prerogatives.

Fractor (5): Close associate of Anganctus, third in power. Holds title of Second-Equal.

Gallenda Ryan (4): Jon's daughter with Kayla Beckzel.

General Saunders (1): Hardscrabble original head of Project Ark.

Gollar (5): Home world of the Fenptodinians.

Gortantor (6): Leader of the Jinicgus at the time of Molly Hatcher and Jon's mission.

Groombridge-1618 3 (1): Original human name for the planet GB 3, aka Azsuram.

Gumnolar (1): Deity of the Listhelons. Very demanding.

Habitable zone (1): Zone surrounding a star in which orbiting planets can have liquid water on their surface.

Haldrob (4): Faxél version of hell.

Havibibo (3): Commander of the Berrillian fleet that attacked Azsuram.

Heath Ryan (2): Descendant of original Jon Ryan, entered politics reluctantly.

Indigo (1): Second and final wife of the original Jon Ryan, not the android. They have five children, including their version of Jon Ryan II.

Infinity charges (2): Membrane-based bombs that expand, ripping whatever they're in to shreds.

Jane Geraty (1): TV newswoman who had an affair with newly minted android Jon. Gave birth to Jon Ryan II, her only child.

Jason Kaserian (5): Chief assistant to UN Secretary General Bin Li.

Jinicgus (1): Tiny sausage-shaped natives of Luhman 16a 2.

Jodfderal (2): Son in Fashallana's second set of twins. Name means *strength of ten*.

Jon Junior, JJ (2): Son of Sapale. One of her first set of twins. The apple of Jon Ryan's eye.

Jon Ryan (1): Both the human template and the android who sailed into legend.

Jon III and his wife, Abree (2): Jon's grandson, via the human Jon Ryan.

Julregar (6): Captain of Berrillian ship *Color of Blood* after Anganctus.

Katashi Matsumoto (2): Fleet Admiral in command of the UN forces when the Listhelons attacked and later the worldfleet defenses.

Karnean Beckzel (4): Pirate captain of *Desolation*. Shanghaied Jon.

Kashiril (2): From Sapale's second set of twins. Name means *answers the wind.*

Kayla Beckzel (4): Sister to Karnean and first officer of *Desolation*. A real looker.

Kendra Hatcher (5): Jon's teammate on his mission to Revstok.

Kelldrek (3): Second, and hence mate of, Havibibo. Captured by Jon.

Kendell Jackson (2): Major general who became head of Project Ark after DeJesus left. Forced to become an android by Stuart Marshall.

Klonsar (2): The Uhoor name for Azsuram, which they claim as their hunting grounds.

Lilith, Lily (2): Second AI on *Shearwater*. Al no likey!

LIP (1): Abbreviation for Local Indigenous Population.

Listhelon (1): Enemy species from third planet orbiting Lacaille 9352. Aquatic, they have huge, overlapping fang-like teeth, small bumpy head, big, bulging eyes articulated somewhat like a lizard's. Their eyes bobbed around in a nauseating manner. His skin is sleek, with thin scales. They sport gill a split in their thick neck on either side. Maniacally devoted to Gumnolar.

Lornot (3): Female Deavoriath who used to be a political leader.

Luhman 16a (1): The second target of *Ark 1*. Called by the natives *Reglic*. Eight planets, only one in habit zone, LH 2. Two sentient species are the *Sarcorit* that are the size and shape of glazed donuts and *Jinicgus,* looking like hot dogs. Both are unfriendly be nature.

Luminarians (5): Species recently transformed into a non-corporeal being. They are basically sentient balls of electrical energy.

Manly (2): Jon's pet name for the conscious of an unclear nature in the vortex. He refers to himself the vortex manipulator.

Mary Kahl (2): UN Secretary General at the time of the human exodus from Earth.

Matt Duncan (2): Chief of staff for the evil President Stuart Marshall. Became an android that was destroyed. Marshall resurrected him in the body of Marilyn Monroe. Matt no likey that!

Maxwal-Asute (5): Advanced species brought in to help fight the Last Nightmare. Fire hydrants with toilet plunger heads. Real tough cookies. Home world is named Ventural.

Molly Hatcher (6): Captain and Form. Daughter of Amanda Hatcher and Kendra Hatcher. Form of *Expectation*.

Monoz (4): Port city on Deerkon and home base for Varrank Simzle.

Nmemton (3): JJ's first born, a son.

Noresmel (2): Fashallana's daughter, twin of Almonerca. Name means *kiss of love*.

Nufe (3): A magical liquor made by the Deavoriath.

Offlin (2): Son of Otollar. Piloted ship that tried to attack Earth and was captured by Jon.

One That Is All (2): The mentally linked Deavoriath community.

Otollar (2): Leader, or Warrior One, of Listhelon. Died when he failed to defeat humans.

Owant (2): Second Warrior to Otollar.

Oowaoa (1): Home world of the Deavoriath.

Oxisanna (5): Wife of Yibitriander

Pallolo (4): First destination for *Desolation* after shanghaiing Jon.

Palquir (6): Domesticated meat-producing animal on Berrill.

Peg's Bar Nobody (4): Dive bar on farmship *Granger* where Jon misspent a good deal of time after Sapale's died.

Phil Anderson (1): TV host, sidekick of Jane Geraty.

Phillip Szeto (2): Head of CIA under Stuart Marshall.

Piper Ryan (2): Heath Ryan's wife.

Plo (2): First Uhoor to attack Azsuram.

Prime (2): Pet name for the android of Carlos De La Frontera.

Proxima Centauri (1): Last system investigated by Jon at the end of his *Ark 1* mission. PC 1 is where he met Uto.

Quantum Decoupler (4): A weapon given to Jon by Kymee. It pulls the quarks free in a hydrogen nucleus, hence it overcomes the strong force. That produces prodigious amounts of energy. Big boom.

Quelstrum (4): Planet of origin for some of Varrank's guards. Really big, tough guards.

Rasraller (6): Berrillian female, captured near death on LH 2.

Reglic (1): Sarcorit name for the planet Luhman 16a 2.

Revstok (5): Planet held by the Berrillians where Jon and Kendra tried to plant a story to test the security of the broken Berrillian code.

Rigel 12 (6): Home world of the Luminarians. Their name for the planet is Beftil.

Roaquar (5): Berrillian commander of outpost on Revstok.

Sam Peterson (2): Chief Justice at the time of Earth's destruction. Member of Stuart Marshall's inner circle, The Four Horsemen.

Sapale (1): Brood's-mate to android Jon Ryan. From Kaljax.

Sarcorit (1): Tiny donut-shaped natives of Luhman 16a 2. The dominate species on the planet.

Seamus O'Leary (2): The pilot of *Ark 4*, discovered Azsuram.

Shearwater (2): Jon's second starship, sleek, fast, and bitchin'.

Sherman Collins (1): Secretary of State to President John Marshall when it was discovered Jupiter would destroy the Earth.

Space-time congruity manipulator (1): Hugely helpful force field.

Stuart Marshall (1): Born human on Earth, became president there. Before exodus, he downloaded into an android and became the insane menace of his people.

Tersfeller the Huge (1): Sarcorit ruler of LH 2. A tiny bully.

Tho (2): The head Uhoor, referred to herself as *the mother of the Uhoor.*

Toño DeJesus (1): Chief scientist in both the android and Ark programs. Course of events forced him to reluctantly become an android.

Tralmore (1): Heaven, in the religion of Kaljax.

Uhoor (2): Massive whale-like creatures of immense age. They feed off black holes and propel themselves though space as if it was water.

Uto (1): Alternate time line android Jon Ryan, possibly…

Vacuum Energy (5): The energy of a complete vacuum. It is not zero, though the net energy is zero. Basically, virtual pairs opposite particles that blink into existence and then annihilate in a timespan too short to observe. Hey, it's real, seriously, I didn't make this one up.

Varrank Simzle (4): Insanely cruel crime boss on Deerkon.

Vhalisma (2): From Sapale's third set twins. Name means *drink love.*

Vortex (2): Deavoriath vessel in cube shape with a mass of 200,000 tons. Move instantly anywhere by folding space.

Vortex manipulator (2): Sentient computer-like being in vortex.

Wolf 359 (1): Third target for *Ark 1*. Two small planets WS 3, which was a bad prospect, and WS 4, which was about as bad.

Wolnara (2): Twin in Sapale's second set. Name means *wisdom sees*.

Worldships (1): Cored out asteroids serve as colony ships for the human exodus.

Wo-woo-loll (5): First among equals and spokes individual for the Fenptodinians.

Xantrop (5): Head of the palace guard and a confidant to Anganctus. Rank title is First-Equal.

Yibitriander (1): Three legged Deavoriath, past Form of Jon's vortex.

Zantral (5): Assistant to Dolirca.

Shameless Self-Promotion
(Who doesn't look forward to that?)

Thank you for joining me on the Forever Journey! I hope you enjoyed the saga. All six books in the series are available now.

There is a sequel to *The Forever Series* now. *Galaxy On Fire* begins with *Embers*. Once you finish this series be sure to check out the new one. Trust me, it's even better.

The third series in the Ryanverse begins with *Return of the Ancient Gods*. The first book is *Return of the Ancient Gods*.

Please do leave me a review. They're more precious than gold.

My Website: craigrobertsonblog.wordpress.com

Feel free to email me comments or to discuss any part of the series. contact@craigarobertson.com Also, you can ask to be on my email list. I'll send out infrequent alerts concerning new material or some of the extras I'm planning in the near future.

Facebook? But of course. https://www.facebook.com/Craig-A-Robertsons-Authors-Page-943237189133053/

Wow! That's a whole lot of social media. But, I'm so worth it, so bear with me.

Well, *vayan con Dios, mis amigos* ... craig

Made in the USA
Lexington, KY
24 March 2019